I0673376

LADDER TO THE SKY

ETTORE LUZZATTO

Edited by Kfir Luzzatto

PINE TEN

Pine Ten, LLC
205 North Michigan Avenue
Chicago, IL 60601

This is a work of fiction. Names, characters, places, and incidents are either the product of the author's imagination or are used fictitiously. Any resemblance to actual events, places, organizations, or persons, living or dead, is entirely coincidental.

Fist publication, March 2021

Copyright © 2021 by Kfir Luzzatto.

All rights reserved. No part of this book may be used or reproduced in any form without permission, except as provided by U.S. Copyright Law. For information, please address Pine Ten, LLC.

ISBN: 978-1-938212-99-4

Contents

PREFACE

When shortly before his death, at almost 97, my father charged me with keeping and curating several boxes of family documents, I was overwhelmed. I kept those boxes in my basement for a few years before I resolved to honor my father's wish. One of the folders I fished out of a box was a brown thing with *Ladder to the Sky* handwritten on it. I put it back in the box, promising myself that I would read it soon, but I did so only recently.

Ladder to the Sky turned out to be much more significant for me than I had initially guessed. It reads like fiction—and some of it is fiction—but in essence, it is an authentic, autobiographic relation of how a bright, young man's life radically changed when, in 1938, Italian Jews overnight became an inferior race.

My father left Italy for the U.S.A., naturalized there, enlisted in the army, and fought the Japanese in the Philippines. After the war, he returned to Italy, and 22 years later ended up in Israel—a real Wandering Jew.

The dramatic events recounted in this book shaped my father's life, ideas, emotions, and much more. In reading the manuscript, I realized that it provides rare insight into how becoming a refugee from your home will change you. Generations that have not had to suffer a similar fate—at least not so far—have much to learn from it.

Based on various clues, I know that my father wrote the book in 1971-1972. At that time, he had not yet reassumed his American name, Edgar, which he did in later years, so the author of this book remains Ettore Luzzatto. At first, I wondered why he had never published it, while he had published other books both before and after that time. A simple reading of the manuscript gave me the answer: this book exposes my father's soul for everyone to see; when he relates events that took place during the war and after, it reveals his most private thoughts. It also lays bare some of his most intimate feelings that he never shared with us, but knowing my father as I do, I can tell that they are genuine, not fictional.

My father had a strong personality but was also incredibly self-conscious. I believe he kept the book in his drawer simply because he was too reserved to let the world know him too well. And he also took "precautions" to protect his family. The children he describes in the book have nothing to do with his real ones, and while he had to tell in detail events that affected my mother, who narrowly escaped death in the Holocaust in which she lost her father and most of her family, he depicted her as the opposite of who she was. My mother was petite, delicate, and a teetotaler, so he described her in the book as a large, almost beefy, vulgar woman and a drunkard.

The manuscript was a finished book if you consider the many handwritten additions and changes in it. My father had written them with the minute and thin calligraphy that only he and I could read. Nevertheless, it called for some heavy editing to remove repetitions and bring paragraphs and sentences to a more palatable form for the modern reader. Every change I made (and I made many) required a soul-searching process. Each dilemma reminded me that my father is no longer here to advise me and argue with me—that I truly am on my own.

I hope that the result is one he would have loved.

Kfir Luzzatto
Omer, Israel
November 2020

CHAPTER ONE

My twin sons insisted that I take them to Beth-El. We stood at its highest point, beside the road, the Arab village of Beltin to our left. We could see all the way to the Lebanese mountains, far to the north. All of that hill is rocky ground, and sheep and goats graze stubbornly on the weedy patches between rocks, as they always have. Who knows why men have chosen it as a place where to worship God.

My sons wondered why the Torah tells us that Jacob took a stone and placed it under his head. "What's the meaning of it?" they asked. "Perhaps if his head had rested on anything made by man, he could not have seen God?"

Well, he had come from Be'er-Sheva and was exhausted from the long, harsh journey through the awful barrenness of Judea. He lay down on the ground and rested his head on a pillow of stone, a pillow as unyielding and merciless as his destiny, and then he dreamed. He saw the ladder set on the earth and reaching to the sky and angels climbing up and down, and the Lord standing over it. I believe I know that Jacob climbed that ladder, but of course, he couldn't tell about it; he could say no more than, "This is the gate to heaven." No man can tell the things he faced utterly alone. Jacob was alone before the ladder as one is in birth and death and any passing over.

The sun was setting; we decided to wait for the night. It came with a swift darkening of all colors in the sky and a rising chill in the air.

"The stars in Israel are brighter than elsewhere," said one of the twins. "See, they're not pinpoints. The bigger ones look like studs, and in each one, you can make out a tiny circle of light within a crown of rays."

"The biggest of them all will rise shortly before the dawn," I said. "In Latin, it is Lucifer, the bringer of light, and you should know its Hebrew name, which sounds like an endearment is *Ayelet-Hashachar*, the doe of dawning."

"Let's stand a while here in the dark," they begged me. I didn't ask them why; I didn't need to.

On another night, a long time ago, while we slept, we Italian Jews changed into something not quite human. Not bugs like Kafka's Joseph K., no, something more handsome and nobler but still not human, like heads of big game. No other group of men underwent so sudden, capricious, irrational, so stupid a transformation brought about by such utterly inane means. As we slept, newspaper presses printed an idiotic little paragraph claiming that an "Italian race" existed and that "the Jews did not belong to the Italian race." When we woke up in the swelter of an August morning, our metamorphosis was complete. So little was required to cancel our rights in a country where there had never been any more assimilated, diluted, camouflaged, unrecognizable Jews.

At first, no one realized what had happened. It took many months and the piling up of laws and regulations to crush us down so low that any coward could kick us for fun. But a trick of the memory foreshortens the months as if it all had happened in the span of that morning. It felt like a single flash of instantaneous universal awareness, with the sudden appearance of the look of betrayal—that "stay away from me" look in the eyes of friends and lovers.

When I was a child, teachers excused me from religion classes because I was not a Christian. Neither my schoolmates nor I had a clear idea of what it meant to be a Jew. It was quaint to be one, though not very important because religion classes weren't so many. Besides, all I could do at those times was to pace the school's interminable corridor, made gloomy by its brick flooring, and walls colored the shade of decaying mushrooms. Occasionally, I gazed through the corridor windows and watched a girl airing rooms in another house across a courtyard. When she leaned down to fasten open shutters to the wall, her hair cascaded over her brow and hung down like Melisande's. Then I fancied that I stroked that hair warm from the sunshine, and she sighed at my touch. In reality, she didn't know I existed; she never saw me, a small shadow in a gloomy corridor across the courtyard. Sometimes our principal passed through the corridor. He stopped before me and placed his hand gently on my head. He never said anything, but I felt tenderness and puzzling compassion in his gesture. He was very old, white, and stooped, and they said that he wore a hair shirt next to his skin. He caressed me lightly and went on his way without ever talking.

Mine was a private school and very exclusive. It took only boys who were sons of aristocrats or wealthy industrialists or professionals. We all lived in the same section of Milan, where I had been born, a few hundred yards from the Scala theater. A canal, the Naviglio, once ringed the city's heart, and then they covered it up. Nevertheless, all true *Milanese* remained very conscious of its flowing underground like an ideal moat. It sheltered the only space where *i signori*—the gentlefolk—could feel at home. We considered it a disgrace to live outside its enclosure. We clung to the space within, to our old houses with their clean-lined, ochre-painted neoclassic facades, high-latticed wooden ceilings, and cobblestone courtyards, and monumental granite stairways.

Some weeks after that August morning of metamorphosis, I ran into my best friend in the street. We had graduated from high school and talked about the university, what courses we should take, and what profession we should choose. We spoke in a vacuum because I was leaving Italy, and he knew it. Still, we pretended that nothing had happened, that there was no such thing as an "Italian race" to which Jews "did not belong." But it didn't come off. He kept squinting up and down the street. I guess he was thinking, "I hope no one notices my being friendly to a Jew. But hell, how can I cut him, my oldest and best friend?"

We had been schoolmates since kindergarten. We had passed through the age when a trace of homosexuality colors all friendship between boys. After he turned eighteen, I had told him, "It's high time you went with a woman." I had been initiated long before and felt like an expert. I escorted him to the most expensive brothel in town. It was a sedate, almost stuffy establishment. Even the stained glass door, then the brothels' trademark, looked borrowed from a church that they said was patronized by members of the royal family. I picked the youngest, freshest girl for him. Later we walked off the excitement of his first manhood together.

Now he kept looking and squinting up and down the street, shrinking from my contagious disease, that of being persecuted. But it didn't matter; I had already lost much more than a friendship, so I talked to him in a vacuum, and then I let him go. I watched his hurrying away from the Jew.

There were also Jews running away from themselves. They simpered with gratification when somebody told them that they didn't look Jewish at all. "Do you think so?" they would ask hopefully. "I do have rather a small nose and light-colored hair." They would stare into a mirror with swingable side panes, which they adjusted this way and that, to reassure themselves that they looked equally un-Jewish from all angles.

Catholic children of mixed marriages could qualify as "Aryans." They were required to prove baptism at birth, but that was no problem—you could buy a retroactive baptism cheaply. Still, their status remained precarious. But if the Jewish parent was the father, they could improve it: all they had to do was to swear they were not their father's son. It was particularly convenient when the mother had died and was not available for questioning. A little holy water and branding their dead mother a bitch bought them safety, or rather the illusion of safety.

Most Gentiles were sorry. They tried to console us. "It won't last," they said. "The Duce is very humane. He's been forced into this by those cursed Nazis, but it can't last—mark my words. Why, there are no better Italians, no greater patriots than you Israelites. You were never different from us, never different at all."

What they said had been true of people who no longer existed, who had ceased to exist on that August morning. But what did it matter? What does it matter what they were like? What do I care about what I was like, and have stopped being like so long ago? Yet somehow, I do care. I keep creeping up stealthily on my youth, watching, and trying to understand myself. But it's no use; nothing comes through but a sense of loss, a strange mood of despair, like a plaintive cry perceived from a great distance of which I know neither the source nor the meanings.

Our house was built over the remnants of an ancient convent. Carved granite holy water bowls still protruded from the bottom of the walls. The walls bore giant fresco portraits of Dante and Petrarca, weathered to blots of faded colors, though not as old as the bowls. From the ground floor, we could walk out into what had once been a garden. Still, no longer—houses and dividing walls had grown all around it. Now it was but a patch of sickly weeds, with two tall trees in the middle sheltering a family of blackbirds. At one corner stood a strange one-story construction, the purpose of which had long since been forgotten. The trees were decrepit. I saw them as two gaunt, gnarled centenarians. I fancied I heard their catarrhal coughing outside my window in the dead of night. Somebody had taught me a popular rhyme in Milanese dialect about blackbirds and winter. I remember only a cruel verse in which winter threatens mother blackbird to freeze her little ones to death. On cold winter mornings, I would scan the garden ground for little blackbird corpses, but I never found any. Either my blackbirds didn't breed, or they bred tough offspring.

In the summertime, I slept with my bedroom window open onto a balcony overlooking the garden. Sometimes the moonlight woke me up, and then I got up, stepped out on the balcony, and leaned on its wrought-iron railing. I looked at the back of other houses, the higher stories, even garrets, where the poorer people lived, and I thought I saw their faces at the open windows. But I wasn't sure; all I could make out were whitish blots, and even when I watched for hours, they never budged; they looked no more like faces than the moon does.

There was a deep silence in that tight enclosure within ancient walls, although the city surrounded us. As I listened keenly, the silence changed to a rushing sigh and then resolved into a spectrum of small sounds. One of them was the sound of someone's crying, not like a child but like an adult who chokes his sobs into a pillow. Children cry to call for help, but who can help an adult? Only God and God never bends down to a tight enclosure within ancient city walls, where someone chokes his sobs every night. Only I can hear them as I stand on my balcony till the chilly hours of dawn.

My father was a widower and quite a ladies' man. Sometimes I ran into his mistresses, fluffy, sweet-scented, elegant, obviously married ladies. To me, they looked pretty much all the same, and all seemed worried that I had seen them. Once I heard my father reassuring one of those women.

"Don't worry, darling," he said, "he's no chatterbox; he's a strong, silent little man."

Then she gushed over me.

"Of course, the poor motherless kid! D'you remember your mother at all?"

I shook my head.

"Strange, isn't it?" my father commented. "He was no longer a baby when she died."

He always sounded annoyed that I didn't remember her, but what could I do? I didn't. All I knew about my mother was what she looked like in some stiffly posed studio photographs, and somehow I felt that I had never met a woman who looked like that.

My father was kind; he never punished me, but then I was a quiet, respectful boy. When I visited his offices—he was a lawyer, and I liked the dusty smell of old files—he pinched my cheek and gave me small gifts of money. But when he talked to me, his eyes didn't quite focus, and I suppose mine didn't either. We didn't really look at each other until it was too late, and perhaps never at all. He called me a "strong, silent little man" because I never cried when I got hurt. He was proud of it; he didn't pause to wonder whether it might make the pain sharper.

When I neared thirteen, and I astounded him by demanding to have a proper Bar Mitzvah, he balked and grumbled that he was against "the clergy." We were a family of free thinkers, he said. Why, he himself wasn't even circumcised. Finally, he gave in, and then he even defended me against angry, scandalized relatives. Still, he drew a breath of relief when it appeared that my bout of religion had been nothing but a whim, soon forgotten. I didn't know any Hebrew then, and I was spared the disgust of understanding that our rabbi was praying for the compassion, *rachamim*, of the state.

Then, life stretched ahead of me like a straight line without bends or kinks, already drawn out to its full length. The plan was clear: I would be a successful lawyer like my father, inherit money, lead my social life in a high bourgeoisie with a smattering of nobility, marry an attractive rich girl, probably a Catholic, whom I would abundantly cuckold, and who might deceive me, now and then, in a discreet manner. I would father an uninteresting but reliable son and give him small gifts of money when he visited my offices, and pinch his cheek. At the same time, we would look at one another with unfocused eyes. In the end, there was room for me in the family chapel in the smart old Monumental Cemetery; no danger of having to travel to the huge unexclusive newer one.

Of course, I had read about antisemitism. I was shocked by such Nazi slogans as "death to the Jews." Still, antisemitism concerned a very different kind of Jews—it concerned ignorant bigots with long whiskers and funereal caftans, ugly black beetles crawling over the snows of Russia and Poland, or fat businessmen, who insisted on controlling all banking and commerce in Germany. Still, I understood that there was no excuse. The Nazis were brutes, and my father donated generously to refugee relief. Antisemitism had nothing to do with me because I was an Italian gentleman, I had a classic education, and I came from a line of patriots.

Occasionally I met students from Hungary, Romania, or Poland, sad-eyed youth with names like Friedman, Meyer, Finkelstein. One of them was Yuhasz, which he told me was Hungarian for Schaefer. He winked at me as he said it, and I wondered what the wink could mean. I often asked them, "Why do you come to Italy? Aren't the schools adequate in your own country?"

They would shrug evasively. They didn't confide in me. Although they knew I was a Jew, they didn't acknowledge me as such, and I certainly felt no instinctive, revealing kinship to them. I hadn't the slightest suspicion that we had anything in common. I found them unattractive, *antipatici*. I thought they had furtive manners as if they were afraid of being found out in a lie, which in a way was not untrue—their lie was to hope. I wonder what they thought of me, how many have survived, and if any of them finally went to Palestine and fought for our freedom while I was lost in my personal maze. I should like to ask their forgiveness for my dislike of them and tell them how I have paid dearly, nearly as much as I deserved. But I remember what countries they came from. I expect that I could only ask forgiveness of the smoke long since scattered and of the ash long since swallowed up in the earth. Those sad-eyed hopeless young people with the names that meant nothing to me had become smoke and ash.

Milan, the city in which I was born, is full of sadness. It nestles in the countryside of pastel colors and heavy winter fogs swirling up from canals and ditches. There are shadows in the fog, a host of shadows that float about and hover above hedges and fields. Of course, they are nothing but refractions of light in the tiny water droplets of the fog, and still, dogs howl at them. Why should dogs howl at refractions? But they do, and the mournful sound drives the shadows away. I was only a boy then; all I could do was stand at my balcony through the night, watching white face-like blobs in the windows of the poor, and listening keenly enough to make out the sound of someone's sobbing.

When it rained, I liked to walk the streets in purposeless roaming walks. The rain smelled clean and chilled my face pleasantly, but sometimes there was a bitterness to it. Then I would stand still and shiver while the sidewalks glistened, and small streams ran in the gutters. I would raise my eyes to windows shuttered against the rain, feeling out of everything and lost.

The Milanese were proud people. They kept their sorrows locked behind slatted shutters and heavy wooden doors, but I felt those sorrows— the rain seemed to wash them down and soak me with them. I wished I were one of those boys who can cry; then, I would have stood in the rain and wept for their sorrows beneath their closed slatted shutters.

I wanted to walk into one of their houses through the arched stone-framed gate that was wide enough for the carriages to drive through. I would slowly climb the stone staircase, listening to the rain crashing down on the skylight, filling the stairwell with its steady roar. Then, I would knock on a door and watch it open slowly to let me in. I could imagine an end to loneliness only through the sharing of a burden, the sharing of pain. But after that August morning, I knew that the door would open only a crack, and a voice would whisper through the crack: "Go away, life's harsh enough as it is, go away, Jew!"

CHAPTER TWO

In school, my greatest distinction was being my grandfather's grandson, the grandson of an Italian hero. It was hard for me to identify him with the personage the teachers read about, and by that time, he had died, and I couldn't ask him, "Grandfather, is it really you they read about?"

He would have smiled and answered, "Of course it is I—except that I was eighteen then and am eighty-five now. It's I as much as an eighty-five-year-old man can be the same as a boy of eighteen."

He was very fond of his grandson, and he kept trying to bridge the vertiginous gap of years between us. He liked to talk about his battles, and when he did, his face lighted up with a tender fierceness because he thought of his country. I was very young, but I haven't forgotten. Although I was too young to understand the meaning of patriotism, I caught his love for Italy, and it's a kind of love one never grows out of.

The teachers read from the diary of one of Garibaldi's volunteers, the *"Mille"* They read how grandfather had run away to join the *Mille.* In those days, if you were a kid at eighteen, you had to run away if you wished to fight. When the teacher read about my grandfather, my schoolmates stared at me, and I felt very proud, but I also felt a constriction in my chest. I almost cried from the love of my country, which may sound silly now that so much has happened. People would laugh at me, especially young people. "How corny can you get," they would say, and I admit it makes a corny picture, the proud little boy basking in his schoolmates' stares and nearly crying from the love of his country. I admit it, but I don't give a damn.

Garibaldi commissioned grandfather a lieutenant. Later the Italian government validated the commission. When the First World War broke out, grandfather campaigned for Italy to join the Allies, and when she did, he volunteered for the front. He was seventy-two, and they asked him if he was crazy. He was the oldest fighter in the Italian army, perhaps in all the armies. Prisoners gaped awe-struck at encountering this patriarch in the front lines. Once a shell burst next to a group of prisoners he was escorting to a rear zone, and the prisoners broke into a run. He drew his pistol and shouted, "Stop! Nobody runs away when he's with me!" then added ruefully, "Besides, I'm too old to chase you."

He wasn't aware of having a Jewish sense of humor. His generation saw things in black-and-white: what wasn't right was wrong; what wasn't good was evil.

Because grandfather had been a great patriot, we, father and I, were "discriminated." Discrimination meant the contrary to what it seems to suggest—we were supposed to be exempt, to a somewhat imprecise degree, from anti-Jewish discrimination. But it was a concession, not the recognition of a right; the hand that had given it could take it away.

"Besides," I said to my father, "what would *he* do if he were alive and they told him, 'See how generous we are, we grant you full citizenship ... well, almost full. After all, there's a limit'. What would he do? You know damn well what," I said, feeling excited at the thought of my grandfather's reaction, "he'd spit in their eye. We are men, and we can't accept our manhood like a handout."

But my father answered that he saw no sense in being theatrical. He wanted to keep working and owning property and hiring Gentile help, and as long as he could, he would. He knew it wouldn't last forever, but while it did ...

When I told him that I should leave Italy, he merely nodded. He was fifty-six then, I thought of him as elderly, but he was still handsome. He hadn't run out of fluffy, smartly dressed, sweet-scented ladies, and antisemitism had a hard time getting past his bedroom door.

My rebellious great-grandfather and all his people had been silk merchants and growers, though, of course, you don't "grow" silk. You grow silkworms, and you feed them on tender mulberry leaves. They synthesize the silk polymers in the nauseating little factories of their bodies, and they spin it into a cocoon. Then you kill them and unwind the cocoon. At least, I suppose you do; I don't really know a thing about it. When the silk market was up, my people bought real estate, and when it was down, they sold. You could draw a bull and bear diagram for silk from their real estate transactions. The men were stocky, heavy-muscled from helping to wrestle silk bales, the women petite, pretty, and stubborn. They all knew how to deal with sharecroppers and silk mill girl hands. They were a cheerful, down-to-earth lot, with a simple job to do and quite firm about doing it. But my grandfather ran away from them when he was eighteen.

In the days of the Republic of Venice, the Doge used to call on the Jews for loans to finance wars. They say that once a Doge got very angry at the Jews' reluctance and shouted at the Jewish delegation that they should be ashamed. As the story goes, one of my ancestors interposed, "We were coming forward, but your Excellency's so quick at soliciting loans that he beat us to the punch." Then the Doge laughed, and friendliness returned. But I don't like to recall that anecdote; I'm not so proud of my quick-witted forefather. Although it happened over two hundred years ago, his quip reminds me too much of the gesture of a runt dodging a blow and pretending it's all in fun.

The Jews fared well enough in the Republic of Venice. However, the ghetto, its name, and substance were invented there. That was because the Republic wished to keep its Jews in the face of Counterreformation pressure. So, they found a compromise: we'll keep the Jews, but we'll restrain them. Jews and Venetians got along well enough, though. There were ups and downs, but the Jews could stand them, and after the Republic died, its tradition remained. Grandfather's people were never troubled. They felt at home; sometimes, they were elected mayors. All they had to worry about were silk prices, and I suppose spurring the worms to do their job, assuming that there are ways to influence silkworms.

I wonder if I would have found it hard to turn away from the peaceful façade of a moneyed house in my grandfather's place. To leave behind the silkworms, the pert black-haired cousin who would be good in bed, and the peace, which no one seemed to threaten. I know now that to accept that kind of peace is flight, that when grandfather ran away from home, he kept a *rendezvous* with himself. I, too, went away, toward a small man's small destiny.

CHAPTER THREE

I landed In New York on a Sunday. I'm not a good sailor. The ship had tossed a lot in the winter storms, and I had been seasick nearly all the time and still felt weak at the landing. I found a room, unpacked my suitcases, and went for a walk through my new world. It was a gray, cold January day. On the nearly deserted pavement, a grim, middle-aged woman in a mink coat shouldered me out of her path in the almost deserted street.

I entered a coffee shop. "May I have a cup of coffee?" I asked.

The counterman weighed my respectfulness against my good clothes, the clothes lost. He growled, "Yeah, if you pay for it."

I gave him a dime.

In those days, beggars used to chant, "A dime for a cuppa coffee ..." What do they beg for now? Two bits? Or more? It's so long since I have seen New York except at night when it becomes a stand-in for hell. Nor am I likely to see it again soon; it has grown as distant from me as the stars. I had never been a free man before. It's hard to explain how it feels to meet freedom for the first time on the nearly deserted sidewalks of New York on a January Sunday morning.

My room was off upper Broadway. One of those decaying brownstone houses that long ago, I believe, were the rich's houses. One mounted a few steps and came into a dark-paneled hall. The phone booth was in the corner, over there was the door to the super's suite, and then a wooden staircase with a worn red carpet still able to muffle the steps' noise. One heard very little noise in that house. The roomers never spoke to one another and whispered when greeting outsiders in the hall. My room, almost a garret, was on the fourth floor. One reached it through a narrow, steep staircase beginning where the main one ended. A small electric range and a sink occupied the landing. The room had two beds. It was large and luminous and had a glass door opening inanely and dangerously onto the roof's sloping tar-papered surface. It was comfortable enough, and most importantly, it was cheap.

Years later, I returned to that house. The new super was a man of color—only people of color lived now in the neighborhood. He eyed me crossly, but he let me in. The room hadn't changed; it could never change. It would go on forever, housing the same melancholy and yearnings under different skins. There's something elemental about young men poor and alone, haunted by the same primary frustrations, driven by the same basic wants, and each believing in his uniqueness. I shuddered, and I ran away before the room became aware of my presence and reached out at me once again.

Sometimes I couldn't sleep. I sat in an armchair, my feet on a spot of a rug worn threadbare by other feet, a bottle of blended whisky on the floor within reach. I had never drunk much; I didn't enjoy it. My rare drunken bouts were usually followed by a desperate sickness and the same kind of shame that comes after masturbation. Now and then, I went out; I kept going out and coming in most of the night. The journeys up and down the stairs were soothingly long. When I reached the bottom of the upper stairway, I pulled on a string that ran upwards through hooks set along the wall and controlled the landing light. The string was long and stretched under tension; only when it was taut enough would the light overhead snap on or off. It was an awkward contrivance, which I found vaguely symbolic, but of what, I didn't know.

The crowds on that part of upper Broadway were fascinating in those days. Each hour had its own crowd. Only the cabbies and a few prostitutes watched over the whole night, their permanence making them superior to the mere passers-by. I felt a kinship with them. As the night deepened, I felt lighter and freer and that I belonged. Only sheer exhaustion could finally drive me back to the house, the dank hall, the dangling string, the click of the light overhead, the threadbare spot on the rug.

The days blur in my memory, but it's easy to remember the nights. In remembrance, the nights of nearly three years merge into one long night, one long, cold, crystal-clear night. I sat through a double feature in the neighborhood movie house, came out with the last movie crowd, and went into a cafeteria. Once I had paid with a twenty, believing it to be a one-dollar bill. The cashier had guessed my mistake and had short-changed me. I had gone hungry for a week, but I hadn't minded because it had been a good lesson—it had driven into my head the fact that I was now poor. Hunger, something I had read about as a child in fairy tales about woodcutters and widows who took in washing, was something real and sneakingly near; it was like those companions who have a trick of walking one step behind you and never catch up, but neither fall back, no matter how fast you walk. At night, I counted my change with special care. At night, I recognized my poverty more clearly. Every condition is more itself at night, and perceptions are keener, things invisible by daytime glow in the dark like cats' eyes.

In the cafeteria, an old man and a girl sat at the next table. The girl was pale, and when she spoke, she exposed long whitish gums in her mouth. She wore glasses with cup-like lenses ground down at the center from an enormously thick edge. The old man wore his hat. He ate fiercely, glaring at his plate while the girl was talking.

"And so he said, take off your glasses and read there. And you know, I couldn't read a letter, not a single letter, not even the great big ones on top, without my glasses."

She was pale as a slug, and her skin had an unhealthy mucous moistness. Men would cross her in the street, and there never would be a stirring of desire in any one of them. There would be no awareness of her; she didn't really exist. Her pale eyes behind the cup-shaped lenses were wide with the question, "do I exist?" And she had found her pitiful answer: "I exist because I have this extraordinary, this matchless short-sightedness. There's no one as short-sighted as I; therefore, I am unique; therefore, I am a person, and I exist." Descartes in an upper Broadway cafeteria—but then, most of everybody's life is spends looking for words to precede *"ergo sum."*

The old man sat with his hat on and ate with growling noises. She kept looking at him, her pale eyes, her wonderfully, matchlessly short-sighted eyes, clouding with doubt at his silence. Then he raised his head; he wiped his mouth and smirked. He looked greedy and evil. He said, "My wife can't see the big letters on top, even with her glasses on."

The girl made a small wan gesture with her hands.

I got up and walked away.

I beckoned to a prostitute who had her post near the corner where I turned off-Broadway. She smiled, stretched out her hand as if to touch me, and then she let it drop and fell into step beside me. I had not wanted to turn in alone. Sometimes I had the feeling that going up to my room was the last leg of a journey in an upside-down world where climbing meant falling.

Up in the room, I gave her a drink of whisky. She thanked me. Her voice was without resonance, a subdued helpless sound. She was younger than I had guessed, and her clothes were cheap but not garish at all. Had I not been one of the all-night crowd, I might have taken her for an office girl a bit down on her luck. She had beautiful large gray eyes and fair brown hair. I told her so, and she shot me a worried look. I remembered the coffee shop man and his distrust of my politeness.

"Don't worry," I said, "I'm not trying to bum your sweet favors."

She smiled doubtfully, not quite understanding, but reassured. When she started to undress, I switched off the overhead light. At my age, I measured a woman's body against an ideal of perfection in Pentelic marble. A slight blemish could freeze me tight, at least in an occasional cold-blooded encounter. But I couldn't avoid perceiving that her breasts were small and empty. They were discouraged undernourished breasts. Her skinny limbs had an unpleasant sort of flexibility as if her bones were soft and filled with rubbery marrow. I was thankful that she restrained her motions and kept her breathing light. She didn't gasp or moan; she didn't make the usual lugubrious pretense to pleasure.

I felt pity for this young woman and a glimmer of tenderness; I didn't think of her as of a whore at all. I had needed a woman, but the intercourse left me dissatisfied, unappeased, and slightly nauseous at the same time. I thought that I might as well have made love to that slug-like girl in the cafeteria, and it wouldn't have been much different. For one moment, I had the nightmarish sensation that I had done so, and I snapped on the light. The little prostitute lay quietly beside me, her lovely brown hair framing a pinched youthful face, not repulsive at all.

I asked her if she was in a hurry. She said no, these were hard times, very little money about, and she wouldn't find another customer tonight. We lay beside one another in silence. I wanted very much to talk about myself—I hadn't spoken to anyone about myself in a long time. Maybe I was changing from day to day and slipping away from myself. If I didn't talk about it, I might forget my past and therefore be unable to understand my future. The very thought gave me a drowning feeling. I ached with the need to talk about myself. What good is intercourse if you can't talk afterward? It's like uncorking a bottle and pouring its contents on the ground. But I could not.

We lay in silence, and from time to time, we slept a little. Then the dawn came at my windows, a wilted sooty big city light, but still, the dawn. We got up, and we made coffee, we drank it, and I paid her.

She said, "It was no good, was it?"

I patted her head. "Don't worry about it," I said. "You were fine; you're a fine girl."

Strangely, it sounded like saying good-bye on a pier. We went out, and it was bitterly cold but somehow soothingly so. I watched her walk away. I wondered why she had made no remarks about my being a Jew. I started to walk, aimlessly, in the opposite direction.

I have a recurring nightmare about New York. Only it's not really New York; I think I know what it is. The dream runs like this. It's evening; I know it's Friday evening because I feel the emptiness of the whole weekend stretching ahead. The weekend is a dead time, falling like a stone in stagnant waters, a time removed from time. One feels that the live, real time, will never return. I have no one to talk to. I walk the streets. They are like tubes set in a dimly lit room, no glare of sunlight at their open ends, only the twilight of a brass-like, artificial-looking surface which is the sky of my dream. I'm crawling like an ant, too small ever to hope to reach the tube's ends and not really wanting to. That brazen twilight is somehow too hostile, too threatening. People are walking beside me and toward and away from me and crossing my path, but I cannot address anyone of them. If I did, they would turn empty orbits on me, answer my appeal with a lipless grin, and be on their way. Perhaps not even that would happen; maybe my voice is as soundless to them as their bustling motion is to me. Perhaps it is my eyes that are empty orbits. I don't wish to find out; it might be too frightening.

The twilight has deepened, an opaque dusk is settling, and it's cold now. Sheets of wind flap against me and choke me. Suddenly the streets glitter with prickly pinpoints of light, and I know I can't stand it any longer, I must get inside, but the very thought is oppressive. "Inside" does not sound like "shelter" but rather like "tomb." There is terror in imagining myself inside the house where I live—I can't see it in the dream, I don't know what it looks like, but I feel it's reaching out at me like a big rotting hand.

No, I can't go inside, not like this. Then I remember that I have a friend. I have a friend in New York. A woman, I don't think of her as of a "girl." She isn't important to me, and I mean very little to her, yet I believe that she would hear my voice, and I would hear hers, and even in silence, she would be a benevolent presence. Suddenly I yearn for that presence, but I haven't thought of her for a long time, and now I have forgotten where to find her. I walk into a store; I look her up in the phone book. It proves incredibly difficult. For a while, I forget the spelling of her name, and when I remember, it seems that I can't turn the pages; they stick together under my stiff fingers. For one panicky moment, I fear that that page has been torn out of the book, but no, there it is, and I find her name, or rather ten, one hundred names that could be hers. I have to eliminate the wrong ones, one after the other, in a sweat of concentration. But the store has no telephone. The storekeeper turns empty eye sockets on me and grins a lipless grin. Of course, like all the others, he has no voice; he rejects me soundlessly. Then the store vanishes. A row of benches runs along the walls, high benches, much higher than my head, and people sit on them, unmoving stony statue-like people, quite out of my reach. I find what looks like a telephone. I try to dial her number, but my fingers slip, and the disc clicks back. I try repeatedly. Finally, I succeed, only to discover that I have dialed nothing but a meaningless set of zeros.

Now I am frightened. It's getting late; surely she'll be going out on a Friday night; she won't come back tonight. I can't even think beyond tonight, to the bottomless, empty, dead time of the weekend. Suddenly I succeed. The line is clear. The phone is ringing at her home. It rings and it rings. There's no answer. I hear myself screaming. Then my nightmare world bursts and dissolves in a shower of light, and I wake up.

But my nightmare isn't really about New York. Now I know what it's about: it's about hell. Why does New York signify hell in my oneiric world? It's so damned unfair. New York is a wonderful city; I love it, and I'm grateful to it. So, why hell? Maybe the Greeks were right; maybe there can be no Paradise after death, only hell, my kind of hell. Try to imagine Paradise, and you'll see. Paradise makes no sense at all, but hell does; hell makes a lot of sense if you take the devils and the gnashing of teeth and all the stage property out of it. It makes so much sense that you could just round a corner and run into it. I run into it at night now and then, it doesn't last long, but while it lasts, it's horrible enough.

Yet my life in New York was not unhappy. Dreary, sad, at times, but on the whole, not unhappy. Nor even lonely. It seems lonely now, in retrospect. From a distance of years, the eye goes through things that looked solid then, bulky things that took up space and had substance, and now they have become transparent. The eye goes right through them and sees a nothingness underneath. From a distance of years, the people who filled my days have turned to mere outlines. It's hard to recall the color of their eyes and the sound of their voices. It's hard to remember that they had eyes and voices at all. So there's nothing in the space which they once took up. I stand alone in the middle of all that space, there's no one near me, and it is useless telling myself that this is a trick of the memory. My reality is as I see it today, and the way I felt then is but something out of a tale, a tale I know well, but still, only one that doesn't concern me anymore.

CHAPTER FOUR

When I had no money left, I found a job.

I ate my lunches at the German's. I never learned his name. The German nests in my memory like a polished nodule of some hard foreign substance. Enduring because of its irrelevancy, its lack of sense, and of purpose. A fat, obsequious little man.

"You don't hate me because I'm a German?" he asked me once.

I didn't hate him. "A German" is only an abstraction, and he was a very concrete, fat little man. We faced each other across an enameled tabletop; we mirrored one another, paired like two pieces of flotsam imperceptibly bobbing up and down in not quite stagnant backwaters. It didn't matter that we bore the tags "Jew" and "German." But that is how things usually go— someone puts tags on people. The people look at the labels, and each discovers that the other is hateful and evil and lunges at him. It's all supremely stupid, but we were two insignificant men marooned on the banks of the Hudson, well past caring about our tags.

"We had a lovely act," he told me. "The two of us. Acrobats, acrobatic cyclists, you know, riding bicycles on a high wire. It was sensational. You wouldn't know it to look at me. I was slim and quick, like a coiled spring."

"Really ..."

"Oh, yes. And not long ago. A man goes to seed awfully quickly. My partner fell and got killed, and I ... I just lost my nerve. I tried, but I couldn't go up there any longer. So, what was I to do?"

The German occupies a corner of my memory that I could put to better use, but I shall never get rid of him.

"We have a fine soup today," he crooned. He smiled as if this were great news. "Eat your fine soup."

He fed me an aqueous emulsion of rancid fat, later a thin, leathery slice of meat, potatoes, a chicory brew, every day the same, for thirty-five cents. These little details still force themselves on me, as overbearing as a crowd of unwelcome guests. Someday a dazzling light will come in through my windows; the day will shine bright to my failing eyesight; my children will be clutching my hands as if to keep me from going away alone. There will be so much to forgive and to ask forgiveness for, and so little time in which to do it. I shall be mumbling about the German, how he lost his nerve, and what he fed me, and how we faced each other like two pieces of flotsam.

The German's place was next door to the laundry plant where I worked. The plant belonged to a linen supply company; therefore, we washed its own linen, and there was no nonsense about it. The stocky, cigar-smoking Irishman who managed it was obsessed with the knowledge that a greater weight of work came in each day than went out. Where did the difference go? How could matter disappear like that?

"But listen," I tried to explain to him, "the incoming linen is merely weighted down with excess moisture and dirt, that's all."

He stared at me with small blue eyes, china pig's eyes. I felt in him a distaste at my difference, amounting almost to hatred. I could read his thoughts: *You've been hired as a porter, see, a goddamn unskilled laborer, and a fucking poor excuse for a porter you are, at that, and you would tell me things, would you?*

Near us, the big machines gaped, belched steam, swallowed loads of dishtowels fetid with corrupted blood and serum. I wasn't permitted to load them, much less to run them; that was skilled work. The plant was in a building that had once been a stable. The steam rose from the machines at the ground level through the loose planking of a floor put in to exploit the building's height. It rose, and it stewed the workers above. The workers were all girls, and in summer, they kept fainting, and someone carried them to one side to recover. They fainted more willingly when I was near them and ready to support them in a strained embrace. They were mostly heavy, hefty girls.

"Bruno, d'you think there's too much flesh on me?" one asked.

My job was to drag the trucks full of wet linen from the elevator to the dryers. Damp linen is heavy as water, and the trucks' wheels rusted fast, so it was a backbreaking job. The girls felt sorry for me because I wasn't quite strong enough, so they kept calling me over to the shaking table where they unknotted the aprons' strings.

"Come over here, Bruno, give us a hand," they would say.

Their pale faces shone with sweat. The room was low and broad, like an enormous shelf. We were small creatures, something like anthropomorphic mice living a precarious life of hiding and scurrying from danger. Our was a species doomed to extinction because I was the only male and the females so unfetching, their skins glistening gray and green whenever they came into a shaft of light. The light itself was gray and green—maybe the Hudson colored it as it struck its surface, then it came in through the windows but didn't stay far from them.

At night, I staggered home, broken with fatigue. On the way, I bought a hunk of pumpernickel bread and a can of soup. I heated the soup at home, sat in my armchair with my feet on the threadbare spot of the rug, switched on a small radio, ate, and listened to "Amos 'n' Andy." It was reckoned an amusing program, but I remember it as bleakly melancholy drivel. I finished my soup and my bread, switched off the radio, and went to bed. That was the end of my day. Sometimes in the whole day, I hadn't thought a single thought worthy of a man.

Then there was the day the refugees from Germany came.

"They're trying to sell some fucking detergent concoction," The manager said. "We can't buy any, see? The cheapest kind of plain soap is all we can afford in this business, it's all, and if they find anything cheaper, that's what we'll buy. But the owner says he's sending these guys out; they speak only German, you've got this Italian fellow, he says, maybe he speaks a little German, So okay. You talk to them, and you get nicely rid of them."

The Germans were respectful to me. They thought I was a powerful man—a man who could buy or refuse to buy their *Seife*, their fantastic, quick-acting, whitewashing, patented *Seife*. They had frayed clothes, genteel manners, a darting, don't-hit-me-please way of looking at people. I wondered what they had been before. Perhaps the older one had been rich, and the other one—who was fat and had a pinched petulant mouth but must have been handsome once—had married his daughter.

Yes, there must be a daughter-wife somewhere. That would explain the desperate tenacity in the old man's manner and his contempt when looking at his partner. ("I have no money left, but I'll still look after you both; you help me, and you'll see," the older one would say. "Yea, Father," the younger man would call him "Father," he looked stupid and dependent). I wondered what the daughter was doing now. Probably nothing, probably sitting in a shabby room somewhere in a seedy section of town, sitting with her hands in her lap, now and then crying quietly at her uselessness. I wondered what her name was, probably Lotte or a more utterly un-Jewish name, maybe even Brunhilde. Yes, there must be a daughter somewhere. I sensed in the old man the heartbreak of one who has promised: "Don't worry, your daddy will see to it, your daddy's old, but he's all there, he knows his way around," and it's all nothing but sound, like crooning a lullaby to a doomed child.

They were two men weak and lost, with frayed clothes, trying to make a living by selling unsaleable stuff in a foreign tongue. I could picture them discussing this company—the owner is a Jew, so ... reckoning how much they would sell. The company had several plants; so much percent commission, running to so much money, would mean food and perhaps cheap new clothes. But more than that, selling meant achieving at least a minimal status in society.

We stood on the concrete floor, our feet in puddles of scummy water—the floor was too uneven for drainage. The workers walked by and spit into the puddles; the machines groaned and puffed and choked us with clouds of steam. The younger man opened a cardboard suitcase, took out a heavy package of detergent.

"Be careful; it's the only one we have," the older man cautioned.

"Yes, Father."

He put it on top of a machine, and the old man gave me his sales talk. He talked cleverly, like an educated man who has never had to fight for a living. He was trying hard to charm and convince me; he believed I was an important man, and I felt like a cheat. We discussed the test we would run, we turned around, and there was the package, fallen off into a puddle, soaked through, useless. The old man got red in the face, he trembled with rage and disappointment, he slapped the other's wrist, the other cowered and whimpered. I felt sick.

"Don't carry on like that; it makes no difference," I said, "the company would never have bought your detergent anyway."

Suddenly the old man began to cry. I let him cry for a while, then he calmed down, and I took his arm and led him out into the street.

As I came back, the manager said to me, "You got rid of those guys? Then get back to work."

When I scanned the newspaper on the morrow, I half expected to read that an old Jewish refugee had jumped from his window, but there was nothing, at least that day. But this didn't lessen my feeling of shame, of being somehow responsible for an old man's tears, an old man's loss of dignity and courage. And even now, whenever I hear about the Jews' being the salt of the earth, about the Jews' mission being to participate in and enrich other nations' cultures, I see once more that package of detergent lying in the scummy water. I wish I could paint it; I wish I could make everybody see it as I do, such a meaningful, a conclusive sight.

Yet I saw that sight, and what did I do? I took the old man's arm and led him out into the street, and then I came back. The manager said, "get to work," and I went upstairs. I went back to dragging the rusty, immensely heavy trucks of wet work. I did it because I needed to make a living, somehow, anyhow. I was sick with shame, but still, I needed it. I strained my inadequate arms and back and waited for the girls to call, "Bruno, come here, Bruno, what's the matter with you, are you ill?" their voices soft with pity.

Later the German said, "What's the matter with you? Are you ill?"

"No."

"Then eat your nice soup."

"It isn't nice soup; it's piss."

His mouth puckered; he looked hurt.

"Forget it, it's not your fault, even lousy cooks like you have to live."

He drew himself up.

"I'm not a cook, I'm an acrobat. I did an act on the high wire."

But on Saturday night, sometimes I ate well. An Italian couple had turned their Little Italy apartment into a restaurant. Illegal, no license, but who cared. It was good and cheap. Someone said to me, "you'll feel at home; they are a northern people anyway, none of that greasy garlicky stuff."

The wife was tall and spare, and with her black hair braided about a pale, severe face, she looked like a peasant Madonna. She cuckolded her husband; I couldn't decide whether he knew it or not. Whenever I came in, she gave me a meditative smile that seemed to rise slowly from great depths, and she let her shapely work-roughened hand linger in mine.

The customers were always the same. One of them cried in his coffee every night.

"I worked in Russia," he told me, "I'm an engineer, you know, I built a dam there, and … oh, other things, too, I worked a long time. And I married a local girl. I loved her very much. Then they told me, get out, go back where you came from, get out right away. And she? No. She stays. I've never seen her since. I keep writing to Stalin, and it's no good."

They served thick, sweetish red wine, not fine imported wine that was too expensive anyway, but strong wine. He kept drinking; his face became flushed and oozed sweat.

"And the worst of all, when I think about her, everything blurs, I cannot remember what she looked like—looks like, if she's alive. I never get any letters, so she's like dead to me. Maybe she's alive, and maybe she's dead, you understand."

They brought his coffee, and he cried into it.

Another one was a White Russian, a gentle, sweet, bewildered fellow. He had probably looked on the bloodiest pogroms in his youth as a most appropriate, if somewhat coarse popular entertainment. He told me a story about three White Russians who are exchanging memories. One says, "I am now a taxi driver, but in Russia, I was a duke." The second says, "I am now a waiter, but in Russia, I was a prince," and the third says, "You see my

Pekingese? In Russia, he was a greyhound." He looked proud when telling the story. I suppose he meant it to prove that it isn't only Jews who can tell jokes about themselves. I asked what he had been when in Russia. He smiled his gentle bewildered smile and didn't reply. I had a feeling that he didn't remember.

Nobody there seemed to remember much.

There was a journalist who claimed that Pope Pius XII wore special ceremonial headgear made of aluminum. He said it was "Because he suffers from headaches, frightful headaches, he cannot stand any weight on his head. Those are neurotic's headaches. Oh, he's a neurotic all right. And what is a neurotic?" He lowered his voice as if imparting a secret: *"Un'anima dannata!"*— "a damned soul!"

Every time he said it, somebody would snap back, "Don't be a fool! What about us, then? We're all neurotics."

A group of Italian expatriates talked of nothing but fascism and what they called their struggle against it. Their struggle consisted of shouting around the dinner table. As they drank more wine, the shouting grew louder, and this satisfied them completely. They had never done and would never do anything riskier.

We were a depressing collection of people, gathered together like a heap of inoffensive human rubbish that somebody had hastily swept out of the way for the time being. Futile, frustrated people, capable only of watching life flow by, a life of evil, cruel and hateful, yet for all that, life. Whenever I came in, the woman gave me her meditative smile and let her hand linger in mine. One night I arrived very early.

"Why are you so early?" she asked.

I didn't reply.

She nodded, "I understand."

She took me into a bedroom.

"Don't worry about my husband," she said. "He never comes into my bedroom without knocking, and he knows when not to knock. He's a good man and very obedient, not too stupid to know that he's stupid and needs me."

I started to speak, and she hushed me.

"Don't talk now; talking is for afterward."

She had a fine body, still youthful and firm, with slim shoulders and swelling, plump breasts. She had a lithe body, a smooth skin, pale with a warm ochre hue, a Gypsy's skin, *cutis amasado con aceituna y jasmin* – a skin kneaded with olive and jasmine.

"I'm old enough to be your mother," she said, "but you see, I take good care of myself. In the countryside where I grew up, women of my age are old cronies while I'm still desirable. I see it confirmed in your face, but you're only a boy. You're clean, not like those old lechers who patronize this place only because of me. Kissing you is like drinking cold water in the heat."

Afterward, she said, "My first man was your age, but I was just a child. He took me where the wheat was high, and later you could have seen our marks in the crushed stalks, if you stood on a rise, from miles away."

Her meditative smile rose slowly from a great depth, from that field of wheat far away.

"I wish that you could be the last, that I could let myself grow old all of a sudden," she said. "But we would lose our customers, and besides, I couldn't deny my poor stupid husband, so I might as well go on for as long as anybody wants me."

She lay nude on the bed, lazily stretching her beautiful peasant woman's body with the olive and jasmine skin. I could imagine the obedient husband biding his time behind the closed door. I knew that I couldn't face either of them, ever again, with their too wise knowledge of each other and me.

I had nothing in common with them. My Italy was not their Italy. Perhaps mine didn't exist at all, but whether she did or not, I understood that there would be no going back for me. The sudden inexplicable loss of hope made me achingly aware that there had been hope. I realized that I hadn't believed in the truth, in the finality of what had happened to me. I looked at the lovely nude body stretching on the bed. I wanted to touch it once again for the last time, but she shook her head. She got up gracefully, her peasant Madonna's face framed by the braided hair, suddenly severe. She stood in front of me, utterly unapproachable now despite her nakedness. It was easy to understand how she could subject a man, and if the man was weak, make him bide his time behind a closed door.

"Another time, when you come back," she said.

But I wasn't coming back.

CHAPTER FIVE

"*Shabbat*" in Hebrew is feminine. Of course, Jews endow everything fine with femininity. Here we put our best tablecloth on the table, to receive the Shabbat, and set two candles in the Yemenite candlesticks. I must admit that they are not very fine; they are what we have in Israel. We were used to much finer ones elsewhere. Most Jewish families in other countries set out much finer tablecloths and candlesticks.

The sun has just set. The horizon still glows from its drowning rays. It is light blue; the wake of a jet plane lies bright pink against the horizon where the blue gradually turns dark and compact like a stone's color. This sky is deeper than any other, like an immense hand cupped over a cradle. The wind carries scents of salt and blossoms and tough desert plants overcoming one another like children capering to attract attention. The surf breaks in its obstinate, soothing rhythm; at high tide, the beach will be alive with tiny insects scurrying away from the rising water. We are supposed to be careful about walking over its unguarded stretches because there might be mines. Still, the beach is lovely at sunset, and we don't worry about the mines. It's easy to receive the Shabbat as she should be welcomed here. It doesn't matter that our best tablecloth and our Yemenite candlesticks might look a bit shoddy.

But my first *Kabalath Shabbat* was very different. It meant nothing to me. I might as well have been witnessing some quaint Ainu ceremony, except that this was supposed to have something to do with me. Like many Western Jews, I felt that someone was thrusting membership in an alien culture upon me. It was like being stood in front of a crazily distorting mirror and being told, look, that's you. And it wasn't all my fault.

At my first *Kabalath Shabbat*, I sat in a dark, musty room with traffic noise below the windows, among mean shopworn people who had carried with them their mean shopworn daily thoughts. The whole proceedings were embalmed in blind deference to a tradition, not of bright suns and kneading one's bread. The cold grayness, huddling like vermin in moldy corners, required mumbling phrases that had lost all significance and turned to a mere hypnotic drone. The sky looked too dirty for snow, but it was bitterly cold, and the windowpanes grew ice incrustations. It was easy to imagine Cossacks too far away to be heard but closing in at a gallop. It made you shiver with the chilling apprehension of danger and to drop back into the days when Jews hid behind an easily torn gossamer screen of rites and resignation. Then blood would run down the gutters into the sewer.

Everything on the table was probably clean but managed to look filmed over with some unpleasant substance. One expected crumbs of bread and stains of egg yolk in the old man's beard who recited the *Kiddush*. I can't stand a filthy beard on a Jew; it reminds me of that vile verse from William Shakespeare's *The Merchant of Venice*, "You that did void thy rheum upon my beard." I become white-hot with rage thinking of it; it's a vile verse in an offensive play; shame on the culture that boasts of it. If Jews will wear beards, let them be flowing, silky ones, shiny prophets' beards.

The old man's beard was dull. Surely, it would attract breadcrumbs and egg yolk stains in a little while, and it would look like a beard that someone had spit upon. The beard muffled his voice, muffled that Hebrew, which I did not then understand, pronounced with that thick Eastern accent, which I have never ceased disliking.

My host's daughter's name was Violet, and she was my mistress.

"What's this," she would protest when I used that word, "am I a whore yet? Call me your girlfriend."

But I thought "girlfriend" juvenile.

"You sleep with me, therefore you're my mistress," I said.

"Mistress" had a pleasant tang of sinfulness. Now I realize that this was an assimilated attitude, the acceptance of the Catholics' idea that sex for pleasure is sinful and, therefore, brave and glamorous. Thus today's kids smoke pot or take trips, as I believe it's called (nothing dates a man so obviously as trying to borrow another generation's slang). To challenge disapproval that has no teeth in it is what youth likes best.

I could feel the old man's hostility like physical pressure. I could read his thoughts: *He is not one of us, he has no respect for me, he is nothing but a Goy, woe is to me.*

The old man mumbled his blessings and his prayers. I paid no attention. I thought, *What am I doing here? I am a free thinker; what do these formulae and incantations mean to me?* I tried to imagine my father at the head of the table, wearing a *kipah* of Como silk. He would have had a *kipah* specially cut to size and embroidered for him if he ever had worn one. No doubt, he would have languidly read the *Sidur* in his musical voice with his blurred French "r." The image was ludicrous. I smiled, and the old man shot me a murderous glance. It was not a success, my first *Kabalath Shabbat*, and I did not take part in another one for many, many years.

After the Saturday night meal, Violet and I usually went to a movie and then "home." She made me think of my dismal room as a home. She wasn't a housekeeping sort of girl; nevertheless, she made the room into a home by the way she came into it. She walked deliberately and proudly, proud of herself as a sex object.

"Home," she would say, "is where you go to bed with your woman."

She always climbed the stairs ahead of me. I had explained to her that this was wrong, that the man should go before the lady when entering a public place and certainly when walking up a stairway, but she shrugged all that aside.

"So you see my panties, so what? You know them by heart anyway."

I hated that kind of talk. I have always hated coarseness in women, but she shrugged my protests aside; it was her way of proving to herself or me how uncomplicated she was. When I met her, I had been a knot of hunger, and her big, somewhat rawboned body had promised appeasement. When she lay down, she made me think of a benevolent sea monster. She looked somehow immense, a bottomless, boundless source of hunger-appeasing things. Her long limbs were muscular, her breasts small and supple, and she had a fair, stern face, with the handsomeness that comes from good clean lines of the skull, smoothed over but not hidden by the flesh. Whenever she relaxed, her firm body could lie lazily still for hours. Sometimes after sex, I fell asleep in her arms and woke up to find her smiling quietly down at me. She hadn't slept at all. I felt forlorn and consoled; she didn't give me happiness but consolation for unhappiness. It was not enough, but it was something painful to give up.

We had met in a Zionist group. She asked me questions, and I told her, "Jews like me are difficult to explain."

One day not long ago, a little Sephardi asked where I was from; I told him. He gave me a puzzled stare—I didn't look like anything he found familiar—then he shrugged, his face lit up; he had found the answer.

"It's all right. We're all Jews," he said confidently—*"Cullanu Yehudim."*

That, I thought, is the answer to all questions. Of course, it's an answer with different implications depending on who gives it, but all the truth is in it. I wanted to hug the little Sephardi. Little insignificant Jews have a trick of reaching out to a great truth; they do so as unassumingly as they would to a piece of dusty, shoddy merchandise on a shelf of their dusty, shoddy stores. Ill-clothed, uneducated, harmless wonderful little people: my people.

Cullanu Yehudim, but I didn't know it then, as I sat facing that tall, hard-bodied girl whose movements were so sexy. Her very sitting down had been a sexual provocation; she kept her hand possessively on mine, her fingers curled claw-like on the back of my hand. I couldn't have gotten away had I wanted to.

"My name is Violet," she said.

"Of course, your eyes are the color of violets."

"Go on, say more."

She meant, let's get through the badinage and the serious talk, so we can get to where there's a bed.

"Well, Zionism was to me a dubious philanthropic activity to rescue troublesome Eastern people from an obscure plight which they had probably brought on themselves by being pushy and refusing to assimilate. Nothing to do with me. In 1934 they arrested some Turin Jews as Zionists and traitors. It takes very little for 'and' to become 'and therefore.' Of course, they were not traitors, whatever that was supposed to mean. How could they be? Most of them wore old, distinguished Italian names like mine. Antifascists they might be, and that was all right with me. Fascism was any Italian's business, and it might have been worth going to jail about. But Zionism—going to jail about Zionism, about getting some Eastern Jews into Palestine, I thought that foolishness."

"How did it end?"

"There was quite a commotion at first. But it soon died down."

"And the prisoners?"

"I don't know."

I didn't wish to talk about it anymore. I didn't want to recall how ready some Jews had been to help hunt down the "Zionist traitors." Tame animals have always been used to trap the wild ones, and slaves have helped their masters against their free brothers. But domesticated animals and slaves have no choice.

These Jews published a newspaper: *"Nostra Bandiera"*—"Our Flag." It called the roll of dead Jewish patriots ("Gold Medal Giulio Blum!" "Here!"), But Gentiles don't have to call the roll of their dead. If it becomes necessary to do it, then it is in vain; if you have to shout, "me too," you are excluded—childishly simple truths. Yet there are always Jews to wave a flag, black then and red today, against other Jews. They will join in their Gentile master's hunt, baying dutifully thoroughly tame, crawling, boot-licking Jew hounds.

If the commotion hadn't died out quickly, I might have smelled the scent of danger, and now there wouldn't be the shame of confessing, "I don't know what happened to those prisoners with the distinguished old Italian names, so very much like mine."

"Now, you see, the tables have been turned," I said. "I'm the one who comes from far away, who has no roots, who has to beg for shelter. So perhaps Zionism now applies to me."

She shrugged, "I don't think so. It's all right to attend the meetings, you'll find a bunch of nice kids here, but you'll settle down. This country's fighting Hitler, isn't it? Well, then. You'll do your share."

Suddenly she squeezed my hand hard, almost painfully. She leaned toward me, and there was a slight twitching in her cheek.

"Let's go. You have a room, haven't you?" she said. "Let's go," she repeated.

It was raining hard. We ran from the subway station to my door. Now her brown hair was soaked and hung limply; cold rivulets ran down her neck, she was hot and laughing. She reminded me of a filly with her hide steaming after a hard run under the rain. She climbed the stairs ahead of me. With her proud aggressive steps, slowly, the long muscles of her limbs playing under the wet, clinging fabric of her dress. Her legs were okay, a bit too lean perhaps, a bit too rawboned, but fine clean-lined legs.

Months later, she told me, "Do you know why I always climb the stairs ahead of you? Everything this gal does has a purpose; you should know that by now. I'm big and tough. I'm not the clinging vine type. I have to scheme and bull my way through life, and even a little thing like walking ahead of or behind you can be important. Now, I know that I look good from behind— a body like mine's at its best in motion. I may be a bit too much when standing still, but I move sexily, so by the time we get to the top of the stairs, you're pretty horny, and that's the way I want you."

"Don't be vulgar, please," I said.

I had started to learn about Zionism; that's what my evening was about. I had been looking for new ideas, for some transcendent meaning to put into my daily life, and see how it was ending. She had told me that she attended the meetings because the members were nice kids. I wasn't so sure about myself. I had said that Zionism applies to me, and perhaps it was true in a painful way. Maybe it was a truth I wanted to forget. It was easy to forget it while watching a handsome girl's rippling backside, knowing that at the end of the ascent to my garret room, there would be a bed waiting for us. I was grateful to her, yet I was also resentful, as a boy is when parents laugh indulgently at all the things he's going to do someday.

Still, how long since I had a girl of my age—not a whore, not a wise woman with a skin like a Gypsy—a girl. My room was full of the soothing rush of rain, breaking on the tar-papered roof. Violet opened the window and stood looking into the blackness outside. The house in front was dark, the street was dark, only from the corner of the avenue came glistening glimmers of light. It wasn't far to the corner, but they looked like lights out on the sea.

"It feels lonely up here. It feels kind of desperate," she said.

"Yes, I know."

"I wonder, did anybody ever jump from this window?"

"You couldn't jump," I said. "You'd have to step out onto the roof and let yourself slide."

My words surprised me; they conveyed a thought I had never been aware of thinking. Suddenly she clung to me, and I felt her tremble.

"Are you afraid?" I asked.

She drew back. She laughed. "What of?"

I touched her skin. It was cold now, and I felt her shiver at my touch.

"I believe you are."

"Oh, don't be silly."

She stripped off her clothes. She lay down on the bed.

"Come on, let's fuck," she said simply.

"Don't be vulgar."

"Oh, come on!"

Afterward, I fell asleep in her arms and woke up at dawn to find her smiling quietly down at me.

CHAPTER SIX

I wanted to go to Palestine. I couldn't drift aimlessly along anymore. I wanted to fight. This is what I told myself, and I believed it, but it wasn't true. Had I wanted to go, I would have gone. I should have said, "the hell with all the advice and the argument and the excuses, I'm going, and that's that."

"Who wants your Zionist state?" Violet's father said. "Thank the Lord there'll never be one, and what would be Jewish about it, anyway, I'm asking you—a state of Jewish Goyim, a state without religion. What's so great about a state, anyhow? Let the Goyim have states: us the Lord will lead back to the Land in His own good time."

It was useless to argue. His mind was a tightly locked, empty safe, and we quarreled. When I left, he screamed after me.

"So go ahead, go to Palestine, such a Jewish Goy you are already!"

But of course, had I really wanted to go, I shouldn't have been talking so much about it.

Once upon a time, as the story goes, on a Shabbat evening, a holy rabbi was walking with his pupils in the hills near Tzfat. The rabbi said, "Let's fly to Jerusalem; the Messiah is there."

The pupils began to argue. Some were ready to obey, but others objected: "Why, are we birds that we should fly? Anyone knows that men can't fly; the rabbi must be going soft in his old age, and Jerusalem is far, far away over the hills. Even if we did fly, we should never reach her before the sunset brings the Shabbat. In any case, it's too dangerous a journey to be undertaken like that, at least let's take leave from our wives and children."

They argued back and forth for a long time. The holy rabbi listened patiently. Finally, he sighed and said, "What a pity, while you were arguing, the Messiah went away."

Oh yes, the Jews are very fond of arguing in times of emergency.

There was always a reason not to go.

"We should go to Palestine? But look here, the British have limited immigration so drastically, let those in danger go."

"Dose in danger come foist,"

"We should like to go, but we're more useful here. What would happen if we all left our posts?"

"At my age, what could I do there? I'm too old."

"I'd go if my family went. But I'm too young."

"Of course, there are those who have no choice."

I didn't go to Palestine: therefore, I didn't wish to go.

I didn't work in the laundry anymore because I had found a clerical job in a lawyer's office. My boss was talking about giving me time off to attend law school.

"You should," Violet said, "but don't be grateful. Law school in your spare time takes a long time to go through. He's just figuring a way to tie you down at a low salary."

True, my boss had a squint to his eyes and a slippery mind.

The girls in the laundry had been sad to see me go.

"You'll get better help, a big man with big hands who can do a lot of work," I said to them, but they shrugged this off.

"Who cares about the work? We liked you, Bruno, it's good for you that you're getting out, but we'll miss you; we liked you a lot."

"Your small hands were awfully good at shaking aprons," said one of them.

It was a nice thing to say. Nobody had said anything nicer to me in a long time. Suddenly I felt that I was losing something I had never known I possessed. They hugged me. Some kissed me; some wiped their eyes. What was I taking away that they should miss? Perhaps the scent of a life they would never live—old polished wood and leather, pine smoke, expensive wine, choice silk, money, and leisure—the scent of it still clung to me.

The steam of the washing machines rose through the loose flooring matching the fog out on the Hudson; a dispiriting, nauseating smell of dirty linen hung in the steam. The girls had pale moist skins and stringy hair. They stared at me out of hopeless eyes and waved their chapped hands.

"Good-bye, Bruno, remember us."

I walked out.

"Remember us, Bruno, call on us once in a while."

Louse that I am, I never did.

Violet was happy about my new job.

"Now you're settling down. You'll go to law school. You're brilliant, I know. You'll go far. And I'll be the smart suburban wife of a rising young lawyer."

I told her that I couldn't stand her people. She didn't look offended.

"What is it that you don't like about them?"

"Everything. The smell of garlic. They'll wear hired tuxedos at morning marriages and maybe take their coats off. Their speech is as thick as their greasy soup; they smack their tongues over awful fish jelly; they're incredibly ignorant. They're either bigoted or foolishly imitative. But above all, they're insecure, and their souls are as ingrained with fear—causeless, pure, self-sustaining, vacuum-packed fear as coal miners' hands with black dust."

I said all this, and I didn't quite mean it, but she laughed.

"All right, we won't live among them. There are better social circles." She watched me cunningly to make sure that I had caught the "we." "But those are Jewish defects, you know. In Palestine, you'd be among exactly that kind of people."

Soon I became sick of all the planning about jobs, a career, fine social circles, maybe finding our way into places where Jews are not wanted. I preferred to talk about Palestine. Palestine was unreal, a thin, unsubstantial dream. But life with Violet could become nightmarishly concrete.

"Don't you want nice things?" Violet asked.

"I'm a snotty bastard."

"I know."

"Then why stick with me?"

"Could be I'm in love with you."

It hadn't occurred to me. I stared at Violet and saw that her eyes had a sick, hurt look. Their color was indeed the color of violets, the kind of violets that grow bashfully on edges along country roads—apologetic flowers, slightly dusty from the nearness of traffic. Her eyes were too bright, moistly bright. *God help me*, I thought, *it's true*. More than anything else, I wished I could say to her, "I love you too." She was waiting for it, ready to believe it, willing me to say it, but I could not. After a while, she sighed and turned her back on me.

She stood in front of the open window. We were in my room, and I remembered her standing on the same spot, our first night, and saying, "It feels lonely up here, it feels kind of desperate," but all was different now, now it was springtime. There was a hum in the air. Walking in the city streets, one seemed to perceive a life vibrating under the city pavements. It was like an infinite number of tiny lives stirred, pressed against the hard concrete shell to break through to the sunlight. The sunlight flowed between the rows of houses, in the narrow cleft of the street, like a warm honey-colored stream. We had felt a little tipsy walking side-by-side, so close that our hips rubbed together, then she had run upstairs ahead of me, her fine clean legs dancing up the steps, and I had become tight with desire.

But I wouldn't tell her the lie that she wanted to hear. She turned around, walked to the bed, took her clothes off.

"Come on."

I felt ashamed of making love to her, but I did.

"We should go away, to someplace where life's still simple, where you lie in the sun, and when you're hungry, you climb a tree and pluck the fruit," I said afterward.

"I bet I'd be the one to pluck the fruit," she said.

"No, I shouldn't allow you to do any work at all. You're nothing but a sex object. You'll eat the fruit, run and swim, make love, sleep."

"What if civilization caught up with us?"

"Then we should just die. Why twist ourselves into the crazy frames society dreams up for us?"

A shaft of sunlight came through the window. Particles of dust and lint floated into it and lighted up. It was an early Sunday afternoon, a spring afternoon tepid and bright, and we couldn't sleep. There was a card near the door on the floor. I hadn't noticed it; it must have lain there a day or more. We had stepped on it, but it was intact and very readable. It was a draft card. She took it out of my hands, looked at it for a long time, and then she laughed harshly.

"The U.S. Army riding to the rescue?"

I shrugged, "Sooner or later…"

"I bet you're glad."

"All right, I'm glad. Because I'll be active, finally."

"Take me home," she said.

It was a long ride to her Bronx station, and we didn't talk. We went out of the station, walked up to her house, and stopped at the door. We looked at each other. There was a hard shell of silence around her that I wanted to pierce.

"What about tomorrow?" I asked.

"Is there going to be a tomorrow?"

"I don't know what to say."

"Is there anything to say?"

"There should be. You've meant a lot to me."

"Then tell me one thing. Are you coming back to me?"

I didn't answer.

"Answer me! Are you coming back when you get out, a year or two or five years from now, however long, are you or are you not?"

"I don't think so. I'd like to say yes," I answered. "I know it would be the thing to say, but honestly, I can't. Honestly, I don't think so."

Then she slapped my face, her hand as hard and heavy as a man's.

"You lousy bastard!"

My eyes stung with the blow.

"Don't feel bitter about it," I said, "it wouldn't have worked out."

She began to cry. She cried stonily, without expression, tears running down her face's fine hard lines like drops of rain. I remembered the raindrops on her face the night we had met; the first night we had made love when we had run home. She was flushed and hot like a filly steaming from a good hard run in the rain. Now her face was stony, the skin pale and tight on its delicate bones. I put out my hand and touched my fingertips to her cheek, and it felt ice-cold. I wished she would turn her back on me and go inside, but she stood there; I had to walk away and leave her standing there.

But I didn't go home. I knew it wouldn't be my home much longer, but it still had the power of making me uneasy when I was alone, and now I felt very much alone. Something had gone out of my life; something had been shattered. I had shattered it, and there was nothing left but debris. I ate, I went to the movies, I killed time. It isn't easy to kill time alone in New York on a Sunday evening. Then it got dark. I walked the streets; a chill had set in with the evening; I wasn't dressed for it, and I shivered. I shivered, and I thought, *what is all this about?*

I didn't love her, but we had made good love. She was a capable girl, a tough girl. It's good to be tough, and she would have helped me. She would have managed me a little, but perhaps I needed managing. She would have turned a low-paid office clerk into a rising young lawyer with a fine suburban home. I would have been socially and financially successful, moving in the best Jewish circles and someday in circles in which acceptance is a great prize for a Jew indeed. What was wrong with all that? Oh, I knew damned well what was wrong, but had I any better hopes? Of course not.

Then why, in the name of God, why had I not told her, "I love you, I'm coming back to you someday, in a year or two or five, who knows, if I live through the war, I'm coming back to you."

Why?

I wandered through the darkened streets. It got chillier, and I shivered in my inadequate clothes. I saw a man lying in an unlighted doorway. I walked up to him and touched him; he felt rigid and cold. I struck a match. Now I could see that the man was dead. I stood looking down at him. He had been a small man, thin-boned and skinny, his clothes frayed, a stubble of beard on his receding chin. He lay there as if he had gone to sleep and forgotten to wake up. He looked brittle and light, lying there, like a fallen sparrow.

As a boy, I'd seen farmers shoot down sparrows. They fell and lay like this on the ground, brittle and light, but the ground was grassy and fragrant earth, not a hard, sooty, artificial surface. I had a crazy thought. I felt like picking the little man up and cradling him in my arms. I could have done it without effort, he looked so light, and I was sure that nobody would miss him. Little men like him disappear from the city pavements like coins dropped through a grate into the sewer, so I could carry him away from the city and lay him somewhere on grassy, fragrant earth. As spring grew, he would gradually melt away into the ground, and by summertime, he would be in the grass blades and the flowers of the grass, in bright, live, fragrant things. But it was against the law—so many acts of love are against the law. I went into a bar and called the police, and then I started to drink. Soon I was quite drunk. I hadn't been drunk for a long time, but now it seemed the right thing to do.

I lay my arms on the table and my head on my arms. I fell into a half-conscious stupor. Memories came to me, fuzzy, puzzling, drunken memories, with a lot of light and sound to them. Children running, scuffling, monkey chattering. Footprints in wet sand, the surf coming in, sucking the sand from under my feet, the tingling feel of the sandy water running out between my toes. Foam riding the crests of waves as they neared the shore. Birds screaming against the sky, their screams half complaining, half summons. When was all this, and where?

"Bruno!"

Who's calling me?

"Bruno, come here!"

I don't want to answer. I don't want to go back; I want to get away. There's a sharp blue line out there and infinity beyond it. But I can't swim, and I don't have a boat.

"Bruno!"

I can only hide. I'll dig into the sand and bury myself, only my face sticking out, so nobody will ever find me, but I'll be able to look out to sea. Now I'm hiding, but someday I'll get away.

See if I don't.

CHAPTER SEVEN

One of the tricks my memory plays on me is the story of Herman. This story has been with me for a long time, and I know everything about it, except whence and how it has come to me. First of all, I see Herman getting out of his bunk before reveille. His equipment rifle, canteen, mess kit, gas mask, and all the rest have been very neatly laid out, but by someone else, because really old soldiers like him are seldom neat. Herman stands a while looking at his bunk, listening to the others' snoring. Then he shuffles out of the pyramidal tent into the shivering darkness of an unfinished night. It's cold outside, cold and damp; the tent has been pitched on the slope of a wooded foothill, under towering fir trees. Herman curses under his breath. He curses the woods' rheumatic dampness and the tangled roots that make digging so hard. Even digging a shit trench, narrow enough to be straddled by a short-legged man, is a pain in the neck, in this kind of ground. He curses the pine needles, which are so ready to ignite that a soldier cannot make a fire to warm his hands or roast a slice of beef if he has gotten hold of a bottle of moonshine and needs to steady his stomach. Most of all, he curses the chiggers, which get under a man's skin, making it break out in hard itchy, burning sore welts that one cannot help kneading and scratching. The only way to kill the chigger for sure is to cut the skin with a razor blade, a deep cross-shaped cut, and pour iodine into the cut.

Herman stands there a while, shivering and cursing under his breath, and then he smells coffee. He walks into the kitchen tent. The Sergeant of the Guard is drinking coffee from his canteen cup. The Mess Sergeant is cooking himself a breakfast of pancakes and bacon. The bacon curls and browns on a hot plate, giving out a pleasant fatty smell, which overcomes the fir trees' dank night scent. It's warm and comfortable, standing in front of the stone rubbing one's hands.

Herman says, "Boy, this is the day, I'm going to blow this Goddam outfit to hell unless my discharge comes through pronto."

The Mess Sergeant sighs, "Yeah, sure."

"It's been so many years, and everyone else who was drafted with me, every last sonofabitch but me, has gone home long ago. Hell, it feels like they'd chucked me down a fucking well and covered it up."

"Yeah, sure, Herman, you're right, we old-timers feel for you, but sometimes ... Well, I don't know about these things, but I guess no one here can do much about it. Maybe your papers got lost somewhere on the way to Washington or got into the wrong pigeon hole. It could be hell to straighten it out."

It is evident that this conversation has been repeated many times. Perhaps it's repeated every morning before reveille, and to the Mess Sergeant, it has become as monotonous and inevitable as his breakfast of pancakes and bacon. Then reveille sounds. The men stir in their tents, come outside rubbing their eyes, walk in turn to the water faucets and the latrines, cursing the cold and the dampness.

Later Herman watches the roll call, the calisthenics, the morning chow, the drill. He does not take part in any of them—he's a privileged character. He stands to one side, leaning against a tree, almost sunk into the bark of the tree. The sun rises slowly and shines between the branches; an early sun casts long, deep shadows. Herman is almost invisible in those shadows. Herman's name is not on the roll. Sometimes he does line up, but he stands anywhere he pleases, and no one seems to notice. He does it just for the hell of it. Herman hates foot drill; he has never been good at it; he doesn't like hikes either. He doesn't have to do any of those things; he's a veteran from way back and has shed his blood; he has a Purple Heart.

"Come on, get the head out of your arses, let's move!"

The whole company goes on a hike with full gear, and only the First Sergeant stays in. He's a career soldier and as much of a veteran as Herman. Herman is happy he doesn't have to go, but he doesn't like the mournful quiet, which descends on the camp when the boys have gone. Indeed work's hell, but while you are working, you don't think, and as soon as this quiet descends, you realize that you are trapped in a quagmire which does not suck you down but holds you fast. All you can manage is to keep your head out and breathe, stand still, and breathe. Trees, too, stand still and breathe, but they are built that way, and it satisfies them.

Most of the boys will go home soon, and they don't feel trapped, but others have to stay because they have nowhere else to go. Or, like Herman, because their papers have been mislaid somewhere and their discharge doesn't come through.

Herman barges into the orderly tent. The First Sergeant has white hair, precociously white, and his skin has the red-gray hue of California red pine wood that has been out in the weather for some years.

"I want my discharge," Herman says.

"Herman, Herman..."

"How many years is it? Twenty, thirty? I even forget how many years of this stinking life. All the others come and go, only me ..."

"Herman, we keep saying the same things over and over. What can I do? You know I can't do nothing. Your papers are in Washington,"

"You sure you sent them through?"

"Herman, I'm your friend," the First Sergeant sighs.

Herman leaves the tent. The camp is oppressively silent now, so silent he can't stand it one minute longer. He walks away, gets into the thick of the woods, wanders at random, but driven by urgency, almost running. It's the only way not to think, and after a while, a kind of numbness seizes him, everything blurs, he forgets his discharge, which is not coming through, and that the others are going home. He forgets where he is and his age, even his name.

He goes on like that for a long time. Nobody looks for him—he's a privileged character. When he gets back to camp, the men are in from the hike. Herman notices a young recruit, who reminds him a little of himself when he was a boy. The recruit looks hot and tired, he's drinking greedily from a beer bottle, and that's a mistake.

"Hey, you," cries Herman, "cut it out!"

The boy turns around, drops the bottle, and watches Herman with popping eyes.

Someone laughs. "Don't you know our Herman?"

The boy nods.

"Don't drink so fast; you'll puke," Herman says.

The boy walks away, but Herman follows him and talks to him in a ... kind way. He feels a sudden liking for this boy and wants to help him. After a while, he's telling stories about the Second World War, especially about Okinawa, the last place, the last battle he remembers.

"You've been around ever since?" the boy asks.

"Oh, sure, I could tell you the name of every officer and soldier this Company's had since Okinawa. But my discharge will come through pretty soon. And then I'll go back ..." he falters, "I'll go back ..."

"Back to what?" the boy prods him.

Now Herman is annoyed, he shouts, "To what I Goddam please! It's my own fucking business! I remember ..."

But in truth, he doesn't remember anything, he doesn't know what he can go back to, and because he hates to admit it, he stalks away angrily, mumbling to himself. The boy stops the First Sergeant who's passing by.

"Sergeant, can't you do something for Herman?"

The First Sergeant looks at him in silence.

"Do what?" he says after a while. "Can I get a discharge for a soldier who's been dead twenty, thirty years?" Then his voice softens. "And d'you think he'd know where to go if he could, poor old Herman?"

That is Herman's story. Where does it come from? Did I read it or hear it from somebody? I don't think so. There's an element of identification between Herman and myself. Of course, I'm not a ghost, and I did get my discharge. Yet, I am Herman, no doubt about it. The identification between Herman and myself is too strong for the story to have originated outside me.

A dream, then?

But dreams are never so clear-cut, so consistent. Once the act of dreaming is over, they become pliable, their details are easily blurred, and they change. At the same time, Herman's story remains itself, immutable even in the minor details. It is immutable in its locale (I'm sure it's the North Carolina fir woods). However, it seems to drift along in time as I grow older. I have no control over it. I merely watch it happen, in obstinate pedantic repetition, again and again. And why the name Herman? It carries no significance to me. I never knew anybody by that name. I certainly can't associate it with myself, and such a prosaic name, right for a German shopkeeper. How absurd to be haunted by a ghost called Herman.

Once I thought I could get rid of Herman if I wrote a book about him, that by so doing, I would gain mastery over him and finally exorcise him. I imagined an American army unit somewhere in a war zone, say Vietnam or Cambodia, the men in it seeing Herman and talking to him. Of course, Herman doesn't exist; he is the projection of each man's frustrations and yearnings, of his sickness with military life, of his rebellion against the war. And I asked myself, what could one do with a unit like that? Herman might well be dangerous, the germ of some disruptive contagious disease of the soldier's soul. The only thing would be to march the unit off to the hottest combat zone and have everybody in it honorably killed off. I got excited thinking about all this. If I knew Herman, this was a book that would write itself.

I talked to a friend in the publishing business. He told me, "It's a fine idea, the book could be a success; it has the only feature needed today, you can turn it into a 'hate America' book." He said, "That's the way the wind blows. If you hit out at America, you'll make many friends—people who feel that way and people who don't but have learned that there's a lot to be gained and nothing to be lost by it. America doesn't hit back; indeed, her policy is to court her enemies and to hell with her friends. They're her friends already, and that's that, but her enemies must be courted so they'll be a little less mad at her, she hopes. And this," he said, "has been going on for a long time. Our young people have never read a magazine or a book or watched a movie or a TV show that didn't knock the U.S.A. Americans do it to prove that they are liberal and have open, self-critical minds. Our young people have been told that there's white and black in this world, and the black is the U.S.A. They have been told so, day in and day out, by people who don't believe a word of it but are ambitious or merely have families to support. And what do you expect after such daily brainwashing? Oh yes, write a 'hate America' book, and you'll do all right for yourself. So you owe the U.S.A. some gratitude, so what? Every European does, more or less, but is this stopping anyone? Should you worry about being fair to America, if she herself does not?"

I heard him, and I did not write a book about Herman.

CHAPTER EIGHT

Like Herman, I camped in the Carolina fir woods, and like him, I got up in the shivering darkness of unfinished nights. I never slept well, and in the morning, I walked over crunching carpets of dry pine needles toward the smell of early coffee. I liked the cold hour before dawn because it was my own. It was an hour ignored by the military routine; that routine, like the endless repetition of a falling drop, can wear away a stone or drive a man crazy.

Yet, at the time, I felt that I fit in. I was different from the others only because mine was a Southern outfit, and I was a damnyankee. It didn't matter that I was a Jew and an Italian, but my being both puzzled my comrades no end. I had to fight for furloughs on the Jewish holidays ("Go on, who're you trying to snow," they would say, "you're no Jew, you're a Eyetalian"). But my being Jewish and Italian was secondary. The sore point was my being from the North, and the others kept a sharp lookout for any sign of "niggerloving" on my part. They were a tough, violent bunch, and it was dangerous to cross them. But I had been silent enough. I had been afraid enough and hid enough, back "in the old country." Here I refused to yield even a shred of my dignity.

Sometimes at night, we sat about a fire in a clearing of the woods. We had swept the pine needles as far away as we could and gathered them where we could make them into thick, springy rustling mats to lay our bedding upon. We drank hard out of jugs of colorless fiery moonshine. We stuck thick slices of beef on the tip of forked branches and cooked them over the fire, the fat dripping and crackling in the flame. Someone always had marshmallows to roast; roasting marshmallows seemed to be a most incongruous occupation for these violent half-drunk men. After a while, fights would break out over nothing at all. At dawn, we would pick up the battered dregs of the fights, unconscious blood-encrusted men snoring breathlessly in puddles of dry vomit. "Let's see who's the better man," they cried when squaring off against one another. Because to simple men, all customary phrases are magic formulae and create reality, the stronger man was the "better" one and his victory, the proof of his right. They had been fed on popular fiction, in which the hero is always stronger than the villain and proves his goodness by the battering impact of his fists.

Nearly all the men in my outfit were Southerners, from the Carolinas, Georgia, Tennessee. Some were mere kids. One of them kept telling me how he had watched Superman fly over a dam, which had burst, and put it right. He was not stupid at all, but he was only a kid and had not yet broken away from fairy tales. There were many like him. When we sat around the fire, sooner or later, the talk would veer to Negroes. Every one of them had reminiscences of fabulous sex with a "high-yellow" girl. Most of them had a sister, a Negro had just looked at her, and they had beaten him up.

"I nearly killed that sonofabitch," one said.

"Wasn't that a little excessive?" I said.

"If he'd gone within ten feet of her, I'd have killed him. What're you anyway, a fucking nigger-lover?"

"Oh, he's a damnyankee."

They all stared at me, a circle of hard, hostile, moonshine-bleared eyes, menacingly lit up by the dancing glow of the fire.

"Say, maybe you think a nigger's as good as a white man."

I didn't answer.

"By God, you've got to answer, you damnyankee, yes or no?"

Well, I thought, this is it.

"I believe that any man is as good as any other," I said.

A dead silence fell, a motionless expectant silence. I heard the pine branches snap and crackle in the fire, the tang of rosin dame sweet and sharp to my nostrils. I remembered the woodchuck I had freed from a trap that very morning and how its muzzle had twitched as if it were trying to perceive some faint distant scent. I felt my lips twitching in somewhat the same way. Then one of the older men, a master sergeant, spoke.

"We'll let that pass because we know you. You're a good guy; you're not really a nigger-lover, you just don't know niggers," he said.

Someone laughed, everybody stirred, the moonshine jugs were passed around, my blasphemy was forgotten. Later I thanked the master sergeant.

"Mac, if you hadn't spoken up when you did, all it needed was for someone to lift a hand, and there wouldn't have been one sound bone left in my body," I said.

He nodded. "Yeah, they didn't want to do it, you know, the men like you. That's why I could stop them. I don't think anybody else could have gotten away with it. They didn't want to, but they would've had to do it. What possessed you to make such a damnfool statement, anyway?"

"They asked me a question."

"I see. Well, it took guts, but it still was a damnfool thing to do."

Mac was an old-timer; nobody knew his age. He had a fleshless, wizened, wiry body that might have been forty or sixty. He was an outstanding soldier but a drunkard; he would keep sober for a while, shoot up in grade, and then go on a roaring drunk and be broken down to private.

"Let me tell you something," said Mac. "You're a Jew, and maybe you think that because your people have been discriminated against, they should feel for the Negroes. Well, don't you make any mistakes: if the Negroes become emancipated, they'll turn against the Jews. The better off they are, the more antisemitic they'll become. You Jews may be full of sympathy and fellowship toward them, but believe me, that won't cut no ice. People who have been oppressed—between us, I'll admit that the Negroes are oppressed. I ain't no ignorant bastard like the others, though I understand them, too, mind you, they have their reasons—people who've been oppressed don't turn against their oppressors, their oppressors are too distant, too invulnerable, they turn against those closest to them, those who are just a little better off than they."

"Mac, I understand all this," I replied. "Maybe you're right, but it doesn't make one bit of difference. Listen, once I was out on a walk and I came to a railway crossing. There was an old man, a white man. I fell to talking with him. After a while, a Negro came walking along the tracks. I think he was looking for junk, scraps, anything he could salvage and use or sell for a few cents. As he neared the crossing, he picked up an empty bottle. The white man saw him, called out to him, 'Boy, come here,' the Negro pretended not to hear. The other called out again, 'Boy, I'm talking to you, come over and give me what you just picked up.' The Negro shuffled over, reluctantly, handed over the empty bottle. The white man said, 'Go on, go away,' and he went away. You see, it wouldn't have been so bad if the white man had walked over and taken the bottle, but no, he made the Negro bring it to him, as one would whistle to a dog to fetch what it has retrieved. By so doing, he robbed the Negro of all human substance. I couldn't stand his callous bullishness and the Negro's submissiveness. As long as that Negro is denied his manhood, I'm not sure of mine. Maybe someday he'll become my enemy for no reason at all, as you say, but I don't care. I don't want to be spared an enemy at such a price."

"You're a damned fool," Mac said.

He never revealed much about himself. There had been some tragic violence in his past, at which he only hinted, yet he was a gentle man. Before being transferred to our company, he had served a long sentence for shooting at another soldier. After we had become friends, he told me about it.

"The captain called me in and asked me, 'Where were you when you shot at the man?' and I answered, 'We were sitting on a bench next to one another.' And he said, 'You were sitting on the same bench and didn't hit him?' 'Yes,' I admitted. 'Man, you're a lousy shot.' That's all he ever said about it. But you know, actually, I'm a very good shot. The truth is I didn't want to hit the man, though at the court-martial, they tried to make out that I couldn't shoot straight because I was drunk."

One day he received the news that his mother was dying. I found him sitting on his bunk, and he was crying. He told me he had refused a furlough.

I asked him why.

"I can't damn you, I can't go home," he shouted. Then he rushed out of the barracks.

The next morning, I heard that he had been taken into custody and would be court-martialed on charges of inciting men to desertion and insulting an officer. He pleaded not guilty to the first charge and guilty to the second.

"Tell us what happened," they asked him.

"Yes, Sir. I was coming back into camp with other men. We had drunk more than was good for us, perhaps, and we were noisy. We ran across Lieutenant O'Hara, and he said to me, 'Take my advice, Sergeant, go on in and sleep it off.' And I said to him, 'Sir, you can take your advice and stick it up your arse.' I'm sorry I said it, but at the time, with all respect, Sir, I thought he had it coming."

"What do you mean by that?"

"Well, Sir, consider that I had drunk a little, and Lieutenant O'Hara's a very young man. Of course, he could have given me an order, he's an officer, but I didn't think he was qualified to offer advice to a much older man like myself."

"An officer is always qualified to give advice to non-commissioned personnel."

"I was only relating what I thought at the time. Sir."

"Did you incite the men to desert?"

"Certainly not, Sir."

"According to the prosecution, you said, 'Men, let's go.'"

"I meant, let's go to the PX and have a Coke. I felt very thirsty, Sir."

Defense counsel gave Lieutenant O'Hara a hard time.

"What do you mean by saying that the accused incited other men to desertion?"

"Well, he did say, 'Let's go,' and he enjoys a lot of prestige with the other men."

"The accused stated that he meant, 'Let's go to the PX and have a Coke.' How do you know he didn't mean exactly that?"

"Well, it didn't sound that way to me ..."

Mac was acquitted of the first charge and found guilty of telling the Lieutenant to take his advice and stick it up his arse. After six months in the stockade, he was back with us.

CHAPTER NINE

At the bottom of an old wardrobe trunk, I found a stack of letters I forgot to destroy. They are almost thirty years old, dry, and discolored like a camphor-scented bouquet fallen from the folds of a grandmother's wedding dress. They are written on a liver-colored paper that was once azure, they are neatly dated, and they are neatly signed "Sue." The seal of a girls' college is engraved at the top of most sheets.

"Dear Bruno," one letter says, "Although I haven't the time to write a complete letter, I took advantage of tonight's few idle hours to say 'Hello!' I'm sorely disappointed that our date continues to be postponed until, perhaps, the 'clammy locusts' (?) are in season! (And please inform me when they are, for I have no idea)."

Well, Sue, you have me there. I certainly couldn't tell you. I have completely forgotten what the clammy locusts are and what I wrote to you about them—some nonsense, of course, to amuse you, so that I could picture your fresh young mouth blossoming into laughter. I wonder if you guessed that I should postpone "our date" forever. I suppose you did; it should have been apparent that I couldn't do otherwise. Oh, you tried your best, and don't think that your naive seductiveness was not fetching. Often it was irresistible, but luckily for both of us, I was far away, at times many thousands of miles away across the water, always in an altogether different world from yours.

But the letter continues …

"Even if I do succeed in getting married by then, I will never turn down the date I have with you. Even if it causes divorce or other family disruption, I'd forfeit, gladly …

"Have you ever really watched a Carolina moon? Last week that ole celestial ball was a sight to behold. It is never so pretty as when seen coming through a Carolina long-leaf. I saw it for 16 months climbing Ga. mountains, but it looked bare and out of place even at that. I know of a favorite haunt that I frequent when the moon is full. Shall I show you that too—when?"

We had a weekend leave, and one of my boys (I was a buck sergeant then) was going home. He asked me to join him, he was from a North Carolina town, but we were camping out in Tennessee at the time. It wasn't such a short trip, so we arrived in the early morning and sat down to a breakfast of eggs, sausage and grits. His parents asked if we should like to attend the Sunday church picnic. The boy shook his head warningly at me; I said, "No, thanks," but I was disappointed.

"What do you want with a fucking church picnic, anyway," later he explained. "There's a honky-tonk right out of town where we can get plenty of hard likker and a couple of women."

I could picture the "women" blowzy, or sallow-skinned, sagging whores.

"You go to hell," I said to him, then I apologized to his parents and told them I should love to go.

I met Sue at the church picnic. But it was such a fleeting encounter that I have no visual recollection of it. All I know about what she looked like is from the letters I forgot to destroy, and there were some photographs too, but those must have crumbled away a long time ago. I think that we barely touched hands and exchanged a few words. She had heard about me from the men in my company. I have a vague recollection of a pleasant smile on an unmade-up face, a bunch of black curls, a sturdy quick-moving body.

"Do you miss your family, your old friends?" she asked.

"There's only my father, and we were not close," I said, "and I've never had friends. When certain things happen, you don't lose your friends; you find you never had any."

"I'll write to you if you like, and if you'll write to me," she said, and she turned suddenly away. There was a shyness in her, which doesn't come through her pert letter writing, and that was the end of our one meeting. I left for overseas—the Solomons—soon after that.

Once I sent her a grass skirt.

"Made some snaps in the grass skirt," she wrote provocatively, "but damn! The wind blew too much ... I'll try again."

And later she wrote again. "The grass skirt adorned every hip in the girls' room. They all borrowed it toward commencement to take shots for their boyfriends. I'll have one for you later. Don't be too disappointed, please. Any defects are due entirely to the skirt or the camera, not to my body!!"

I wanted to send her a pair of Philippino carved wooden sandals, and I jokingly asked if her size was seven and a half. She sent back an indignant inventory of herself.

"How grossly mistaken you are, concerning the measurements of yours truly. You must be correct in a woman's figure. You know, I now weigh 120, much to my regret. I've tried hard enough to reach 127 again and remain there. I have acquired a 39" expansion of hips (darn!), and instead of a neat 25" waist, it's a husky 26". My feet are big, but not that big, I assure you. I wear a 6—and not a 7 1/2, of all sizes! I stand 5'5" even—and wear a 6 ¾ hat. Now don't be so negligent again (or should I say erroneous) about my measurements. You must have had someone else in mind."

I wonder if she was aware of the mating call underlying that playful list of sizes. It was as if she meant me to picture her undressing slowly before a mirror and taking narcissistic stock of herself, calling out, "Come and stand beside me. I am young and desirable; let us admire and fondle me together. You must be hungry for a woman, but that's all you are permitted to do. I will tease you until you are ill with desire, and I can feel your suffering and frustration caressing my skin like the surf of a hot sea." It might have been a wicked game, but it was so ingenuously done that it became innocent.

"Dear Bruno," she wrote in another letter, "I'm on the brink of a six weeks literature test tonight, but I couldn't concentrate on it, somehow. My mind is constantly wandering to the South Pacific—inconsistently, for I 'came to' only to find myself right here in this dull, dreary, drab room of mine, in this hard, uncushioned chair, on such a lovely spring night. I could really be romantic this evening if a proper subject were available for my affections. However, I suppose I can continue dreaming of one inhabitant of the South Pacific and just pretend.

"The night is windy and lonesome as hell, but much warmer than it has been. I like to be at home on nights when the wind blows so fiercely angry. I can go stand out in it and think, think, think. If I've never told you a lonesome wind and penetrating rain are my thinking incentives, I have no other!"

The "clammy locusts" letter is her last. I was back in the U. S. by then, back in New York, at my old clerical job. She set a time and a place for our long-postponed "date."

"Hoping that you may have 'hi-jacked' your bosses into that vacation before the locusts bloom and fade out, I'm going to be bold enough to ask of you a magnificent favor, but one that can be comfortably granted. On March 10, the College's Freshman-Sophomore classes have their traditional banquet at the College. There are several Army camps close by, and I could choose from plenty of escorts, but I prefer one specimen from Upper B'way. So, if a vacation looks promising, will you consider my request? I can think of no other way to entice you southwards than as a banquet escort, I mean!"

I sat a long time with that letter in my hands, staring at it, rereading it, again and again. I thought, why not? Suppose I accept; we don't really know one another, perhaps we shall find that we are two polite strangers who have come together for one evening but perhaps not. We might fall in love, and it might be for keeps; what would be wrong with that, two sincere, honest young people, why not?

Making love to a girl with no ancestral memories of tragedy would be fantastic. She's a girl who has not been born with the crushing' weight of monstrous injustice on her shoulders, who must only forget the harm her fathers have done, not that which they have suffered. How simple, how easy and refreshing, making love to a girl like that. No problem, but to find a job, make a little money, feed one's family blissfully uncomplicated, painless minor issues.

I could picture myself sitting next to her at "the banquet of the Freshman-Sophomore classes," talking about the war. People would be asking about it. It would be ungracious not to answer. Besides, she should wish to be proud of her escort. There is no harm in pleasing her by exaggerating a little by inventing a few plausibly brave deeds and escapes from thrilling dangers. My accent was excellent by then. They wouldn't think of me as of a foreigner but as of a damnyankee. And if they remembered my origin, it would merely lend me a touch of the exotic. Oh, yes, I should have to show off a little, my classic education, my knowledge of languages, my experience in gracious living, to try to charm the other girls. And I thought I could, for one evening at least, so that she could preen herself on having captured me and triumph over her friends who could only boast of home town escorts with crew cuts.

It would all be very innocent, very jejune and not a little silly, but so gently refreshing to my twisted, bruised, aching self. Later we'll walk outside and find some quiet, dark corner to be alone in. We'll watch the moonlight coming through a Carolina long-leaf and be very self-conscious because, after all, we are strangers, though intimate friends in a way. I'll be cautious not to say anything that could embarrass her or hurt her feelings. I'll be very quiet, but this will embarrass her too. All the flush of her social triumph will drain from her cheeks; she'll look away from me and giggle and nervously scrape the ground with the tip of her size-six party shoe. Suddenly she won't know what to say or do; all the pertness and seductiveness bubbling in her letters gone from her, leaving an inexperienced small-town girl standing alone in a quiet, dark corner with a redoubtable stranger from outer space.

Then I'll kiss her. Perhaps she'll tremble a little, though she expected it. I'll feel her clean youthfulness under my hands—is she a virgin? Somehow I think she must be. It would be rather wonderful if she were; it would make it easy for me to tell her that I love her. I have never made love to a virgin, and it might be absurd for me to want to, but I do want to. After that first kiss, everything will be simple. Somehow that kiss will cancel all of my past.

Suddenly there'll be no more weights on my shoulders; it will be so very easy to stand straight and walk confidently among people.

I thought now I knew what has charmed me in her letters, what I had sensed in them that is so precious and rare. I couldn't have named it until now: purity, an absolute purity that is freedom not so much from sin as from pain and rancor. I couldn't explain this to her—one can't explain simplicity any more than one can cut up a single crystal into component pieces. But I'll take her inexpertly manicured hand. She'll try to wiggle it free because she chews her fingernails a little, but I won't let it go. I'll raise it to my lips and kiss it, and that will be all the explanation I can give. She won't quite understand; she'll stare at me with her clear, earnest eyes, now round with surprise. How strange to kiss a girl's hand after you have kissed her mouth, but some of my emotions will get through to her, and then her eyes will mist over, and it will be the sweetest moment of the night.

Yes, I sat a long time with that letter in my hands. But I didn't reply to it. And she never wrote again. I wonder if she cried a little. I hope that she did. I wonder if she ever found out what the clammy locusts are and when they bloom. Are they really things that bloom? And if she ever thought of me when the clammy locusts' blooms were fading. I have forgotten so much; the photographs she sent me have long since crumbled away. It is the merest chance that I found a stack of her letters at the bottom of an old trunk.

And of course, it was impossible. It was in a moment of weariness that I dreamed of it. For a moment, I was weary of looking down my road. For a moment, I imagined that I could escape. All of us Jews have a favorite illusion that they can escape; every one of us has dreamed of it at one time or another; every one of us has asked himself, why not? But it never works.

The purity of being born without a burden of pain and rancor, without the ancestral memory of man's inhumanity, without a burning hunger for justice and an inescapable dedication to justice—that purity is not for us. We find ours, if we have the strength, at the end of our road. We can't look for heaven unless we have first gone through hell.

No, Sue, I couldn't have escorted you to the banquet of your college's Freshman-Sophomore classes. It wasn't "a favor that can be comfortably granted." You might as well have asked me to sprout wings and carry you in my arms in a flight to the stars. And deep down, I didn't want to. I wanted to go all the way down my road. It's mine, such as it is, and even then, confused and tired as I was, I accepted it by walking away from you without looking back. I am only sorry that I didn't get to kiss your inexpertly manicured hand, for a fleeting instant, and see your clear, earnest eyes go round with surprise.

CHAPTER TEN

One night, a Japanese pocket submarine torpedoed one of our ammunition ships in a lagoon off Guadalcanal's shore. Ten thousand tons of TNT burst with a shattering roar, and the compression wave hit us in our tents. The pyramidal tents stretched over frames of two-by-fours in a grove of coconut palm trees. That kind of compression wave has a stupefying impact. It's like a fist striking one's temple; a fist encased in a huge, padded glove making the blow all the more stunning. We dove from our beds in a daze. Coconuts jarred off their high perches in the trees came caroming down and bouncing off the canvases, and bouncing off the skulls of those who had run outside too hastily.

It had barely stopped raining, and frogs croaked lustily in fresh puddles. Drainage was inadequate in that part of the island—rainwater seeped down to some underground impermeable surface and stagnated on top of it. We had become animals of the muck, sloshing our way in a thick layer of slime barely more consistent than quicksand. It soon crusted over, when the sun came out, with sickly crumbling skin, so that our feet mired in the mud while dust flew in our eyes. But, as an Army cartoon character explained, "dat's da conditions dat prevailed."

I was a master sergeant by then, and I had responsibility. I ran out and

LADDER TO THE SKY

began rounding up the men who walked about in a daze. Some had put on their good khakis, had tied their neckties nicely, had forgotten their shoes but not their rifles. Their faces wore the stupid earnestness of the drunk about to pass out,

"Christ, what was it, what happened, Sarge?" one asked in confusion.

"Nothing happened, just a little bang, nothing to do with you, get back to bed," I said.

I had guessed at once what had happened. I pictured a cloud of fragments of steel and flesh scattering about the lagoon. Would there be survivors? Of course not, unless some of the crew happened to be ashore. I had noticed the ship the day before, and it must carry a crew of about seventy. Seventy dead is only a trifle. Still, this is a lousy way to die when you have gone to sleep thinking of unloading the cargo tomorrow and then sailing straight home.

Strangely I thought of New York as "home." I had nothing and no one there, very nearly nothing and no one anywhere. Still, my throat tightened when I heard talk of "home." It was so far away, thousands of miles of water, that it had taken us so long to get here zig-zagging about the ocean to escape submarines. We had been told, "We have no escort but don't worry, boys, with our two engines, we can run faster than any damned Jap submarine. No submarine is going to catch us unless it happens to be sailing across our bow." But right out of San Francisco, one of our engines had broken down, and since then, we had crawled along at twelve knots, zig-zagging crazily like a maimed insect.

I bunked way down in the hold, so far down that the hull flared inwards within reach of my hand. I lay deep underwater, and I could feel a thick slab of sea pressing down on me. When I slept, my chest muscles, the whole machine of my body strained and labored against the imaginary pressure. It would take me a full hour to get on deck in an emergency, so if a submarine caught us, I could never outrun the rush of water through the cloven belly of the hull.

Yes, it had taken us very long, and yet going overseas was a journey downhill, and back home was uphill. Therefore, back home was merely a dream, a thin wisp-like malignant dream to visit you when you couldn't

. 65 .

sleep, to visit you, and sit on your chest choking you.

"Sarge, there's a man lying there, must've been hit," a soldier cried.

"By a coconut, you horse's arse! Were you afraid the Japs had come back? I'll take care of him; you get back into your bunk."

I felt my responsibility, taking pride in being calm, and having understood right away what had happened. Our camp had been set up nicely by the Seabees. The canvas of the tents stretched taut over the wooden frames. The frames reached outwards with their low eaves. I kept butting my head on them—my hair was cut short, and I split my scalp every time, so a network of scabs crisscrossed my scalp. Short ribbons hung from the underside of the canvases to assist in tying them up when folded. We hung bunches of bananas from those ribbons to save them from the rats. But, it was no use—the rats climbed to the canvas and let themselves drop onto the bananas, there to feast at leisure. They were tough, combative rats. We kept a small tomcat, but he was no match for them; he only protected us from the dragonflies, which he cleverly hunted and devoured. Even domestic dragonflies I find disgusting, but the tropical ones are giant. The sun and humidity of the tropics swell all insects to absurd proportions. Tropical insects are thick, rangy, fleshy monsters, nightmare stuff, flies like moths, and moths like birds. Any organic waste turns to maggots at the blink of an eye, to giant tumbling maggots encased in disgustingly serrated skins.

When the Seabees had pulled out, they had left the camp in a mess. Their latrine had stood in the middle of it, and they had pulled it off, leaving a cavernous hole full to the brim with excrement. There was an argument, how to cover it. I suggested laying palm trunks across the pit and piling earth on them, but our First Sergeant said no, a mound of dirt in the middle of the camp doesn't look neat, and he had a better idea. He brought over a dump truck full of loose earth and had the earth dumped into the hole, and of course, it sank to the bottom, and the shit bubbled up and overflowed.

"What do we do now?" he asked in dismay.

"Only one thing we can do," I said. "Let's dig another hole close by, and then send somebody down with a pick to bore a gallery. Part of the shit will flow into the fresh hole, and it will level down, then we can cover everything up with palm trunks and earth."

"Who do we send down?" The First Sergeant asked.

"Someone you don't like," I said. "Tie a rope around his waist, haul him up when he hollers, and maybe we'll be faster than the shit."

What an episode to stick in my memory. But life in a theater of war becomes pretty empty when the enemy has moved away. Its emptiness grows into you like the fingernails in the closed fist of a fakir, it grows into your flesh, and its bite drives you crazy. It's like a Chinese drop torture with acid drops of ever-increasing strength. You feel that you are being robbed of every day that passes. You have been cut up into many thin slices of time, and they are being picked up one by one by a callously indifferent hand and thrown away to rot and turn into fat tumbling maggots. Sometimes you wish there were no more slices left, but no, there are so many, there's such a lot of you to throw away, and it will be all thrown away, slice by slice.

Then, even an ammunition ship's blown up in the lagoon is a change. You ought to be ashamed of yourself, but you aren't sorry that it blew up because that shows things can still happen, and not all the thin slices of time are exactly alike. Covering up the shit hole, that is a landmark too, perhaps, in the flat boundless wasteland of your futile time.

"I wonder what those pocket submarines look like," a soldier said.

"They're fat little things, like pigs made of sheet steel, with two little yellow men inside. They say they lock those men in so they can't get away, to make sure they'll accomplish their mission," another soldier answered.

"They couldn't get back to their mother ship anyhow. Those things haven't enough autonomy, and if they torpedo a ship, the concussion kills them, so they're fucked coming and going."

The island of Guadalcanal is shaped somewhat like a bean, pointing north, a ridge of mountains running along the middle. To the north lies the island of Malaita, where you can find head hunters and cannibals, or at least you could once. We had brought some men over from Malaita and turned them into a team of laborers. Their foreman carried a human head with him. It was a Japanese soldier's head, which looked unnaturally large; it had a shock of wiry black hair, and its face bore an absurdly contented expression. He claimed the Japanese had been a major, but perhaps he was boasting.

"See, these boys know who's gonna win the war; they cut the Japs' heads off!" I commented.

At this, the foreman smiled a glassy smile. Perhaps he did understand. He never laughed; he was a very earnest fellow.

On their first day on Guadalcanal, an ammunition dump blew up. The men from Malaita took to their heels. We found them days later at the northernmost tip of the island, looking wistfully out to sea. We brought them back. They were ugly fellows, their skins dull dark mahogany, their teeth ebony black, and their saliva crimson from chewing betel. Their lives were ephemeral: at thirty, they were old men, and not much later, they died. The shortness of their life span somehow deprived them of full human stature. Had I been told that their mothers didn't bother to carry them for a full nine months, I shouldn't have been surprised. Mosquitoes pricked them and filled them with diseases—sometimes their testicles swelled to the size of watermelons. I asked what did they do then, and I got no answer. I suppose they cut them off.

They were the first primitive people I had ever known. It comes as a shock when one meets primitives. How little is required to make up a man, into how small a space can man's likeness to God be compressed. It takes an act of faith to accept that we are the same animal; that it isn't a question of "what" but only of "how."

We talked with the natives in pidgin English. If they wanted to find out how far it was from where we stood to the beach, they would ask, "Suppose we lose 'eem here along too-light, bye-'n-bye sun 'ee stop where, now we come up along beach?"

Time to them was only an arc, the travel of the sun in the sky. Their time stood still when the sun set and began again at its rise. At sunrise, the cock crows—they said, "Number one pigeon, 'ee cries"—man stands up from his couch of dried leaves, it's time to act once again. Man's actions are tuned to the rhythm of the sun's travel in the sky. In a rhythmical, pulsating time, each moment is self-contained, its happiness or unhappiness enclosed within it. If one feels pain or hunger, one gets up and goes in search of relief. Perhaps that's how man was meant to live, in serene disjointed successive cocoons of time, and that's the Garden of Eden.

My Malaitan friends had a name for man as food—the "long pig." Of course, the foreman said, they didn't eat long pig anymore; it was a thing of the past. He bared black fangs in an ingratiating leer, coughed, and darted a jet of crimson spittle. I wondered whether he was lying, whether somehow he felt I should disapprove of his eating long pig. As I was a member of that powerful body, the U. S. Army, he bowed to my prejudices. But as to human heads, he was quite sincere about them. Obviously, he couldn't even conceive that anyone might disapprove of his collecting things so valuable, imbued with strong magic.

"Come on," I teased him, "be honest. What happened to the body that went with the head you're carrying? Don't tell me it went to waste."

Oh yes, he claimed, though, of course, it was a pity. If you eat a good warrior, you assimilate his virtues; therefore, women should never be eaten. Captured women should be tied to a tree and allowed to die by themselves so as not to pollute their conquerors. Of course, such things were done a long, long time ago, now no more, on Malaita, he assured me. My Malaitan friend had undoubtedly solved the problem of the owner of the head he was carrying, to his if not to the head's satisfaction.

Sometimes he eyed me speculatively. Army food had filled me out, and I looked like a fine long pig indeed. But the Americans were too strong, and one dared not attempt to solve the American problem by assimilation.

At night, I stood on the shore of the lagoon and watched men fishing the pieces of the ammunition ship's crew out of the water. They looked like morsels fallen from a giant cannibal's jaws, shredded, chewed-up lumps of tissue. The fish had been at them. The stench was unbearable, and the pieces were quickly dumped into big trench-like graves and covered up. It was useless to try sorting them out. A fat, cheesy, low hanging moon shone a sickly yellow over the proceedings, putting a rancid hue on the beach's crushed coral. The coral crunched resentfully under the wet boots of the men who climbed from the shore to the graves, grunting and swearing under their grisly loads. They had been allowed to drink on this job and kept taking deep gurgling swallows from flat whisky flasks. They were all volunteers doing it for the sake of a day off. I admired their steadiness (or was it callousness), but there's something obscene about a mortician's job. It reminds one of Shakespearean clowns coarsely jesting from newly dug graves. Handling dead flesh defiles it, and no man should touch it—it should revert to earth in mysterious remote isolation.

Somewhere, off in his tent, the Malaitan foreman fondled his Japanese's head, grooming it, crooning to it. Then he would carry it outside and hold it aloft, and the moon would lean down to mirror herself in the head. Up north, on Malaita, the heads were stuck on poles about a chief's hut, tilted to expose their gaping orbits to the moon, and a subdued humming, like the vibration of tight wires in the wind, came from their gaping mouths. The chief's hut nestled in a shell of power; the village warriors dreamed of a day when they too would be surrounded by humming heads tilting their orbits and mouths to the moon.

I thought of the pocket submarine floating somewhere, suspended midway between the bottom and the surface of the ocean, a fat sheet-steel pig carrying two small dead yellow men in its belly. The big bulldozers sometimes dug up Japanese bones already dried and polished like fossils. Some soldiers cut and ground themselves rings from the hip bones. It wasn't as disgusting as it sounds because those bones seemed to bear no relationship to anything that had ever been alive. Perhaps the sub had sunk to the bottom, but no, probably it had floated to the surface instead and been washed by the surf onto a deserted stretch of coral beach. I wondered how the two dead men inside looked by now. Probably they were slumped over whatever controls were inside, their bodies leaning over only as much as the cramped space allowed. Blood had trickled from their mouths and nostrils out of blood vessels shattered by the impact of the concussion wave. Their eyes were bloodshot and glassily staring at a host of unasked unanswerable questions. The sub nestled in a sheltered cove; wreckages always wind up in calm waters, slowly gently rocked by a lapping edge of the surf. The bottom of its piggish belly rested on coral sand, such as the sand under my feet, beneath the same fat, sickly yellowish moon.

The tide was retreating, leaving a litter of trash behind it. Among the debris, I saw a man's hand, torn off barely above the wrist. The tear was jagged; shreds of skin, filaments of tendons, and blood vessels trailed from it. I picked it up. It was a large left hand, brown work-roughened fingers hooked in a futile grasping gesture, a big opal ring on the ring finger. I carried it up to the graveyard.

"Here's one more piece, boys," I told the volunteer morticians.

"Hey, Sarge, what're you doing here? Bucking for the strong stomach detail?"

I shrugged. "I'm not sleepy."

"Oh, we thought maybe you were a fucking corpse lover," one said.

When I lay down to sleep at night, my heart always began to hammer, and it thumped hollowly as loud as a drum beat. It shook my chest so much I couldn't breathe; I gagged, the blood rushed and crashed in my ears. Finally, I had to get up, dressed quietly, and sneaked out of the camp,

I took long walks, went to the beach, sometimes I undressed and dove from a rock. I knew it was dangerous because malaria mosquitoes came out at sundown. Still, somehow malaria seemed a minor threat. We were supposed to swallow atabrine tablets, which dyed one's skin saffron yellow. I had turned out to be an exception—I urinated out all the coloring matter, and my skin stayed pink. From some medical report, I had understood that atabrine merely suppressed symptoms which would appear as soon as we went back to civilian life. So I quit taking it. If I happened to catch malaria, I wanted a discharge for it; I almost wished I should catch it.

But I had my good nights too when I went to bed so tired that I slept, never quite until reveille but almost. Then I got up at the first dawning, the first seeping of gray light through the foliage and between the palm trees' trunks. At the end of the company street, the cooks were beginning to prepare for breakfast, and the warm, pungent smell of coffee wafted through the distance to me. At that hour, I didn't wish to talk to anyone; I walked away, deep into the grove, and sat on the trunk of a fallen palm tree. The wood of the palm tree is massive; it's tough, stringy wood. When the palm tree is uprooted, it tears at the bottom, it gives out a rending snapping sound, and it crashes down, leaving a cup-shaped remnant in the ground, its surface covered with torn tentacle-like fibers. Sitting on the trunk of a fallen palm tree, one feels its weight and its stringy toughness, the bark pitted and rough under one's rump. It's an uncomfortable seat, but somehow one doesn't feel guilty about the fallen tree.

Life is quite still at the moment before dawn, yesterday's time has long passed away, and today's time has not yet begun.

"Suppose we lose 'eem ere along too-light ...'"

It's not yet too-light. The men from Malaita are still asleep, drunk with moon power. All's quiet down by the shore; the surf laps the shore as mechanically as a person twitching in sleep. The fishing for human debris has been over a long time. The trench-like graves have been filled up over their pell-mell contents, and the night breeze has washed away almost all the festering stench. Only the cooks are stirring, but army cooks are a breed apart. I wished I knew why I could not sleep like everyone else; why my heart hammered in my chest as if I were straining myself to an almost unbearable degree. It was as if I were running, running in a blind panic. Only a panicky run can make a young man's heart pound away like that, so what am I running from when I lie down to sleep?

There's no sense in running away; I have no place to run to. I talk like everyone else about getting away from here, "Boy, this is one hell of a shit hole, I want to go home," but it's all talk; this is as good a place for me to be in as any other.

There was a shortage of infantrymen up north to where the fighting had moved, and a call had been issued for any engineers who felt like it to transfer to the infantry. They needed replacements—those boys were getting killed too fast, or else they broke down. A man can stand just so much patrol duty in the jungle and no more. I had volunteered, and they had called me in.

"D'you know. Sergeant, that you'll be broken down to private if you transfer? Lose your rank and your pay?" the interviewing officer asked.

"Yes, Sir, I know."

"And you're willing?"

"I'm willing, Sir."

"But why?"

"Well, I wish to serve ..."

"You're serving very well where you are now. When we asked for volunteers, we didn't have highly trained senior non-coms in mind."

"Still, Sir ..."

"Come now, Sergeant, out with the real reason."

"If you'll excuse me, Sir, I'm just bored as all hell."

"All right, Sergeant, that'll do. We don't know what your angle is, but you must have an angle. We'll put it down that you're indispensable where you are right now."

I couldn't tell them I'm trying to run away. The front line is one hell of a funny direction to be running away to. Who would believe me If I told them that I wish to run away to the front line?

Suddenly the grove comes to life. Clouds of waspish little parrots swoop down, screeching from trunk to trunk, streaking to tiny rainbows, kindling to flashes of color as they cross the ribbons of sunlight piercing through the foliage. The sun has come out as abruptly as it set last night. The air tingles with sudden warmth, and the little parrots chatter their delight, their short fluttering wings unafraid of brushing my face.

Why are so much brightness and motion, the tingling warmth, the flashing colors in the grove's green nest, the chatter of flitting mercurial life, time starting its course in its daily cocoon, the wake of languor and the drowsy expectancy of early morning, why are they so yearningly, wrenchingly triste?

Number one pigeon, 'ee cry.

CHAPTER ELEVEN

There's something about sheltering oneself from the rain with leaves, which calls to mind a picnic. You picture girls squealing at a sudden downpour, soaked clinging dresses, cold water refreshing young bodies hot from running, and sexual teasing. There is a moment of feigned dismay and happy confusion, then searching for discreet shelters, and pretending to shiver from the sudden chill of wetness. It conduces to huddling together and kissing under the flimsy cover of the leaves.

One doesn't expect to find a knot of fear and fierceness kill or die behind a shelter of leaves.

We, a private and I, were on patrol in Cebu's hills when we saw a Japanese officer. He sat under an overhang of stone, holding a fleshy banana leaf in front of his face, his head nodded, he looked half-asleep. We stood still. He hadn't heard us. A rushing drone of heavy rain, a steamy hot weather rain heavier than water, had smothered our approach. It seemed to fall not in drops but in liquid filaments spewed out from an infinity of wide-open faucets. We stood still. I held my carbine; the private raised his Garand rifle. At that moment, the rain stopped with tropical suddenness, and in the sudden stillness, I fancied I could hear the tattoo of stray drops on the banana leaf.

"Hands up!" I called out.

The Japanese jumped to his feet. I saw that he was a captain. He bowed very slightly, his mouth stretched in a grimacing grin, his hand still holding the incongruous banana leaf. Slowly the hand opened, and the leaf fluttered to the ground. He kept grinning, and then his body snapped like a released spring. He crouched and reached to his belt.

The private's Garand spat twice behind me. The Japanese jerked, spun around, and crumpled up.

"You're crazy," said the private. He was breathing hard. He pointed at the hand grenades hanging from the Japanese's belt. "All he had to do was pull one pin, just one. Why'd you call out to him?"

"He hadn't even seen us,"

A Filipino came out from behind the rocks, ran up to the dead man, kicked him again and again, and chanted, "You sonofabitch, you sonofabitch, no more pom-pom,"

I pulled him off.

"Come on, cut it out," I told him.

He pointed to a nearby hill, to fields the size of handkerchiefs laboriously cut out of the steep slope. Above the fields, a bamboo hut with a thatched roof perched on the traditional stilts of sturdier stalks.

"My home. That sonofabitch, no more pom-pom."

Of course, that was it; the Japanese had taken his food and his woman.

"He's dead now. Go on home."

He pointed to the watch on the dead man's wrist.

"All right, take it," I said

Posthumous payment for food and woman. The Filipino snatched the watch and ran away.

"I ought to report you," said the private. "I don't care if you're a master sergeant. You know the orders: shoot on sight. You like to got me killed this time."

"Yes, of course, you're right, shoot on sight," I agreed.

He looked baffled.

Why, he hadn't even seen us. How can I explain it to you? You're a nice, uncomplicated boy with a crew cut who obeys orders, and it's quite easy, after all, to tighten your finger on the Garand's trigger. The Garand is a good dependable weapon with a satisfying report, not like the anemic cough of the Japs' twenty-two.

The Japanese had a fat face. Relaxed in death, his mouth had fallen open. If we left him where he lay, he would begin to rot and soon reach the stage when a face is no longer a face. It's not yet a skull, as a mask in soft clay over which the sculptor has rubbed his palm in a dissatisfied defacing gesture. No—putrefaction melts the features away, more like a wax head that has been forgotten out in the hot sun. I had seen so many faces half-molten from rotting away; we didn't bury the corpses because they were often booby-trapped.

Our handbook taught us to tie a string to the body, crouch down in the nearest shell hole, pull the string, and see what happened. But the Japanese had gotten hold of a copy of the handbook, so they buried the charge in the nearest shell hole and ran an underground wire to the corpse. So if we obeyed the instructions, the shell hole exploded under us. Some maniacs blew up the corpse with dynamite, scattering shreds of human rot all around, but mostly we left them alone.

The faces had no more eyes, only a mucous jelly in the staring orbits. The cheeks looked fused down, the mouths gaped, and I had watched soldiers urinate into those putrefying gaping mouths.

He had not seen us. How can I explain why I'm glad I warned him even if he tried to kill us? That made it a fight. Otherwise, it would have been hunting, not enemies fighting each other, but hunters and prey, the prey trying to get away, having no hope but to get away. Hunting is a horror to a Jew. My father said he liked hunting, but he lied. He wished his Gentile friends to think him a fine sporting fellow.

I wanted to tell the young soldier, "That Japanese was our enemy, of course, and more mine than yours. I'm one of those who would suffer the final solution if we lost, and when I warned him, he jumped up, his hands stole to his belt, he tried to kill us. All he had to do was pull a grenade's pin, so how can I explain to you that in the fragment of time when the bullet traveled from the Garand's muzzle to his chest, I identified with him? By warning him and I can reason it out, I can shake off this identification. If I hadn't warned him—if I had stood by while he sat unknowingly shielding himself with a banana leaf and you tightened your healthy uncomplicated finger on the Garand's trigger and took away his life—if I hadn't warned him, it would be my face now beginning to rot away to a smeared deliquescent caricature; it would be my mouth gaping wide to be urinated into by some other healthy uncomplicated youngster."

"Go ahead, report me," I said instead.

"Well ..."

"Go ahead. I'll do it again, every time,"

Once I saw my father kill a deer. We crouched in a gully, and the deer soared over our heads. It looked divine and impregnable, soaring against the clouds as the bullet shattered its flight. My father was a lousy shot, and I don't think he ever killed anything much, but we happened in the deer's path. It was a careless young buck, and so close one couldn't miss. The deer fell, and my father stood still, his right hand trembling. The deer wasn't quite dead yet. The fall had broken its matchstick forelegs, and they lay doubled up under him. The white bone stuck out through the brown furry skin, and blood oozed from his muzzle. His velvety eyes screamed with the terror of life's seeping away.

I was a child then. I didn't think many thoughts about it, but I remember wondering at the sheer destructiveness of my father's act. I wondered why he had done it, what was the sense of turning a small throbbing engine of life, bright and light, into that broken carcass lying there?

I understand, and I have understood, now, for a long time, and that understanding welled up in me when I called out to the Japanese. I couldn't help it. I'll do it every time, but how can I explain to you, a healthy, uncomplicated young man with the Garand rifle? How can I make you feel the ancestral remoteness from which the warning came, the long, tortuous way it has run, like a thread stained here and there with red, down to these foothills, below the handkerchief field of the Filipino farmer and his ravished woman, to this overhang of rock and this fallen, now bloody, banana leaf?

The private reported me. I was assigned to the most unpleasant, most dangerous duty then available—demining and neutralizing booby-traps. I didn't mind it; I wasn't afraid of death. I never knew physical fear. But I was scared of killing. I had never killed anyone with my hands; I was afraid of the moment of truth of killing someone I did not hate. I didn't hate the Japanese; I hated what they fought for. I knew they must be killed, I stood ready to kill them if I had to, but I was afraid of the moment of truth. Better to pit my life against deadly inanimate things.

In war, one doesn't get to know the enemy, and it's as well. Soldiers should only see a dehumanized caricature of the enemy, as we saw of the Japanese. Even when the fighting ended and they came down from the hills and surrendered, they remained as bewildering as rare specimens performing their antics behind a thick glass plate.

Many years later, I stood on a road leading to a temple in Kyoto. I walked by a row of tiny open shops, almost cubicles, selling trinkets and charms. It was spring, cherry blossom time. A breeze soft with warmth and scent glided by. Myriads of miniature bells hung in front of the shops, and each had a strip of paper with some blessing or charm written down its length, attached to the little clapper. The breeze took hold of the strips and stirred them, and all the little bells tinkled sweetly in time.

There's a bamboo contraption in the temple's garden, a short length of thick stalk hinged to the ground. The hinge is closer to its front than its rear end, so water dribbles into the open front end, and gradually the water adds weight to it and dips down. The whole stalk swings about its hinges, the water flows out, the stalk regains its former balance and swings back, and then the rear end strikes a rock and gives out a subdued hollow thump. That sound frightens the wild boars, they say. I wonder what kind of a wild boar would run away from the tick-tocking of a piece of bamboo. I'm sure that they aren't frightened at all but pretend to be because the contraption is venerably old, and it must be humored, like an old man shaking his fist at a boy. The boy must pretend to recoil from the feeble threat, out of respect.

My Japanese friends asked me where I was during the war.

"I escaped the service," I replied. "I found a way."

They smiled and nodded at my shrewdness, though deep down, they despised me a little for it. But I couldn't tell them the truth, that I fought them without hating them and called out to one of them, that he should have his chance too. I couldn't tell them that when we trained with hand grenades, we pulled the pin and timed ourselves by rapping out, "One dead Jap, two dead Japs ...." Three short separate syllables time at one second, the proper unit of count. And I watched men urinate into the gaping mouths of their half-rotten dead. I couldn't explain myself to them; they are proud, fundamentally simple people, actually not very unlike the uncomplicated private with the Garand rifle.

They smiled and bowed slightly.

"Good for you," they said, "good for you, Bruno-san. War is awful; better to stay out of it."

But they thought *we did not*.

We squatted on the tatami. A girl sets a tray in front of me, bearing fish and vegetables shredded and twisted into shapes of flowers and a hot stone. I placed a ribbon of fish-meat on the stone, and it sizzled and broiled. The girl prattled away, and I needed no interpreter to know that she was paying me compliments—how handsome the honored guest is, how wise, how kind—ephemeral beauty from ephemeral trifles to deny poverty, and lilting bird-like prattle to keep away the harsh summons of life.

"We hope you are comfortable, Bruno-san."

Their voices were soft and friendly, and I believe they liked me. But I couldn't explain myself to them—they would have thought me a liar or a very foolish man.

When we dug foxholes on Cebu, we dug them in pairs, at an angle like a V. We lay down in them with our feet touching at the apex of the V. One of us slept, and his partner stood watch and could wake him up by kicking at him. I always paired off with Mac; he had risen once more to buck sergeant, so now I was his senior, but there was no grade question between us. He took a malicious pleasure in watching my ineffectual hacking away at the tough coral ground, my pick hardly biting into it. He had already finished and sat smoking, watching me with silent amusement. But he wouldn't help me.

Sometimes a Filipino farmer appeared from somewhere and squatted down beside me.

"Watcha doing, Joe?"

"Digging foxhole, Joe."

"Joe, you dig foxhole here, Japanese two days over hill."

I shrugged this off. The Filipino watched me silently for a long while and then reached for the pick.

"Joe, better let me help you. Japanese be back before you finish."

Usually, both Mac and I slept. The clammy caress of a carabao's lapping tongue wakened us at dawn. The carabao gazed mournfully down at us, its nearly bare hide, mud-encrusted for protection against insects, quivering exploringly. The carabao has an enormous belly, almost trailing the ground. It gets about by throwing its weight out of balance, then stopping its fall by a thrust of short knobby legs. This is how all mammals walk, but the carabao emphasizes it to absurdity. It's a longsuffering, resigned sort of animal, not unlike its masters. The Filipinos exploit its stumpy power for work, feed on its flesh, tan its hide, and make doubtful delicacies from its bowels. Perhaps the carabao licked us, as we lay in our foxholes because we were humans who made no demands on it, strange, wonderful humans who let it alone, good-humoredly shooed away its intrusions and would have gagged on the delicacies made from its bowels.

After they assigned me to de-mining, I dug no more foxholes. I slept in a tent, and that would have been fine if I had been alone. I wouldn't have minded going out every morning to outwit enemies whom I should never see, who had planted booby traps and baited them with painstaking ingenuity. Sometimes the ground was covered with a spider's web of wires, most of them innocent, and you wondered which the deadly ones were. They all looked alike. I went in ahead of my men, trying to make some sense of the maze of wires, but it was useless. Then I grew angry and kicked at them, cursed them: "So blow me up, you bastards! I'm here; can't you feel me kicking at you? What're you waiting for?" I would shout.

My men thought me a little crazy but respected my disregard of danger. They didn't realize that there's no merit in risking something one doesn't care much about anyway. Now and then, I lost one of them. The magnetic detector was no safeguard because then we had to handle what we had detected. Yes, I lost a good many of them, and nothing ever happened to me.

"Sergeant, I don't feel good today. I don't feel like going in there," a private said to me one morning.

"Come now, don't be an ass," I answered. "You saw me going in and coming out, didn't you? I'm all in one piece; there's no danger at all."

I left them at their work and drove ahead to look at the next day's job. When I came back, there he was, lying on the ground with his belly torn off. He had been carrying a handmade mine, a mere tube of rusty iron full of charge. The fuse had been removed, and without the fuse, it was a perfectly harmless object, but the perfectly harmless object had exploded. He was carrying it at the height of his crotch, and the explosion had plowed his belly from the crotch upwards.

"How old was he?" I asked.

"Oh twenty, twenty-one. He didn't want to go in, Sarge, you know, like he felt it coming."

"Yeah," was all I could say.

We got drunk most nights. We drank liquor the Filipinos made. Bottled in the morning, we drank it at nightfall. Some said the Filipinos brought the drink to volume by urinating into the bottle—there was a water shortage, pity to waste organic liquid. Besides, urine has the right color. They put a label on it and wrote on the label: "Fine Old Scotch." Mac always joined me at drinking time; he held the bottle against a light, looked through it, shook his head, and said, "It ain't fine, it ain't old, it ain't scotch, but what the hell!"

Sometimes it rained heavily at night. The rain drummed at the tent canvas, and it was soothing as if the whole world had been engulfed in the immense rushing sound, had crumbled away all around us, and we were left on a tiny island in space. We were in a silly little asteroid the shape of a bread crumb, we alone with our fine old scotch, everything else blurred and forgotten—the half-rotten Japanese with their gaping mouths, the canny booby-traps lying in wait for me in their underground nests, the probable dead of tomorrow or the next day, with his belly plowed up by a fuseless charge which would refuse to be harmless—all washed away by the droning hypnotical rain, washed into utter nonexistence.

But then, the rain stopped. The sky glittered with sudden diamond-hard brightness, and innumerable little frogs let out a deafening croak.

Where had they come from? Could they have led a lethargic existence in the dry ground, or had they burst out from germs borne by the very raindrops they furiously croaked their short lives away at?

Geckos called out and fought their mating battles in the trees. The dream of aloneness, of being the masters of our little asteroid, was shattered. We finished the urinary scotch and stretched out on the cots. I said to myself, "Now I lay me down to sleep." Still, as always, sleep came reluctantly, so reluctantly that the rainwater had time to drain away and the geckos to tire of their fights. In the last twinkle of sinking consciousness, I perceived only a blanketing silence.

CHAPTER TWELVE

There were a few water fountains along the road from our camp to the ruins of Cebu City. In the early morning, the Filipino girls came out of their bamboo houses and washed, standing fully dressed in front of the fountains, sloshing cold water on their bodies beneath their dresses. They were sturdy, plump little girls, with slightly bowed legs and luscious breasts. Their smooth brown skins marred with the pink scars of impetigo sores. They had velvety eyes, not jet-black like their hair, but shaded with chestnut brown and maroon, melancholy, appealing eyes. When they went with the soldiers, and they bent like reeds under their coarse, mostly drunken lovemaking, those eyes never lost their melancholy and their appeal. They submitted their bodies willingly but kept their little confused souls tucked away out of sight. They were not greedy, but there was little food on the island. There was little money and not much of anything else. Even the hogs had a lean, hungry look; probably they didn't mind being slaughtered, for what is life to a hungry hog ...

There was only plenty of coconuts. Green coconuts are protected by a tough husk, which is very difficult to remove. One way is to stick a spike in the ground with the point up and drive the coconut onto it so that the point sinks into the husk, and then tear off slices of husk with a deft flick of the wrists. You need practice for that, but you are rewarded because the green coconut is full of creamy milk that has not yet coalesced into meat. The shell has three little eyes; you punch holes through them and suck the sweet thick milk, but you need practice to do all this; if you merely hack away at the coconut, you get very little satisfaction.

The Filipino girls' bodies were easily conquered. It was no remarkable feat to tear off their flimsy cotton dresses. They wore nothing underneath on their smooth hairless skins. My girl's name was Filomena, and sometimes we sat quite still and silent. We watched the sky washed by recent rain, a strange sky to me, with the North Star down nearly to the horizon. She lay her head on my shoulder and cried a little, for no reason at all. Her head smelled slightly rancid because she dressed her hair with coconut oil.

The irises of her eyes had a smooth velvety texture. She smiled happily when I told her that they reminded me of petals. She was beautiful, and she was proud. The gossips said that she had been the mistress of a Japanese colonel. I had not found out whether this was true, but I knew that she had turned down many other men because they kept asking me, "Why did it have to be you? What's so good about you? Is your prick especially big, or can you fuck twenty times in a row?" It would have been useless to tell them that with me, she could cry a little, for no reason, letting her slightly rancid smelling tresses tumble down my shoulder. One night a pair of disappointed suitors beat me up on a dark stretch of road. They ran away when a truck happened to drive up. I never found out who they were, but I didn't care.

"The Japanese made us feel like butterflies impaled on a board, with a pin through our breast," she said to me. "The Americans clutch us in their fists, they don't mean to hurt us, but they can't help bruising our wings. With you, I feel free, you hold out your hand, and I alight on it. I could fly away at any time, but I never, never will."

She was an educated girl and prided herself on her flowery speech.

"I hate the Japanese!" she cried. "Don't you?"

But she knew I didn't hate the Japanese; she knew I had been punished for granting one of them a chance to defend himself.

We walked along the road hand in hand; sometimes, another soldier promenading with a less desirable girl shot me a hostile look. A Filipino passed pushing a cart. He carried a loathsome reddish drink called "tuba," coconut milk with a red powder in it. The powder was an acetic ferment, and the liquor had to be drunk at the intermediate alcoholic stage, but there was always some acid in it. She wished to drink it, but I said no. There were many lepers on the island; the Japanese had let the less severe cases out to avoid caring for them, and now they roamed freely. At times one met a beggar with a covered face, and then the beggar would bare it to provoke bigger alms; it was a shattering sight. To me, leprosy was still vested with Biblical terror.

Off the road, people gathered to watch the cockfights. Cockfights were big business in Cebu. Some enterprising American soldiers had taken over their organization and were making money at it. Still, most of them lost it in crap games anyway, so the money finally found its way into the skilled crapshooters' pockets, like river water flowing to its ultimate destiny in the bosom of the sea.

Gaudily dressed, brightly painted prostitutes strolled through the crowds. Some of them were hermaphrodites, but it was impossible to tell them from women. Soldiers told lurid tales of shocking experiences in the darkness of secluded huts ("Stretched out my hand and grabbed a fistful of balls!"). One of them claimed to have twisted away in a last-minute awareness and driven his erected penis into a crack of the bamboo flooring, skinning it atrociously; he kept taking his penis out to exhibit its angry ulcerations.

Later we walked back to Filomena's house. It was not far from the camp, and sometimes I spent most of the night there and turned in shortly before reveille. I never slept much, anyway. There was a mango tree a little distance from the house. The Filipinos did not build under the mango trees because they believed them to be the dwellings of hostile or at least unpredictable spirits. She knew I liked to lie under its spreading branches. She shivered a little; she was an educated girl and didn't believe in the spirits of the mango tree. But at night, the spirits are there whether you believe in them or not, and they never go completely to sleep. You can hear them sighing gently in the rustling of the leaves.

She went into the house and brought out a stolen Army blanket, which I had received from an enterprising Supply Clerk, and spread it on the ground close to the tree roots. I took my shirt off. The air was warm, and the moon was low, swollen, and yellow with the day's rain's humid vapor. I stretched my hand out to her, but she stood away from me, outlined against the moon glow of the horizon.

"Do you mind very much that my legs are not long and straight?" she asked. "All the girls in the movies have legs which are long and straight."

I laughed. "We don't live in the movies, Filomena."

"I wish to tell you a secret. I get up in the middle of the night, every night when it's darkest when there is no moon or the moon has set, and I walk to the fountain. I take off all my clothes, and I wash, long and carefully. I wash all my naked body when no one can see me, to make it clean and pure for you. I want you to understand this. I'm not like the other girls who wash in daylight with their clothes on and without soap. And I have no diseases. I know that some of your men have caught diseases from the other girls, but I'm healthy; I have an American physician's certificate to prove it. And my skin is smooth; I have no scars, no blemishes anywhere, you know that."

"Stop it, Filomena," I said.

"No, I must talk tonight. The war is nearly over; there is little time left."

She slipped her dress off. The moonlight tinted her skin to a warm creamy pallor. There was no hair under her armpits or between her thighs. She knelt beside me. I sat up, drew her near, and ran the tip of my tongue lightly along the outline of her breasts.

She smiled. "Yes, you can lick any part, any square inch of me. I'm clean, every square inch of me."

"I said, "But you taste of coconut soap."

"Don't make fun of me!"

"All right. I'll make serious conversation."

I caressed the hairless inside of her thighs.

"Is it true that you were the mistress of a Japanese colonel?" I asked.

"Yes," she said. "I should have told you about that. I found out from another girl that he was one of those men who like to be hurt. So when he wanted me, I went with him. The other girl had been afraid of him, she had beaten him too lightly, and he had not been satisfied. At first, I enjoyed beating him, but I hated him more every time. The last time I beat him into unconsciousness, and when I saw him bleeding on the floor, I became frightened and ran off. They took him away to a hospital somewhere on another island, I think. I hid until the Americans came."

I reached out to her.

"Not now, not yet, please," she said, "I want to talk."

"Talk? Without any clothes on?"

"Yes, please. Hold me in your arms. I know that my body's beautiful and clean, so when I'm naked, I don't feel so inferior."

She lay down beside me, her nude body matching mine.

"I want you to understand what I am," I said. "You look at my features and my skin, and you think that I'm like the other soldiers and that you are different. But it isn't that way at all. I'm the different one. You see, I'm called a 'Jew.' That word's enough to make one different. You've heard it, but you don't know what it means, and it isn't easy to explain. For one thing, it means that at any time, in any place, other people, more numerous people can tell us, 'You've no right here, go away, go where you belong.' And the joke is, we don't belong anyplace. If one doesn't have the right to be in any specific place, he has no right to exist; it's as simple as that. And if the others decide to kill us, they may do it; it isn't against the law if they don't want it to be because they make the law. And when this happens in a country, the other countries say, it's no business of ours, no one should interfere in the internal affairs of a sovereign state, and we're certainly not going to sacrifice our boys for the sake of a bunch of foreign Jews who are probably not blameless anyway.' So you see, you didn't have to take your clothes off. In the eyes of the world, you are superior to me, whether naked or dressed."

"Bruno, I don't care about all these things," she whispered. "They have nothing to do with us. Soon the war will be over. You don't have to go back to all the evil you are talking about. I want you to stay here with me because I love you."

"Shut up," I said. "Let's make love. Let me taste every square inch of your lovely smooth skin that you've made so clean and pure and flavored with coconut soap for me. The spirits of the mango tree are growing impatient. They wish to see some fun. And when it's over, I'll walk away from you, and I won't come back. I've done you enough harm. Find yourself another friend, and don't refuse his gifts as you've refused mine. He won't stay with you when the war is over, so take what you can, and never, never again tell a man that you love him."

Later, when I got up, she began to cry silently. The tears ran down her cheeks and dripped on her lovely breasts. The night had grown colder. The moisture in the air was condensing into dew, a cloud had come across the moon, a cool breeze stirred the mango tree's foliage, and the spirits whispered angrily in the swaying branches. I wrapped her up in the folds of the stolen blanket and kissed her goodbye.

My tent mates asked me why I was no longer going out.

"What happened to your girlfriend?"

"She broke it off. I guess she felt sorry for me, but sympathy stretches just so far."

They laughed.

"Yeah, too bad. Well, get the chaplain to give you a T. S. slip."

"Now this guy needs a T. S. slip written from right to left," one of them said, "and there ain't no rabbi on this island."

We were told there were no transport ships and we could not go home.

"Our generals have temporary rank," the men said, "they'll keep it as long as there are enough troops under their command. They've sent the ships away on purpose. They'll never let us go If they can help it."

The men were getting into an ugly mood. Then someone proposed to convert the Liberty ships to transports as there were plenty of them around. I had a reputation for efficiency and was put in charge of the Liberty ship conversion crew. We put in wooden bunks, exploiting every corner in the holds. They made miserable living quarters, but the men didn't mind. We set up the kitchens on the deck. The latrines were supported at the ends of massive beams and the beams fixed to the deck. The latrines protruded outside the gunwales, and the men's droppings fell directly into the ocean. It was a grotesque arrangement, but it gave us something to joke about. We told each other, "Better keep our shit in when we're drunk or we might fall off, and the barracudas would have themselves a banquet." But we had been through so much, and we weren't quite sure that our meat still agreed with the barracudas.

It took us three days to convert each ship. I was scheduled to leave with the third of them, bound for Leyte. I stood on the wharf and looked back on the island. I could see some of the hilltops which my crews had flattened down to make storage space. I was a little sorry that I had helped mar the landscape. I felt sure that the Filipinos would look at those flattened hilltops and shake their heads, not understanding. I remembered when we were building a road in a hurry. The easiest way was to draw a straight line by repeatedly reversing the transit, so sometimes we happened to sight through a bamboo house, and it was too bad. We roused the inhabitants in the middle of the night and made them carry their belongings away. They stood by, uncomprehendingly rubbing their eyes while the bulldozers squashed down the flimsy bamboo structures. Of course, they received compensation, but I knew they thought us crazy for not bending the road round their all-important homes.

I saw Filomena. Another soldier had his arm around her waist. She looked up at him and laughed a little feverishly. I thought he looked like a quiet, pleasant boy, and I hoped that he treated her well. She wore a pair of elaborately carved wooden sandals; the other girls often went barefoot, but she never did. The sandals were high and heavy and gave her an uncertain mincing gait, but I had liked them on her and had told her so. She had been offended and had protested, "Of course, they make my legs seem longer and straighter, now I know that you think my legs are not long and straight enough," and then she had sulked. But she often wore those sandals for me. Now she was not looking my way; she was waving as if to someone on the Liberty ship's deck, but there was no one on deck, and her companion said something to her. She shrugged and let her arm drop.

I could have remained in Cebu. Even now, it should have been easy to turn my berth space over to someone else and apply for my discharge here. I would have obtained it quickly, and I had a few thousands of dollars saved up, a sum that could buy a lot on Cebu. With such a sum, one could set up commerce or become an impresario of some sort. The people were hungry for all kinds of entertainment, and life was easy here. A man doesn't need very much in a mild climate—a little carabao meat went a long way. The lean Filipino hogs didn't eat much and were easy to raise. There were plenty of fruits, not only coconuts, but pineapples picked ripe from their plants, mangoes, papayas, and at least three kinds of rich bananas, with red, yellow, or green skins. The lepers would soon be under control. Then, one could learn to enjoy the tuba liquor, even make it oneself, and find ways to improve it, maybe procuring a more selective ferment that wouldn't produce acetic acid quickly. I thought *we could even build a house right under a mango tree. I don't mind the spirits whispering in the night, and with me, she won't mind them either. The spirits will be good, discreet company when we are making love. Some day their rustling voices will lull our little brown-skinned children to sleep.* I wondered whether Filomena had made love to someone else on my stolen Army blanket. I hoped not. I had wrapped her nude body in it before I left her—that had been my last, awkward, lingering, repentant caress.

I kept musing. *We'll spread the blanket again in the moon glow of a warm night; I'll run the tip of my tongue lightly along the contour of her lovely breasts and lightly stroke the smooth hairless inside of her thighs. I'll taste the coconut soap flavor of her skin, her clean, pure skin without blemishes, cream-colored in the darkness.*

Life here could be so easy, with its blissfully uncomplicated problems. All I had to do was to turn my berth space over to someone else. All I had to do was to walk up to Filomena and her soldier and say, "Sorry, pal, but that's my girl you've got there." I might have to pull off my shirt because one shouldn't fight with a master sergeant's chevrons showing. I wasn't a very good man in a fistfight, and I might get whipped, but I should come out the winner anyway.

Someone called out, "All right, fellows, all on board."

I turned my back on the island. On deck, I leaned on the gunwale and looked down. I felt like retching, but I had no excuse for it since we were still moored and not out on the sea.

And now there was no one on the wharf. At least no one I cared about.

CHAPTER THIRTEEN

My first love was a schoolmate's sister.

There's nothing so amusingly absurd to a boy as another boy's falling in love with someone as unglamorous as his sister.

"She's an ugly little shrimp," he would say, "why boys go for her is a mystery. But watch out, you're a good guy, and she's an awful cat. She'll tear you to shreds."

She did, but not in the way he expected.

They both spoke disparagingly of my "goodness."

"I can never be sure how I feel about you," she said. "You are so good—what girl loves a good boy?"

That was before Mussolini discovered that Italian Jews didn't belong to the "Italian race." Strangely, I can't remember that my being a Jew was ever mentioned between us until our very last meeting. We were seventeen when we met and eighteen when she told me: "Go away," and I went away.

She liked to complain about her looks that she was too thin and with a sallow complexion.

"The sun's kind to me, and I tan appetizingly, but in the winter, phew! Even my name, Rita," she said, "is thin and shallow like myself."

Then I had to tell her how beautiful she was, that her name was beautiful too, and she glowed at my words and urged me to go on.

I've forgotten what it is to be seventeen or eighteen, and perhaps she really was homely. Maybe her cattiness was defensive, and she never loved me even a little, but only used me as a stepladder to self-assurance. She understood much better than I that lovers are always enemies, and one of the two must prevail and will, or will not, as the case may be, show some little mercy on the other. She understood it very well and made sure from the beginning that I stood no chance. Or perhaps I wanted to stand no chance because, at that age, I was very naive and believed that love implied the boundless undisguised surrender of oneself.

Whenever we met, she held out the pads of her fingertips for me to kiss, and I did kiss them. I was well aware that I looked a little like a dog licking its master's hand, but I didn't rebel; the submissiveness of that gesture gave me a little thrill. Love at eighteen can make you enjoy your partner's triumphs over yourself, even though deep down, you may realize that she cannot love anyone she dominates so easily. But at that age, you don't demand to be loved; you're satisfied with being permitted to love. And that's all she promised me the first time we met.

She was leaning on the railing of a steamboat. We were on a party outing on the lake, and I had teamed up with another girl. The motion of the boat blew Rita's jet-black hair about her pale face. There were no colors about her except white and black and the tan of sunburn. She gave me an almost fierce stare of her black eyes. There are many kinds of black. Black is any color gone dark enough. Her eyes were a thick, intense green, a coldly glowing, merciless color.

"What are you looking at me like a sheep for," she asked, and I replied, "I think I've fallen in love with you." After a while, she said, "Well, if that's the way you feel, I'll let you love me."

She held out the pads of her fingertips to me, and I kissed them. I'm no longer seventeen or eighteen and wiser about love, and I know that she was nothing but a shallow minx. Despite that, I still feel an impersonal tenderness when I remember her fingers, which used to be ink-stained and not very clean generally. She wasn't neat, she seldom carried a fresh handkerchief, and her room smelled of underwear, which has been worn a bit too long. But clean or dirty, her fingers had a fluttering disembodied lightness as if they were airborne. They reminded me of the gossamer filaments which hover on the countryside in springtime and sparkle with iridescent refractions, seeming, rather than matter, vagaries of light.

The girl I had been teamed with came along and dragged me away, so our first conversation was so absurd and so brief—that the next day I didn't believe it had happened. Then I thought I had forgotten her, but of course, it wasn't true. Many months passed, someone mentioned her casually, and suddenly I knew I couldn't keep away from her any longer. I called her up. She understood at once who I was and said, "All right."

"Well, are you still in love with me?" she asked.

"Yes."

"I was wondering. You've kept away such a long time."

I had turned eighteen, and I owned a car, not a common thing at my age in those days. We drove out of town, at random, and reached a hilly country. I nosed the car up the steepest, narrowest road I saw, and after a while, we had to stop. We got out and walked on, uphill.

"I want you to carry me on your shoulders," she said.

I picked her up. She weighed very little, her chest felt brittle and bony under my hands, and I walked up a steep meadow. Even a small weight feels crushing after a while when you walk sharply uphill, but she kept spurring me, "Go on, please go on, as far as you can." Finally, I couldn't make it any longer. I knelt and dumped her on the grass and fell gasping beside her.

"Now, let's see if you can make love to me!" she said.

"Right away?"

"Right away, before you get your breath back."

She wore trousers fastened in a twisted overlapping way, and my fingers had gone unsteady with fatigue, so I fumbled.

"See? More difficulties I've prepared for you," she laughed.

We made love. She was not a virgin. In those days, an eighteen-year-old girl of a good family was expected to be a virgin. Boys inaugurated their sexual careers with professionals—school ships, as they were called—then progressed to semi-professionals, usually working girls who had been conned into making love, the first time, with promises of marriage above their status, and after their disappointment made the best they could out of their virtue's loss. Finally, the men, no longer boys, graduated into a relationship with a married woman or with a girl of some class, possibly an actress or a dancer or a smart "cocotte," which easily lasted into their married lives. Others but not very young men, perhaps for the same reason that only old tigers are man-eaters, made the defloration of naive low-class girls their hobby.

Yes, there were many variations to a man's sexual opportunities, but young girls of your own class were supposed to be clean. You didn't expect a schoolmate's sister to copulate freely. It did happen, but it was both unusual and dangerous unless you were prepared to make things right. And of course, I was prepared; even while I undid her trousers' fastenings, the idea of marriage stood in the back of my mind. When I discovered that she was not a virgin, I was shocked. She expected me to be shocked, she was worried, almost frightened, and she became the weaker of the two at that moment.

She cried; she talked about the "other time." It didn't occur to me to ask her how many times had been "the other time."

"I never understood how it could have happened," she said. "I think I was tipsy at the time, but with you, it's different because I love you."

"What did you say?" I asked.

"I love you."

"*Lo dici male.*"—"You say it badly," I complained.

I had my moment of ascendancy; I should have taken advantage of it. I should have been politely contemptuous. I should have told her that it was all right, that love is a big word and let's forget it. We can have fun together, I should have said, we can be friends. What has happened before is no concern of mine. What's so important about your little hymen anyway? Why should I care? All would have been well had I talked to her that way. She would have laughed and said okay, she would have become my tame pussycat, her claws carefully sheathed, drawn out now and then only as much as was right for play. But I couldn't do it. Because she was vulnerable, my heart went out to her, and I had to soothe her, to make her feel secure again.

I wasn't entirely foolish; I knew I was losing my love fight, but I wished to lose it to her, and I should have wished it even if I had known that this winner would show me no pity. I have come to think that the winner in love never shows compassion because you cannot win if you feel pity in your heart. So I took her in my arms, I stroked her jet-black hair; I skimmed her gossamer fingertips with my lips. I lost myself in the deep green blackness of her eyes. In a while, she purred, not because I had consoled her, as I naively thought, but because she had her claws firmly and finally back into me.

There was a nip in the spring air, in the grass still cool from the night dew, under a sunlight that held more brightness than warmth. The gossamer threads that hovered above us, as light as her fingers, sparkled with a molecular skin of moisture. Because it was cold and she had cried, her nose was running. She didn't carry a handkerchief, so I lent her mine. She blew her nose awkwardly like a child, and then she returned it to me, and I put it back.

There was no reason at all why I should be in love with her. I didn't even realize that she had beautiful legs because I had seen her only twice, the first time so briefly, and this time she wore trousers. I had pulled them down to make love but hadn't slipped them off, and so I didn't know the only beautiful thing about her body. I had felt her bony chest under my hands and touched her irrelevant little breasts; her thin sallow-skinned face had protruding cheekbones, a snub nose, and pale pouting lips. Her only attractive feature were the deep, wild, green-black eyes. I knew many girls prettier than she. There was no reason at all that I should be in love with her, and it was exquisite to be so tenderly, abjectly in love with her. I was eighteen when I loved her in that meadow.

I taught her to drive, rather I tried to, but she was a very poor pupil, and it all ended with her smashing against a wall and wrecking my car. Since she didn't have a learner's permit, we had to keep it a secret. I took her home, it was early afternoon, and luckily, no one else was in. She told me she'd lie down and rest; she'd had a bit of a shock and limped from a blow on one leg. I went home. After a while, the phone rang. It was she; she cried and said that she must have a broken leg, she couldn't even stand up, she was alone and frightened. I rushed over, sick with worry. She looked quite pitiful, lying there with a tear-stained face. She wore a dressing robe and opened it to show me her leg. There was a red mark on it, but it didn't look so serious to me. I made her flex her leg experimentally. It was a very lovely leg, and I kissed it lingeringly.

"What are you trying to do, make it well?" she laughed.

"Will you try to stand up, maybe walk a little?" I asked.

She jumped up and skipped lightly about the room, laughing at me. Then I slapped her face with all my strength. She fell on the bed, and we made love. Afterward, I was repentant that I had hit her.

"Don't be silly, I had it coming, and I didn't mind it," she said. "I wanted you to worry; I knew you would. I wanted you to suffer a little. I like to play with you, to lead you this way and that; it's exciting, like riding a horse that's wild to anyone else but a slave to me, and of course, I expect to be unseated once in a while. There'd be no thrill to it if it never happened. I didn't know you could slap so hard; how can you slap so hard with your beautiful slim, gentle hands? But you were entitled to it, and I'm glad you did, aren't you?"

I didn't answer. We lay in each other's arms in silence.

"What are you going to do about us?" she asked at last.

"I'll marry you, of course, when I finish my studies."

"That's a long way off."

"All right. I'll do it earlier, when I come of age, or earlier still if my father agrees, and I'm sure he will. He won't care one way or the other, and he'll give us all the money we need. He's a good father that way."

"You'll marry me though I am a whore? Because you know I'm a whore at heart."

I didn't answer.

"I will betray you," she said. "If you marry me, you'll be a cuckold, and then perhaps you'll kill me, won't you? You'll place your slim, gentle hands about my neck and squeeze. Oh! It'll be quite romantic. I have such a thin, scrawny neck that will be easy to wring like a chicken's, don't you think? But I don't want you to do that, promise you won't. Promise you'll place your beautiful hands about it and squeeze the life out of me slowly and as gently as you can."

My being Jewish didn't come into account for either of us in the early summer of 1938. That was only a few weeks before it was discovered that there was such a thing as an "Italian race," and it was solemnly proclaimed:

"The Jews do not belong to the Italian race."

Her room was an awful mess, the closets gaped, and heaps of clothes tumbled halfway out of them. Her schoolbooks littered the floor, and the carpet was covered with ink stains, cigarette butts and ash, dirty stockings lay here and there.

"See," she said, "this is my personality; I am as dirty and messy as this room. I'll never be any other way." Then she stood up entirely naked and said, "Now look at me."

Her body was immature, gawky, thin, and bony, the chest almost flat, the ribs outlined sharply under the sallow skin.

"Do you still say you love me?" she asked

"Don't ask silly questions," I said.

She made a funny little gesture with her hands.

"You're the biggest fool on earth. What am I going to do with you?"

That summer, we both graduated from the *Liceo,* the senior high school. The examinations were an exhausting affair, and quite a serious one, at least for me; I wasn't allowed to fail—such things were just not done. For some weeks, we saw less of each other, and then the exams were over. We had been successful and were expected to go on a vacation. There was no way to be together without disclosing our attachment, but it was too soon for that. I had no news of her for a while.

September came. We were back in town, but meanwhile, the Italian race had been discovered. I waited for her to call me up. It was hell to restrain myself, but this time I felt I must. She didn't call me up. But I was her brother's friend, so it was entirely proper that I visit him, and in the end, I did. He and I talked vaguely of our plans as if nothing had happened. The Jews' situation wasn't mentioned at all, and as I got up to go, he said, "Wait a minute, I'm sure my sister wishes to say hello to you."

She came in. We made small talk in her brother's presence, like two polite acquaintances.

"Come on, I'll show you out," she said at last.

On the doorstep, she gave me her hand. We were alone. I held her beloved gossamer fingers in mine. I couldn't let them go, but I dared not kiss them. I had been her lover, and I dared not kiss her hand. After a while, she slipped it away from mine; she slipped it away and rubbed the palm on her skirt.

"Jews have sweaty hands," she said.

I should have taken that hand once more and kissed it as I had done so many times, and then I should have killed her. All it needed was to place my hands about her neck and squeeze. It was a slim, fragile neck, no sturdier than a flower stalk; it would have snapped under my hands so easily, then all would have been concluded for the both of us. But I didn't. I stood still, looking at her.

She laughed brittly.

"Stop dying on my doormat and go away," she said.

I went away.

CHAPTER FOURTEEN

A few months after my discharge, I obtained passage to Italy on a ship that was still outfitted as a troop transport. The crossing took two weeks. Tourist class passengers slept in dormitories, on canvas strips stretched on metal frames, arranged in closely spaced tiers, one over the other. The latrines had urinals shaped like troughs in which saltwater ran continuously. One night the discharge of a drain clogged up. Filthy saltwater spilled and ran over the floor between the men's and the women's dormitories. Fat middle-aged Italian women in their nightgowns waddled from their dormitory with stiff-kneed gooselike gait, screaming at the sight of the water. They thought the ship had sprung a leak.

"Do something," they yelled at me.

I disliked their fatness and their clumsiness. They looked like the mothers who clean-cut American boys of Italian parentage grow away from in the movies, then marry a slim-legged girl with honey-colored hair and a college education.

"What d'you expect me to do," I replied, "stick my finger in the leak, like the Dutch boy?"

At that, they waddled off flapping about and shrieking. One of them fainted in the urine-flavored saltwater.

I didn't mind the hard canvas cots, I didn't mind eating insipid food cafeteria-style out of not very clean metal plates, and that the ship was slow and pitched sickeningly in even moderate swells, but I hated the fat gooselike women, those caricatures, shrieking and flapping about in their unclean nightgowns. Somehow they cast a cloud; it was an ill omen to be surrounded by such ugliness on my return.

We reached Genoa in the evening and rode at anchor outside the harbor the whole night. One of the passengers had a radio. He tuned it in, and we heard dance music and a man's voice singing in Italian. The music was very much like the American music I was used to. The singer tried to sound like an American, and since one-syllable words are not frequent in Italian, he sang the syllables rather than the words. This achieved a staccato effect, which I found somehow pathetic, and in a strange way, moving. It felt as if the singer were putting on a tattered American shirt, not good and not new, perhaps found on a rubbish heap—still a proud thing because a while ago he couldn't have worn it and because it represented a free choice. At the same time, it was a sad thing that spoke of the years lost, of an entire generation ground down by dictatorship and war. Now the best that could be done was to put on other nations' castoffs.

Unaccountably, I felt my eyes moisten. Nearly nine years before, I had left from that same harbor, a refugee. The injustice which I had suffered hadn't been repaired and would never be repaired. Who could replace the years torn from me? I should have been full of rancor and suspicion and of a wish to get even. I should have gloated at the misfortunes of those who had done me that injustice or at least allowed it to be done. But I felt only love and yearning and melancholy happiness. Like returning home where there is trouble and saying, I am here now, with you, everything's going to be all right now.

The song came softly. The radio had been turned down, and it sounded as if the music had shied away from itself, from its daring to be frivolous, to attempt gaiety against this backdrop of wreckage. But the attempt didn't quite come off—it takes a lot of skill to pretend gaiety and not achieve pathos instead. I thought, well, it's all over, and we are beginning anew. I wasn't ashamed of my lack of vengefulness.

The next morning, my father met me at the landing. For the first time since my boyhood, we embraced; when I had left, he had merely shaken my hand. Then we hadn't known what to say to each other. Now, it was nearly noontime; he asked me, was I hungry; I said yes, and he took me into a restaurant where he said we could get a decent fresh fish meal. It wasn't easy; food was neither plentiful nor good. He had come in his car, a little FIAT 500 shaped like a June bug. Gasoline supplies were uncertain, and one had to look for hustlers selling cans at the side of the road. One bought cigarettes from other hustlers, who exhibited their wares in open suitcases set on folding stools. The stools could be folded, and the suitcases closed quickly for a getaway. Of course, all this traffic was as illegal as it was necessary; this illegal traffic was the nation's life-blood, which the police had to make half-hearted passes, now and then, to sever. All this wasn't as squalid as it sounds; on the contrary, it created a happily excited atmosphere. There's nothing Italians like better than a little justifiable lawlessness and making a living by their wits.

My father looked well; he had not aged more than was right. He dressed as well as ever, and although he wore pre-war clothes, they were still smart. I suspected that these clothes, the little car, and eating at a restaurant like this one were great luxuries. I wanted to know how he had managed to escape the Nazis, but he was reticent about it. He muttered something vague about having hidden out in farm country. I suspected that one of his huffy, sweet-scented ladies, had been a landowner and loyal to him in his danger. I asked him how he was fixed for money, and he replied, "All right, there's not very much but enough, for a while at least."

"Well, I'm here to stay. I have returned," I said.

He looked at me curiously.

"Do you really think so?"

"What do you mean?"

He shrugged vaguely and changed the subject. He told me he had sold a small farm our family had owned for more than a century.

"There's a shortage of housing, you know, the bombings, and no building for a long time. So they requisitioned our house for homeless families. I didn't mind that; I wouldn't be living in the country anyway. But they were destructive people. It wasn't their home, and that does make a difference. The house already needed maintenance, they finished wrecking it, and I certainly couldn't pay for the repairs that became necessary and wouldn't if I could. And the sharecroppers had felt so confident that we were all dead, and they could just take over, that my survival disappointed them bitterly. They couldn't forgive me for having survived. All that was very unpleasant, but still ... it had been our land and our house for so long. Then the parson delivered a sermon about me. He said, here are our poor homeless people quartered in a house that is falling apart, and what does the owner do about it? Nothing. Why doesn't the man show Christian charity? Christian charity, by God! That made my gorge rise. I sold the property to a local man. Inside of a month, he had kicked everybody out. He showed them some Christian charity, all right."

"You were never bitter before," I said.

"I never had any cause to be."

"Being bitter isn't going to help. It's all over now. We can make a fresh beginning."

My father snorted.

"Do you think so? You just wait. We haven't seen the end of Christian charity yet. We are told that it was the Germans' crime, no one's but the Germans'. The other nations are talking very self-righteously about it. But is it true? Do you really believe that six million Jews would have been massacred if the whole world hadn't looked the other way? And maybe given a little wink before looking the other way? No, Son, don't fool yourself. Nothing's over, nothing will be over, now or at any other time, for the Jews."

"You didn't think this way, once," I said. "You used to be very confident of the future, to scoff at the Jewish problem; it was the Jews who made it with their own hands," you said. "Don't you think that now you're swinging over too far?"

"I don't know. And I'm too old to care," said my father. "I feel like a sailor who's sailed his entire life by the stars and knows the winds and the tides, and suddenly he's caught in a storm. He manages to keep his boat afloat, but when the storm is over, look, the sky has changed—no more North Star, no more Big Dipper or Cassiopeia, only strange grotesquely shaped constellations, and the winds are all blowing the wrong way, and the water is rising at low tide. What is he to think?' That this is the real world and he imagined the other one? Or that he's gone crazy? Or that God has gone mad? What is he to do? Lie down on the deck, I suppose, curse himself for having survived the storm, and let himself die. There's nothing else left. And this is what I'm going to do someday, lie down, and die. Sometimes I envy those Jews who committed suicide because they couldn't stand persecution, except that it was a cowardly thing to do. I wouldn't die a coward."

I gaped at him, and my father laughed.

"I deserve a kick on the backside! A fine homecoming I'm giving you! Come on, let's enjoy the food."

We had spaghetti with oil and garlic, fried saltwater fish, and fresh fruit. As I cut one of the fruits, a worm slithered out and crawled about the plate. I have a horror of worms; in America, one doesn't find worms in the fruit. I wasn't prepared for this one. I grabbed a passing waiter by the wrist and began jabbering in English. The waiter didn't understand a word.

"Take it away, take that Goddam dish away!" I shouted.

My father laughed. The waiter tried to pull free, my hand crushed his wrist painfully, and he rolled his eyes in protest. Finally, we understood each other.

"It's just as well that it happened. This will teach you to keep a sharp lookout for worms in your fruit," My father said.

We drove to Milan in the bug-like 500. Our old house looked worn and moldy, but it stood undamaged. Some of the nearby buildings hadn't been so lucky. The rickety elevator that rose in the center of the stairwell didn't work. There was a shortage of power. There was a shortage of fuel and everything else. A wood-burning brick stove attempted to heat the apartment, but it was chilly even a few feet away from it. Suddenly I felt exhausted; I said goodnight and slid under humid, slightly moldy sheets.

In the morning, I unpacked with military neatness, drank a cup of coffee substitute, and then went out. It was early, the winter day had not come quite alive, and the streets were bathed in twilight. I felt very much alone, but I was glad to be alone. It began to rain and suddenly got chilly. I remembered the long walks, purposeless roaming walks of my boyhood. When it rained, as now, in the wintertime, and the rain smelled clean, the pavements shone, rivulets of water gurgled in the gutters. Drainage grades were sharp in this section of town, and the rainwater flowed quickly. The cold wetness bit pleasantly on my face and neck, but I stuck my hands in my overcoat pockets. They chapped easily, and I was ashamed of chapped hands; I feared that they would disgust anybody I happened to touch.

This was the street I walked through every day on my way to school. Down one side of it, there was no sidewalk, only a narrow, thick strip of stone with a downwardly sloping surface. I thought of the street as being phocomelic, with one sidewalk and one stump of sidewalk. The strip of stone has such a crazy shape that served no purpose; it must be something that had been meant to be different and hadn't grown as it should. It was difficult to walk on its sloping surface. The boys coming from school ran along it, flapping their arms to keep their balance. Perhaps to them, it felt like flying, or they hoped that by flapping their arms long enough, they would turn them into wings. The flying phantasy excited them, and at the end of the street, they engaged in minor fights.

The strip of stone served no purpose; therefore, it had endured; it should last forever. Useful things may have to be removed to make room for more useful ones, but useless things are irreplaceable, useless things that have survived their makers, and their makers' forgotten intentions are possessed of magical powers.

Further on, the stone ledge of a basement window used to be the post of a very old, very white little man who sold wooden toys. He sat on the ledge, wrapped in the folds of an enormous brown cloak. He took snuff, the snuff splattered the cloak, but it made only invisible stains in the tobacco-colored expanse of fabric. Nobody bought his wooden toys. The bigger boys passed by without looking at him, but the little ones huddled around him and confabulated—about what? Who could tell ... as soon as they grew up, somewhat, they forgot that labile secret and passed in front of the old man without being aware of him. It had been my secret too, and after I had forgotten it, I used to run by, and the old man swiveled his head to my footsteps and smiled as if he recognized me. But he couldn't recognize anyone; he was nearly blind. Perhaps he merely listened to the sound of footsteps and smiled only because he was so ancient. No, he couldn't recognize in the boy running by him, the child who but a year ago stopped to chatter with him and perhaps brought him the gift of a child's paper.

"Thank you, my dear," he said. He opened the paper and read it through a magnifying glass; he couldn't read otherwise.

A roast chestnut vendor set up his little cast-iron oven in a nearby square in the fall and early winter. The children, who had the money to buy a bag of chestnuts, sometimes gave one or two of them to the toy man. "Thank you, my dear," he would say, and eat them right away.

The oven of the chestnut vendor smoked more strongly on cold, damp days. The chestnut vendor was dried-up and sparrow-like. He kept his mouth covered with a woolen scarf, rubbed his hands near the oven to warm them, and now and then, a child came up and handed him a coin. Then the chestnut vendor twisted a sheet of rough yellow paper into a cone-shaped bag, scooped up the sweet-smelling smoking chestnuts with an iron ladle, and dropped them into the cone-shaped bag. The child took the warm bag, warmed his hands on it, ate a few chestnuts, and then remembered the toy man and ran to him.

"Thank you, my dear," the old man said.

Nobody had ever seen him eat anything but those chestnuts; perhaps he subsisted the whole year long on them; maybe they were magic nourishment. He was old, who could tell how old, perhaps as old as the street, like the houses, as old as time. He sat on his stone ledge; children huddled around him, bigger boys and adults walked by without paying him any attention, without understanding. Once they too had known, but then they had forgotten how to understand.

The streets were filling up now, and boys were going to school, and young people were going to work or beginning their daily hustling, their everyday living by their wits. I watched them hurrying by or looking shrewdly about for an opportunity or merely loafing, and I couldn't recognize my memories in any one of them. Not one of them had ever stopped to confabulate with an infinitely old little man in a tobacco-stained cloak, or bring him a few roasted chestnuts out of a cone-shaped bag, or share a secret with him and then forget it. No one of them had ever done or would ever do any such things. They were insecure, hustling young people, sometimes hungry ones, and they might have cold sores on their hands and feet from the inadequate heating of the wood-burning stoves, but for all that, they were lucky. They had paid for freedom and hope but not as heavy a price as the loss of an aching, bleeding, irreplaceable chunk of themselves.

Even as they hurried or sauntered in the cold, wet street, in the lurid light of a sluggish winter morning, absorbed in their mean daily tasks, there was an air of exhilaration about them, the joy of a beginning, of boundless possibilities, of one's control over one's destiny. They had been granted everything I could ever have wished for. True, in life as in fairy tales, men seldom make fair use of what is given them. I wished these young people well, but their youth was not as mine had been. My problems were foreign to them; my story would have bored them; my affection or dislike would have left them quite indifferent.

I had told my father, "I have returned."

And he had replied, "Do you really think so?"

It had taken me so very little time to find out how things stood. Soon it would be Christmas. I was twenty-seven. I felt very, very old. I walked back home. I climbed the stairs, going round and round the square stairwell. The steps and the landings were of *serizzo*, a fine white and black stone worn smooth with prolonged use, an enduring stone fit for funeral monuments. My steps echoed cavernously on it like a mourner's steps in a monumental vault. A pyramidal glass cupola gave light to the stairwell, but it was covered with soot, so the daylight coming through it turned to sickly dusk. Our apartment was on the fourth floor, and as I climbed, I passed in front of other tenants' doors—heavy wooden doors shut tightly, not so much to keep anything out as to shut something in. Each door would have its share of misery to keep shut in. The people of Milan are proud. In a poem about ancient times, their consul calls them *Signori Milanesi*—Gentlemen of Milan. They walk their old streets dry-eyed no matter what, and they shut their apartments with tight-fitting heavy wooden doors. We had a door like that too.

My father was sitting in his study.

"You know," he said to me, "I have quite a bit of practice already. Of course, not all the clients have come back; in fact, very nearly none have. Other lawyers have been busy stealing their absent Jewish colleagues' clientele. It's strange how much appetite people have for carrion, but it doesn't matter; I'm finding new clients quite easily. Perhaps people have faith in a Jew who has managed to stay alive; he has proven that he's no fool."

"I'll have to go to work now," I said.

"There's no need. I have a little money, and I'm working."

"I'm used to paying my own way."

My father smiled.

"Do you wish me to lie down and die right away? Give me a little time, a little more time to feel needed. I've never felt needed before, even when you were a boy. There was too much money then. Besides, it isn't sound business going to work without a degree. You can study law, and then you'll come in with me, we'll be doing quite well, you'll see."

"All right."

My father nodded.

"Fine."

"Perhaps it has been a mistake," I said.

"What?"

"My return."

"You haven't returned," said my father. "None of us has returned. And no one ever, no one ever returns. I don't really know what has happened to us. Times and places don't seem to match anymore, or it's we who don't match the times and the places. We are lost somewhere; we are lost at some unknown point in a space-time continuum."

CHAPTER FIFTEEN

"You and your damned honesty!" My wife used to scold me. "Why couldn't you tell me that I am your first love?" she complained. "Who cares if it isn't true? Who the hell cares? Why couldn't you say so anyway?"

Before we were married, when we lived together, we enjoyed fighting over nonsense like that people fight from happiness nearly as much as from misery. We argued about the truth. Our first months together were the happiest ones.

"Truth is horse shit," she declared.

In her, I didn't mind what in another I should have called coarseness.

"But even if the truth were as important as you pretend," she said, "one couldn't have it all the time. A steady diet of any one food is unbearable."

"Marriage is a steady diet of one food, too."

"So what, I'm not your wife, and I never will be."

"I meant living together. Even a common-law wife stays the same night after night."

It feels strange to be alone in thinking the thoughts we shared. It's as if we have been walking arm in arm along a bright street, quietly together, and suddenly she's no longer here. My arm is still crooked about hers but there nothing in the crook of my arm. The street is as bright as ever and alive with people, but she has managed to vanish in front of all the people, to disappear from my side, slipping her arm away from mine so stealthily that I felt nothing. I had been looking the other way for only an instant; how could I foresee that she would slip away if I stopped watching her for a moment? But she has done it, and no other arm shall be linked with mine ever again.

Each person is unique. God never repeats himself; God makes each person but once in all eternity. If you don't believe this, if you don't know with every fiber of your soul that this is true, the only truth that matters, then you're not a Jew. I don't care if the *Halachah* says you're a Jew; you are not. That's why I shan't mind dying; my uniqueness will go with me and I with it. But I'm terrified of killing what God has made but once for all eternity. And each person is irreplaceable, and each death is irreparable. No person will ever fit into another's place. There's consolation only for the death of those we didn't love.

In my father's time, when any family member died, they shut the door of his room. They left the room as it had been on the very last day and locked it tight, and it stayed that way. We had several locked rooms in our country house, and the country people believed they were haunted and never approached our house after sundown. When the place was taken over, of course, things were different. Perhaps they reasoned that in the mass slaughter of Jews, Jewish ghosts must have perished too, or if they were still around, they could ask no more than to lurk in dark corners. If they behaved indiscreetly, the parson would come and exorcise them. "Oh, we've learned how to deal with those Jews," they would say. "We didn't approve of Hitler, but he had something there!" And there would be a final solution to the problem of the Jewish ghost. Yes, the ghosts must have known all this, and they lay low; there was nothing to fear from them anymore. And the homeless families quartered in our house had opened all those locked doors, had gone in with a broom and swept out our dead and their uniqueness, the labile lingering shadows of those unrepeatable works of God, out onto the rubbish heap.

Thus when someone you love dies, all you can do is to lock up a space in yourself, lock it up tight with everything in it exactly as it was, forever. That's all you can do. If anyone says differently, it's a lie. And you don't know what goes on inside that tightly locked corner of yourself. You're only aware that something in it hurts. Perhaps if you opened it, whatever that something is would crumble to dust, like a mummy suddenly exposed to the sunlight after a long burial, and the pain would end. But you don't really want it to end.

My wife had strong legs, with well-developed calves and slightly thick ankles. She fretted about them. I could never convince her that I liked them as they were.

"Don't tell me that you prefer heavy legs to slim ones," she challenged.

"No, of course not, but that's in the abstract, you're not abstract, and I wouldn't change any detail of you."

She shook her head.

"You're just trying to be nice."

Her tone implied that I was not succeeding. But she added with heavy politeness, "Of course I appreciate it very much."

She meant, "I don't appreciate it at all; in fact, I loathe it."

Why couldn't I persuade her, in all the years we were together, that I did like her legs precisely as they were. How could I be so ineffectual? If I had succeeded, I should have made her short life a bit happier. God knows she needed every mite of happiness that came her way. Even now, I like strong, slightly heavy legs on a woman; I'm attracted to them. I have a desire to stroke legs like that because it would feel a little like caressing her once again. I wonder whether she'd be glad if she knew this. Probably not, probably she'd be annoyed. I don't know why, but I'm sure she'd be upset. She would say scornfully that I have a dirty mind and be immediately sorry that she had said it.

"But I do wish you had been my first love," I said. "At least, I wish it had been a Jewish girl. I remember visiting an office once. The receptionist wore a dress with a low neckline exhibiting beautiful breasts. A gold Star of David hung from a chain exactly in the cleft between those breasts. I think I made some feeble joke about it, and I don't remember what she replied, and it doesn't matter. But I remember that I felt a pang of regret I had never made love to a Jewish girl. My family knew very few Jews. I wished that the first time I had made love, there had been a chain with a Star of David to be slipped off the girl's neck. Perhaps as I slipped it off, the points of the star might have bruised her skin, and she would have cried out, and then I would have kissed the sore spot in the cleft between her breasts and felt her skin react with a shiver at the touch of my lips."

"You have a dirty mind!" she said.

My wife liked to wake me up in the middle of the night to start an argument about anything or nothing at all. I slept very well since my return. I had become quite a heavy sleeper, but she was cursed with insomnia.

"I spend hours and hours looking at you sleep," she said. "Sometimes, you look like a little boy; you make little boy noises with your breath. I caress your face, and this makes you wrinkle your skin the way cats do. I watch you, and now and then I cry a little, out of tenderness. But at other times, I can't stand your sleeping. You sleep in an insolent manner as if you were showing me up, throwing my insomnia in my face. The noises you make are really nothing but snores. You snore abominably like an old man—no, you sleep and snore like a pig, I just can't stand it. I have to wake you up or go crazy, but it's no fault of mine. It's your fault, the indecent piggish way in which you sleep."

She shook me, "Hey, Bruno, wake up!"

"What is it?"

"Come on, sit up, don't lie there, or you'll go back to sleep on me."

I sat up resignedly. She was usually naked to the waist. She wore flimsy, flapping nightgowns, which always managed to slip off her shoulders and bunch uselessly about her hips. She was generously built, with broad shoulders and large hard breasts, which she liked to show off, and pink, very soft skin. She brushed her long red hair a hundred times a day, but each time, after a few minutes, it flew every which way in the wildest disorder.

"Well, what is it this time?" I asked.

"Why not a cross?" she asked.

She looked flushed and angry, her hair had tumbled about her face, and her angry blue eyes peeked through it as if spying through a half-drawn curtain.

"A cross? What the hell are you talking about?"

"I said, why not a cross? A cross has points too. A cross can bruise the skin if you pull it off brutally, as I'm sure you would. A cross could give you as good a pretext as anything else to nuzzle at a hussy's tits. Why does it have to be a Star of David?"

I reached down into my sleep-befuddled mind for the conversation she was referring to.

"Jewish girls don't wear crosses," I objected.

"Little you know. Lots of Jews, men, and women wore crosses when the Germans were around. And anyway, why did it have to be a Jewish girl?"

I had no answer for that, none at all at that time.

Now I could give an answer and a very long one if I wished, a correct answer, but I don't know how meaningful. Some certainties can't be put into words—you have to reach too deeply for them, as if reaching deep tinder the earth's crust, beyond all neat geometrical shapes of minerals, beyond even molten lava, everything that words can translate into familiar images, deep down to a fiercely hot compressed substance utterly unlike any known state of matter.

But at the time, I merely had no answer.

"That's racism, isn't it?" she insisted.

"Oh, forget it," I said. "Come to think of it, perhaps you are my first love, after all."

"But you just said the opposite!"

"Just" had been twelve hours before.

"Women are empty vessels which we fill with our imagination and yearnings, and when the vessel is full, its beauty makes its contents look infinitely desirable. We don't recognize them as our own; we don't understand that what we adore and submit to is nothing but an empty shell, each of them as good as the next, any one containing exactly what we have put into it, and nothing more; that what we call love is a kind of masturbation of the soul. But once in a while, things are not so. Once in a while, the vessel has a content of its own. If we pour anything into it, it overflows and gives us back as much as it receives, and that's love, and the first time it happens, that's a man's first love. To me, it has happened with you, the first and only time, so you're truly my first love."

"That was nice. You've explained it very nicely," she sighed.

"Now, may I go back to sleep?" I said.

She tossed her hair away from her cheeks.

"No, not so soon!"

She threw her arms around my neck. She lay her cheek against mine. Her cheek was moist with sudden tears.

"Please! You know why I keep waking you up, don't you? It isn't that you sleep like a pig as I always say, that's a lie. You don't even snore; you just make little-boy noises with your breath. It's that I love you too much."

"Well, don't love me to death."

"Oh, don't joke about it! When you sleep, you're not with me; you've gone away. I look at you sleep, and I feel all alone, and after a while, I can't stand it, I have to shake you awake. But look, now I feel happy, you've said very nice things to me, now I can sleep, be patient and wait until I go to sleep. I promise it won't be long."

She kept her promise. She slept heavily, her face buried in a mass of wild red hair. Only the tip of her long straight nose came funnily through the mass of hair. I took my pen and stained the tip of her nose blue, very carefully so as not to awaken her. In the morning, she would be angry at me or pretend to be, and we could engage in one of our fights over nonsense.

But now sleep had deserted me. I slipped away from her body, warm and heavy in sleep. The night was clear outside, a warm, clear night, late winter anticipating spring. Our apartment had a terrace; I opened the door to the terrace and went out and stood looking down at the sleeping city.

I had a fantasy as a child, or perhaps it was a dream. I was on a terrace on a warm, clear night and a stranger suddenly stood beside me. I didn't turn around, but I knew it was God, and I said to Him, "I've been expecting you." I could see Him nodding in the dusk beside me, but He didn't speak. I wept quietly, in quiet desperation. God stood beside me and didn't say anything, didn't reach out to me or try to console me, but I knew it was God all the same.

Standing alone on the terrace, now, I feel the same quiet desperation of my childhood, and I am still alone, as I was then. But perhaps some time God will really come and stand beside me, and then for the first time, I'll be able to weep in the dusk of the night.

What point in time is this now? When I open that door and go back, will there be anyone inside? Shall I find her sleeping warmly and heavily in our bed, soothed by the nice things I have said to her, lulled to sleep by my watching her? Some night there will be no one inside when I open that door and go back. Opening and closing doors, going from one place to another, all will be useless because my aloneness will follow me everywhere ...

Perhaps that night is now, and we have had a short time, such a short time. She hasn't even left the print of her body, her warmly, heavily sleeping body, on the mattress; there hasn't been enough time.

She had a generous body, she looked healthy and vital, but it was an illusion. She was little more than a shadow. When she slipped her shadowy arm away from mine, I wasn't even aware of it, I turned around, and she had vanished. Now I will open that door and go back in, and I don't know what point in time this is, but it doesn't make much difference whether the bed is full or empty. I'll look at it with the quiet desperation that I have carried over from my childhood. Or perhaps it reached down into my childhood from my future to teach me that time is a closed circle, and there is no escape.

And you were my first and only love; all the others were empty vessels who have shattered, leaving nothing but shards, little heaps of brittle rubbish in my memory. But I bent over your sleeping form and tenderly stained the tip of your nose blue. One day, sometime after our talk of tonight, I gave you a Star of David pendant to wear in the cleft between your big hard breasts. It had sharp points, it tore your skin and drew blood, and your sapphire eyes misted with happiness at the sharp pain which had come from my gift.

CHAPTER SIXTEEN

My wife's name was Alessandra—Sandra. But somehow, the name doesn't seem to belong to her, or she to it. Using the name doesn't bring her into sharper focus; on the contrary, the name is like a screen blurring her features. She's my wife to me, and nothing else, even when I think back to the time when we weren't married. Some days she behaved in an aggressive, quarrelsome way, which meant that she was worried or frightened.

"I don't want any children. That's one of the reasons I won't marry you," she said.

"What difference would marriage make?"

"It'd make a lot of difference! You'd feel obligated to have children. You'd worry that people might believe you impotent or at least sterile if we were married and had no children. Oh, I know the penis pride of human bucks! But unmarried couples are expected not to want children, to take all possible precautions. Do you?"

"Do I what?"

"Do you take all possible precautions?"

"Hell, you know I do."

"There's no chance that the great, experienced lover, the Don Juan of two continents, slipped up, is there?"

I laughed then. I understood. She was very irregular, and when her days were late, she became frightened. Fright made her sarcastic and abusive, and she wished to quarrel. I humored her, but I didn't take her very seriously. Children would come, eventually, I was fatalistic about it; in fact, I rather liked the idea.

"Why create unhappiness, why bring into the world a doomed child?" she said.

She had lost her father to the German gas chambers.

"We're like everybody else. It's all over now," I said.

But she shook her head, like my father.

"Wait and see."

We were both law students, and that was how we had met. I thought she didn't take her studies very seriously, but then I understood that the trouble went deeper; she rebelled against and hated them.

"They should print all the law books on toilet paper so we could wipe our arses with them," she said, "tearing the sheets off one by one, going through an entire code in one day if I caught diarrhea. I'd like that. My father's friends put their trust in the protection of the law. What nonsense! The law can't protect anybody any more than religion can. The law's crystallized magic, like religion. They write books about the philosophy of law and try to make a science out of it. That's a laugh—law is nothing civilized and lofty, the law is primitive, it comes from darkness, way, way back when it wasn't enough for Joe to wish to sell something and for Bill to wish to buy it. If they stood in front of each other, uttered certain ritual words, and went through a little ballet of ritual gestures, then the title passed from Joe to Bill in the most binding manner. The gods' vengeance struck anybody who did not respect the acquired title. Of course, that was magic—magic means reckoning man as nothing and looking for all power outside of man. So religion's crystallized magic—sometimes not so crystallized, at that."

Another time the newspapers told of a newly married Jewish couple who had been on a honeymoon; the groom was arrested for violating some paragraph of the fascist racial laws. A warrant for his arrest had been issued years before. A copy of the warrant had lain in a police station somewhere near the place of their honeymoon, and a zealous policeman dutifully carried it out. No one had bothered to tell him that the warrant was now void. Of course, he knew Italy had officially repudiated racism, but what of it? It was none of his business.

I thought it an absurd episode, even funny in a nightmarish way, but she disagreed.

"No, it's all natural and proper. It's the way of the law. The law is blind to truth and fairness, it processes men as a machine processes raw matter, and machines don't feel sympathetic or compassionate about the raw matter. Haven't you read Kafka? The law is Klamm, and God is Klamm. This is Klamm's universe. If we came to the door of heaven and peeped through its keyhole, we should see nothing but Klamm taking his daily nap. My father was a good, man," she said. "He was kind and upright, he was pious, he kept on the right side of God and the law, not out of fear but because he believed in both of them. Oh, I'm sure Klamm had himself a good laugh when they stuck my father into the gas chamber."

A fellow student asked us once, "Why are you Jews persecuted?"

I told him to shut up; he didn't know my wife's history. But he insisted, he wanted to understand, he respected the Jews, he liked them. He knew no better fellows than we, but one couldn't get away from this puzzling fact that the Jews had been persecuted always and everywhere. When all's said and done, well, there must be a reason for it.

I would have kicked the fellow out of my sight, but I saw my wife's taut, white face, and I checked myself. I spoke patiently.

"First of all, it isn't true. The Jews have not been 'persecuted always and everywhere.' They were a minority, and a minority's lot is always hard, especially a religious minority's lot, in cultures where religion is dominant."

When the other had gone, my wife said, "See what I mean?" Of course, the man's right. We must be persecuted because we have been persecuted."

I looked at her pale face, and I swore to myself I should never answer that kind of question, ever again. I brought my wife a drink, she gulped it down, and the alcohol brought a flush to her cheeks. I kissed her lightly, I wanted to stop her talking, but I couldn't.

"Now, do you understand why I don't want children?"

"Not really."

"Don't you? Don't you see we can't fight against this sort of thing?"

"What then?"

"They've left us a way out. We may let ourselves die off. All we have to do is to be very careful not to make any more Jews, and then we can painlessly slide to oblivion. It can be pleasant, I think, a little like cutting one's veins in the bath. The Romans thought it was a sweet end and the easiest way out of any serious trouble."

It was useless to argue with her. When I tried, she nearly screamed at me, "Oh, shut up and pour me another drink, a good stiff one, and leave the bottle here!"

There was only one right answer, and I gave it: "All right, I'll join you,"

She bowed, "Be my guest."

We drank hard, in silence.

After a while, she began to take off her clothes,

"What's the striptease for?" I asked.

"I'm not teasing, I'm undressing, it's hot in here," she giggled.

"No, it's not. It's February, the heating's lousy, and it's as cold as all hell."

"Well, I feel hot. I'm burning alcohol; I'm a nice hot engine running on 'fine champagne.' Anyway, I don't want to keep my clothes on. We're not married, and you can't tell me what to do, so there!"

She sat on the rug; she had only her panties on, her red hair tumbled wildly about her broad shoulders, it grew so long that when she leaned forward, it fell beyond her breasts. She beckoned to me.

"Come on, lie down beside me, put your head on my lap."

"What for?"

"I want you where I can handle you."

She laughed without reason. I was slightly tipsy myself, and I laughed with her.

"It'll be so easy," she crooned. "Oh, what an easy, what a wonderful life! I'm quite beautiful, even if my legs are a bit fleshy. It's natural that you should love me. And luckily, I love you too, though I'll be damned if I know why. You're not a very prepossessing fellow, you know, you're quite skinny. Your potency's nothing to brag about, but I do love you, and you can see it's

LADDER TO THE SKY

the truth because I'm telling you now while I'm drunk. And we can make love any time we wish, what more is there to ask for? We can get drunk like tonight and make drunken love, or stay sober and make sober love. Not a care in the world, we can be two people who have only a present, always and forever a present. The past's gone and doesn't concern us, and who cares about the future? There isn't any such thing as the future anyway. All we have to do is wait, and anything becomes the present, and when there's no more present, there's no more 'we,' so who cares then? We'll live this way, won't we? Promise, promise me we'll live this way."

"All right, I promise."

But tipsy as I was, I knew it was no more than a dream, or a nightmare, out of a bottle. I'd dreamed it before, and then I'd risen with a hangover and smashed the dream with its mother bottle into a gutter.

CHAPTER SEVENTEEN

A friend told me he was going to Israel,

"To Palestine?"

He looked at me angrily.

"There's no such thing as Palestine. Perhaps there never was. Anyway, don't you read the papers? Since yesterday there's a Jewish state, and it's called Israel."

He showed me the day's headlines: "Israel and Islam have unsheathed the sword."

"That's a laugh. Israel has no sword," he said bitterly.

"Why do you say that?"

"Man, where have you been all this time? Don't you know that the British have taken good care that the Jews be helpless? That they've made it a crime for a Jew to keep the smallest gun while Arab formations stream into the country in full battle army? Self-defense has been made into a crime for the Jews, and the Arabs have been granted a power-of-attorney to slaughter us. And they can do it because they have the armor, artillery, ships, planes, money, political power, everything, and we have nothing."

"So, what's the conclusion?" I asked.

"That there is no hope."

"But the world cannot stand by ..."

"Oh, yes, it can, and it will. It'll watch the carnage and make clucking sounds, and be secretly relieved that somebody is doing the dirty work once and for all."

"If that's so, if there is no hope, why are you going?"

He stared at me.

"Forget it," he said.

"No, give me a straight answer."

He was silent for a while.

"There is no straight answer to that kind of a question," he said at last.

I didn't understand the Jewish objectivity, then. It is almost beyond understanding and contributes to rendering the brutal truth of antisemitism unbelievable. Even now, the nearest I can come to explaining it is that there's a limit to evil beyond which the soul ceases to react. One might call this sort of evil "ultra-evil." That's it; antisemitism is ultra-evil. No pain is felt beyond a certain threshold, and the Jews overstepped that threshold a long, long time ago. But at the time, I didn't understand all this and didn't believe my friend.

My wife did.

"Of course it's true," she said. "What does it matter that it's incredible. Were the Germans' gas chambers and crematory ovens less incredible? What did I tell you? The Jews are doomed. Once, they could scatter like vermin, and if one got caught, another escaped. Now they've created that anti-semite's dream, a place where one can shoot at random and no matter, it's always a good hit. What madness made them do it? If the earth were flat, maybe they could hide on the underside. But it's round, and what can you do about it?"

"I could fight," I said.

She didn't reply to that.

While we talked, she had been drinking. She often drank these days. Once it had amused me—tipsiness became her, her skin flushed, and her blue eyes sparkled, even her hair seemed to glow a brighter copper-red, and after a while, she wanted to make love. But there was no sensuousness in her now; this was gloomy, aching drunkenness.

"I see that old Moses is reaching out to you," she said, "the damned old phony. We don't even know where he's buried, yet he keeps reaching out to people, damn him. My father used to tell me how Moses threw away his mantle, a prince's mantle embroidered with gold. He stepped down from a gold-encrusted chariot, patted his horse's neck, and that's the only leave he took from a prince's life. He stepped down to bend his shoulders to a slave's labor. My father was a pious man; he thought all that a wonderful story. I used to think so too because I loved him, but now I know it is a story of madness or the enacting of a curse. I wish I had known then what I know now, I would've told my father, and perhaps I might have saved him. We might be together now, laughing at old Moses. My father was a big man. His hands were big but gentle, very gentle; he wore a short beard the color of my hair, soft and glossy like my hair. My hair's beautiful, isn't it? And his beard was beautiful. He stroked it with a big gentle hand, I put my childish hand on his, and he carried it through his soft glossy beard.

"He liked to sit in front of a fire. We had a fireplace in every house we ever lived in. He lighted his calabash pipe—it's a kind of gourd, you know, shaped like a bugle, they set a meerschaum bowl in the flared-out open end and a mouthpiece in the narrower one. He'd smoked it for so long that the bowl had turned brown-black, caked with tobacco tar. It had a villainous smell, but it was a wonderful smell to me. I loved to put my fingers on it when it was hot, and they caught the smell of tobacco tar. I liked it so much that I hated to wash afterward."

Then she couldn't talk anymore. Her eyes went wide and sapphire-bright, and they shed big tears. The tears coursed down her cheeks, flushed with drink. I sat next to her, put my arm around her shoulder, and rocked her as one rocks a child to sleep.

"You won't leave me?" she whispered.

I hushed her. She turned her face up to me, her lips moistened with her tears. I kissed the tears off her lips and felt a stirring of desire, but I couldn't make love to her now. It would have seemed an act of perversion; she was sunk in misery and worry, and in her bittersweet memories, she would have yielded as passively as a puppet. I kissed her mouth again—it tasted of liquor, salty tears, and her.

"I'll put you to bed," I said.

She didn't resist, but she was almost a dead weight in my arms.

"Come, you're no longer a child," I said, "you're a big heavy girl."

But she clung to me. She was feeling the liquor; her knees buckled, her speech had become thick and blurred. I led her to the bed, and she fell on it and went to sleep. She slept with her mouth slightly open, which made the curve of her cheeks seem fuller. Her cheeks glowed a deep pink, but as I watched, the blood drained slowly away, and they became almost pale. She looked very tired in her sleep. I hoped it was dreamless. The pillow was covered with wildly tangled red hair, and a long mesh of hair flowed down her forehead. I pushed it gently aside, and her long, slightly upturned nose wrinkled at my touch. I thought of undressing her, but she was too heavy in her helplessness.

I removed her shoes and covered her with a blanket. It was the middle of May. The night was warm; an early fly buzzed about the bed and lighted on her pillow. I leaned over to chase the fly away. She moaned softly in her sleep. Her broad, smooth forehead had sprouted tiny pearls of sweat, the skin of her cheeks glistened from an invisible film of sweat, and a warm, sweaty smell rose from her. I folded the blanket off her chest, and I stroked the dress where it tightened over her big breasts. Her whole body shivered in protest.

I wished I could make love to her. In the abandonment of sleep, she looked like a doll, a big luscious live doll made for my pleasure, to be played with and enjoyed how and when I wished. It occurred to me that perhaps that was nearly all she was. Perhaps shock and sorrow had stunted her soul, and it hadn't grown to match her body. She had become a big live doll with a tiny soul inside, a crushed childish soul, as irrelevant as the talking voice inside baby dolls.

Suddenly she spoke in her sleep.

"I'll go with you," she said very clearly, and she smiled happily at the answer she heard in her dream.

I wondered whom she had been talking to and what he had answered to make her smile so happily.

CHAPTER EIGHTEEN

"Why didn't you fight in forty-eight?" the twins asked me.

One of the too many questions to which I have no answer. I could give an excuse, though, something like, "Because your mother was expecting a child, your brother Simon." I could say it, but it would be a lie. I have thought and thought about it, and now I'm sure it was the other way around—she had the child because she felt that I didn't want to go. She interpreted my wish and took the odiousness on herself.

I can hear her protesting: "Don't blame yourself; it's I who trapped you, to make sure you wouldn't leave me."

If I believed in life after death, I should say that she's projecting that thought into my brain even at this moment. She's willing me away from the truth, and she's coming between me and the humiliation of knowing myself as I am.

Once I accused her of sapping my will with her motherhood. She didn't defend herself, she merely smiled, and her sapphire eyes shone with secret satisfaction. She had succeeded in shouldering the guilt of my selfishness and cowardice—no, not even that, I'm not really selfish, and I'm not a coward, just an indecisive, muddled little man. She had protected me from the truth (she thought) forever. But no, not forever. The truth rises in time like the inflated body of a drowned man in still waters. It's ugly, I wish I didn't see it, but it floats right under my eyes; it leers at me, it shows me the features of an indecisive, muddled little man.

When she told me she was pregnant, she said, "You can leave me, if you wish. I'll have an abortion."

"We'll get married right away," I replied.

"Don't treat me like a servant girl who's gotten her young master in trouble."

"Oh, for heaven's sake!"

"But do you really want to marry me?"

"Of course I do. I know it was no way to propose, but please try to understand. Every morning when I read the newspapers, it's like living in a nightmare."

"Then stop reading them. This war has nothing to do with us."

"But it has. And it's very hard to read about it and then lay the paper aside and take the law of torts seriously."

"I'm paying the price too," she said. "I never wanted children."

Even after the marriage, she kept coming back to the talk of abortion.

"Let me get rid of it and stay this way," she said.

"Shut up."

"Oh well, I could still have a miscarriage."

The pregnancy didn't show on her; her belly stayed flat for months. On our honeymoon, she dove, swam, and looked splendid in a bathing suit. I insisted on a honeymoon though she protested that it was ridiculous because we had been sleeping together for a long time. A few words from a rabbi would make no difference, she said.

She drank too much, and she tired herself out; she fought against the child.

"It's your fault that I don't want my child!" she said.

But the child cried before birth.

We had been sitting quietly at home; I studied as graduation drew near, and she had been drinking and dreaming. In the gathering dusk, she was an indistinct shadow beyond the pool of my reading light. Her pregnancy showed by then, and she had grown enormous. She didn't have the traditional Jewish pride in pregnancy and felt ashamed of her looks. She never went out, and even at home, she kept in the shadow as much as she could. By daytime, our blinds would stay drawn, and at night, we made no more light than I needed to study by. She mourned her lost figure.

"I'll never revert to what I was. Motherhood is doom to big women like me; we become cows."

There is more than one word to designate a cow in Italian, and she chose the most disparaging one: *"vacca."* She rolled it on her tongue with masochistic pleasure. Since the first swelling, she had rejected any contact.

"Go away; I know I'm disgusting, I don't want sexual charity from you. Go find yourself a slim girl with a narrow backside and nicely arched loins, leave the *vacca* alone."

She wailed about her breasts ballooning (she said) to a grotesque size, "like water bags, we could cross the Sahara on waterbags this size," and she cried in front of mirrors. But I knew it was all camouflage, deliberate nonsense expressing and masking much deeper anxiety.

Then the child cried.

She came over to me and clutched my arm. Her face had gone white, and it gleamed white at the edge of my pool of light. There was a wonder in her eyes and astounded and frightened delight.

"Bruno, the child cried!" she exclaimed breathlessly.

"You're sure?"

"Bruno, he cried!"

"Well," I answered lightly, "it has been known to happen; you're not the first mother in history."

She shook her head.

"You don't understand. He cried. He's alive. He's ... here."

"Of course he ... or she ... is here."

"Bruno, could he ... know?"

Of course, it couldn't. It couldn't know that it had been a pawn in a game, that it had been conceived ... to what end? To protect her from loneliness or me from having my bluff called? Certainly to an end different from its existing. She had said: "I never wanted children," and she had spoken about abortion, and I had said no, not for the sake of the child but on impersonal moral grounds. She had pretended to worry about her figure, but actually, she was lamenting her motherhood. We had hastened to marry but did a few words from a rabbi make any difference? They surely made no difference. We'd been sleeping together for so long, and conception was just an accident—what is conception but a spermatozoa leakage? All this had been going on while it was growing in her belly, so close to our voices and our thoughts, a part of us yet already distinct from us, stealthily watching and listening from its dark nest.

But of course, it couldn't know. What nonsense. It was a tiny throbbing nodule of organic matter, neutral and non-human, a little frog-shaped monster, primitive, germ-like. It could not feel unwanted, rejected before the very beginning of its existence. It couldn't feel anything besides formless, chaotic satisfaction at the warmth, the flow of nourishing blood, the cushioned floating in the waters of birth.

"Bruno, could he know?"

"Don't be silly."

I felt a shiver and was not surprised that her eyes had gone dark and clouded with remorse.

"Bruno, he cried," she whispered. "Will everything be all right? He's our child."

The day the child cried was a turning point. She stopped drinking. She began to knit, but she had no skill, and only nightmare shapes were issued from her needles. She stopped being ashamed of her size, even grew complacent about it.

"For a *vacca*, I'm a handsome one," she said.

"You're disgusting," I joked, "but when you get your figure back, we'll have a second honeymoon."

On the day of our marriage, she had drunk a lot. I had loaded her into my car and driven off, driving until nightfall. We came to a town by the sea and found a room in a hotel. Our room had a terrace covered with wisteria. The wisteria's blooms had long since faded, but their scent lingered.

She went to bed and fell asleep at once. It was a full-moon night, but the moon hadn't yet risen, or it hid behind trees and sloping roofs. It gave off an ashen glow; the window was an ashen rectangle in the room's blackness, and it was very quiet. There was nothing in the night but that ashen rectangle, the sound of my wife's rhythmical breathing, and the sweet scent of wisteria blooms that had faded. The moment was complete, self-enclosed—nothing beyond this room, no anxiety and no regret, a moment utterly peaceful.

After a while, I fell asleep too. When I woke up, the night had deepened, the moon had risen high above the trees and roofs. Its shine fell on the window, flowing through the window in a luminous beam as thick as cascading water. My wife stood before the window, entirely naked, her harms spread away from her hips, and the hands opened flat, one knee slightly bent, her head held high to expose the throat. The moonlight bathed her body, flowed on the skin of her shoulders and her full breasts, on her still flat belly, on the sweet broad sweep of her hips, on her firm, shapely legs. The moonlight gathered in a bright pool about her feet.

I sat up in bed. She didn't move. She must have unlocked the window because a draft stirred the red hair falling freely on her shoulders. In the neutral whiteness of the moonlight, her whole body glowed golden from the red of her hair. I called out to her, but she didn't answer. Then I got up, I went to her, but I didn't touch her. I felt as if she must not be touched, as if I hadn't the right to touch her. I felt as if I should kneel and sink my face between her golden thighs and lose myself in that narrow enclosure of flesh. Getting up, then, would be like being reborn.

"Look, it's me," she said.

There was a big mirror near the window. She was looking at her image in the mirror, watching herself with a kind of dazed wonder, passing her hands slowly over her body, in a hesitant exploratory caress.

"Look, it's me."

"You'll catch a cold," I said.

What a trivial thing to say!

She told me it's me, and I didn't find an answer, I thought.

"It's me" – the unconditional offer of herself, and I didn't find an answer.

It shows that I didn't deserve that offer. But it has been made to me and no other, and that's the way things stand, the way things will stand forever.

CHAPTER NINETEEN

My wife gazed at me as if hesitant to speak.

"I wish to show you something, but don't ask any questions. If you do, I shan't be able to go through with it," she said at last.

We drove to the Lake of Como and followed the narrow road twisting around the lake.

"Step here," she said.

We stood in a little square near the shore. She picked up pebbles and threw them, trying to make them skim the water's surface.

I waited.

"These pebbles aren't flat enough," she said. "There used to be some really good ones. I was quite skillful at it, though I did it rarely because we didn't like to be noticed. I was fifteen, and I wasn't like today's girls who grow so wise so soon. My body was a woman's all right, almost as developed as it is now, but there was a child's soul inside. I dressed in shapeless backfisch clothes; my parents were very old fashioned, you know. I wonder what people thought as they looked at me, throwing pebbles into the water. They couldn't see my childish soul, only my woman's body. I realize it now: perhaps the men found my pebble-throwing motions sexy and dreamed of raping me. Raping a Jewish girl would be no crime, maybe even a kindness, letting her know a little pleasure before they burn her. Indeed my parents were too naive; they didn't realize how exciting my full limbs must have looked bursting from my absurd backfisch clothes.

"I wonder how it feels to be fifteen and not to be afraid. Looking about for suitors, not murderers; laughing aloud, swaggering a little, wiggling one's hips because you are not scared to be noticed. You want to be seen, and you expect the world to smile at your fifteen years. You're a budding creature with the kind of tender strength that allows a blade of grass to grow through stone, a demanding creature confident of the others' submissiveness to her demands. I wish I knew how it feels to be fifteen and unafraid.

"We lived in a villa up there on the hillside, you know, when the Germans came. There's no motor road to it. In a while, we'll walk up ... in a little while. All around us, along the shoreline and in the hills above it, Jewish families huddled in other villas like ours. There were not a great many, I could tell you all their names, but their presence somehow filled the landscape. They were waiting passively for their butchers as Jews have done throughout their history. All of them had devised precautions—alarms, ways to dodge danger—but almost nothing ever worked, and very few of them came back."

She fell silent, and after a while, she dropped the pebble she was still clutching and took my arm. We walked up the sloping streets to the town's edge, and then up a cobbled path between two winding walls that ascended the hillside so steeply that steps had been cut into it. Now my wife leaned heavily on my arm; sometimes, she swayed a little and stumbled on the cobbled steps. We met no one on the path. It was early afternoon, and the July sun baked a crystal-clear sky. Out on the lake, the glare must be blinding; it didn't reach here, but the air stagnated, humid and stiflingly hot, in the narrow groove between the winding walls. Lizards clung drowsily to the walls, cool on the hot masonry. There was nobody around; the people rested after the midday meal, or else they smelled a survived Jew and kept out of the way of my wife's memories.

We opened a wooden gate, broke through a screen of spider webs into a garden that must have been neatly laid out and landscaped once, but now had no design and no sense to it; tough, prickly matted weeds overran everything, and the pungent, nauseating, poisonous odor of the weeds hung in the stagnant air. The house had once been white, but most of the paint and coating had peeled off; chinks of crumbling wall plaster and shattered roof tiles lay on the ground like the rotten bits of a leper's flesh. The leprous house lay dying amid the rubbish and the malignant growth of weeds. A swarm of iridescent bluebottles buzzing about the carrion of a cat rose angrily at us as we climbed the front steps. Inside, the walls were cracked and patched with mold. Festering rubbish from old pillage littered the brick floors covered with a thick patina of caked dust, and a stench of humid decay seized us by the throat.

"See, this is the fireplace," my wife said, "or what's left of it. We sat in front of it that day; father smoked, mother knitted, I was doing my homework—he was very strict about it. They banged on the door. We knew at once who it was. My father said, 'Get away. I'll run upstairs and let them see me on the balcony; that'll delay them a little. We'll meet at the appointed place.' Like all Jewish families, we had made our plans, and we had set a meeting place for when we became separated if we had to run away.

"Mother and I ran into the garden—you've seen it, it's terraced on two levels. We got to the lower level; there's a hidden gate there, but to reach it, we had to cross the lawn in the open, and the Germans had already broken down the upper gate and were inside. They would see us from above, so we froze at the foot of the wall where the garden drops straight down. They leaned over us from above and shone flashlights because it was getting dark, but they didn't spot us.

"We stayed there for hours and hours. It was bitter cold; it was only the end of October, but the season was harsh, and we had only managed light overcoats. We were numb with cold—a merciful discomfort because it numbed our thoughts as well. Then we heard the Germans leave, and we sneaked out. As soon as we were on the path, we met an Italian militiaman. He pretended not to notice us, but we knew there would be others farther off, and none could behave mercifully if he wasn't alone, so we couldn't go on. We rang a doorbell. An old woman opened the door, took one look at us, and motioned us inside. She led us into a bedroom; it was cold there, but she cautioned us against lighting the stove, and it's incredible, but we ate a little.

"She kept us for a week. She fed us though we had no money. She had a daughter who was accounted for a hussy—at the time, she slept with someone from the Customs Police, and through him, we sent messages to friends and learned what had happened to my father. He had gotten away by jumping from an upper story window and climbing the hillside; he was a strong, active man. He hadn't found us at the rendezvous, so he'd come back into town to search for us. It hadn't occurred to him that we could still be in the garden; he'd searched openly, desperately, recklessly, and in the end, they'd caught him.

"After a week, it became dangerous to stay in town. We had received a little money from friends meanwhile, so we went out very boldly. We climbed on the lake steamboat that was crowded with passengers, and we went unnoticed. We landed at another town and climbed up the mountainside to a place where we had long before rented one half of a cottage.

"A couple of Jewish refugees, man, and wife, already occupied the other half. We all used assumed names, we didn't tell each other that we were Jews, and for some days, we lived in mutual suspicion and fear. The cottage stood in a clearing between woods of chestnut trees. I think it must have been a beautiful spot, especially in that season, when the leaves turn golden and red, and the peasants make heaps of them and burn them. Then, the warm aromatic smoke from the fires mingles with the tangy autumn air. It must be beautiful, but to me, it was a place of terror. I lived in a dumb stupor ever since our flight, but now I began to think and understand. At night I thought of my father, and I stuck my head under the pillow to cry soundlessly. I remembered that I had noticed his calabash pipe lying on a table while fleeing the house, forgotten, and I hadn't picked it up. Now it seemed a betrayal, not having picked it up. I felt boundless guilt and cried all the more bitterly when I remembered it. In the evenings, our neighbor played the violin; he played very badly. When I heard the string's whine, it seemed that it was a car approaching and hooting in the distance. An approaching car would've meant death; therefore, I screamed when I heard the violin, and one evening our neighbor came in to enquire and smiled at me and said, 'We are Jews too.'

"For a few days, we fed on a little bread and cheese we had brought with us, and from chestnuts we picked in the woods. But then, it became necessary to procure food, so we told our landlord the truth, and he went and bought food for us. However, we were still in danger; we had to get away, so we left the cottage and climbed down the mountainside to a town where we'd been told we could find a guide into Switzerland. We found no one. The town swarmed with Germans; people took one quick look at us and muttered, 'We don't know what you're talking about.' They told us, 'You'd better scram and fast.' We boarded the steamboat again, and this time there were few passengers. We were quite conspicuous, anybody could read our story on our faces, and there was a policeman on the boat, but he looked the other way.

"We got off at a town where we knew a man who owed my father some gratitude. He refused to let us in. He opened the door just a little, peered out at us through the crack, and waved us angrily away. By now, we were so tired we couldn't go on, our bodies stiff and sore, all our courage and strength drained off. We sat on a bench, my mother and I; we didn't even talk to one another, we thought, it's all over. Then a woman came along and asked us if we have any money; we answered yes, and she told us to go with her. She took us to two men who were professional smugglers, who agreed to lead us across the border for a price.

"We had good luck there because many fleeing Jews were abandoned after their money had been taken. Some were delivered to the Germans or mercifully murdered outright. We had run into almost-honest smugglers; they didn't lead us into Switzerland but at least to the Italian side of the border. They even cut the barbed wire for us. They pushed us out onto the strip of no man's land, then Swiss guards spotted us from their side and hailed us, and we walked over.

"We were so exhausted from the climb in the night to the border and from all we had endured before that we dropped off to sleep on the floor of the room where they put us. But early in the morning, the Swiss woke us up, made us fall into line, and took us for a hike, not a very long one, but we were a sorry mass of human litter. Many of us were very old or small children, some without soles on our shoes, our feet as bloody as our souls. And the guards shouted at us. They shouted their dislike and contempt. We were helpless, broken beings, we were down with our faces in the dung, and if they had to put up with us, if the ethics and the policy of their country made them put up with us, they might as well have a few laughs. Making us march in the streets was one kind of a laugh. Still, they liked it better to call us out and tell us that they were about to send us back across the border and laugh at our fright, but they did this so often that habit and disbelief dulled our reactions.

"But it was a little different for me. I was a handsome fifteen-year-old girl, and I had other problems ..."

She had told her story in a lifeless, stupefied drone, and suddenly she stopped and stood still as if she had run down. Then she shivered. We looked down on the gray-green expanse of the lake. There was a red sail in the middle that hung flabbily in the windless air. The water lay still, heavy and metal-bright like a mass of mercury, yet my wife shivered in the sweltering day, and her teeth chattered. I touched her forehead, and it felt burning hot.

"When we got back to Italy, my mother just stopped living," she said. "She had reached the only goal she could set herself: I was safe, or so she thought. So she stopped living. You can't call that death. You don't need old age or illness to explain it. Living is a task, and when it doesn't make sense anymore ..."

"You're ill," I said, "let's go away. Let's go back home."

She seemed not to hear me.

"You see that red sail? There was one just like it, then. I used to look at it from here, I was fifteen, and I pretended that it was a great bird with fifty wings, which had descended on the lake and stood poised restlessly and soon would fly up to me. I would cling to its talons and be carried away to whatever place the bird had come from. It didn't matter where, but far, far from here. A silly dream, but there are no dreams of happiness for a fifteen-year-old Jewish girl hiding from death. There should have been a brave man to come and kiss the fear from my lips. Could you have done it if you had known me then? Or would you have laughed at my woman's limbs bundled in the backfisch clothes? It's too late now. That was the time to be brave, to laugh at hell. Now it's too late. My lips remained unkissed, and we ran away. I learned what it is to be a hunted beast, a head of game trembling in its lair and drawing its enemies by the smell of fear it gives off. Once you have been that, you'll never be completely a human being again. My fifteen-year-old lips remained unkissed, and now it's too late."

CHAPTER TWENTY

My father had a heart attack. We were working together in our office when it happened. He was talking, shaking the pencil he held in his delicate slim hand to emphasize a point. Suddenly he dropped it, gasped, fell forward with his face on the desk, a little saliva leaked from his mouth, and wet the desk's leather surface. I summoned an ambulance and took him to a clinic, but I knew that he was dying from the very first. I had seen a lot of death, not natural death, but no matter, death and I were old acquaintances; I recognized his approaching footsteps; he couldn't fool me. At the clinic, they gave him a shot of morphia, put him in a bed, and left him there. I sat at his bedside. He breathed raggedly. He was still in pain despite the morphia. His skin had gone yellow pale like that of some plucked chickens. Incongruously I remembered a saying: "You've got to watch the skin, good chickens have yellow skins, don't accept any of that sickly whitish stuff." His beard seemed to have grown with sudden swiftness; I was sure he had shaved a few hours earlier, yet it showed, bristly on the yellow skin. His white hair stuck out from the scalp—he wore a bit too much brilliantine, and that made it stiff— and because I knew how vain he was of his appearance, I smoothed it down with my hand. His aquiline nose seemed to have shrunk sidewise so that it protruded from the middle of the face like the blade of a hatchet having the skull for a handle; his nostrils pulsed with each breath like two parchment membranes of a bellows.

He swiveled his head to look at me, smiled painfully, and gasped.

"It's so difficult to die," he whispered.

"Don't talk," I said.

He stared at me strangely, half-enquiring, half-beseeching, as if willing me to do something but unsure that I would.

"What is it, Father?" I asked, "Anything I can do?"

He didn't answer. He kept staring at me, and his eyes grew brighter. I had a fancy that his stare was turning to solid matter, to a rope, a link binding him to me; that he clung to that link as if to a lifeline over an abyss. His eyes burned into mine, but suddenly he turned away, and the link snapped. Then I knew that he was dead. I looked at him a while before calling the nurse. Lying there, he seemed very different from anyone I remembered. He was a strange old man who must have been handsome once, slim, white-haired, hawk-nosed, very dignified, and supremely indifferent. I had the uneasy sensation that he had been trying to tell me something. I had said, "Don't talk," and he had obeyed. It didn't make any difference to him whether I listened or not because it was to my advantage to hear, so if I wouldn't, I could suit myself. But of course, this was a silly fancy. Probably he had been unconscious for some time, or if not, at least focused inwards on his pain. "It's so difficult to die," he had said. I wondered if it were true; I hoped that it wasn't that it had been easy at the end, at least.

I felt no sorrow, merely an uneasiness. He hadn't occupied a great space in my life; lately, he had been nothing but a clever professional partner. Still, there was some rearrangement to make in my life because of this—I couldn't help thinking of a fussy housewife who rearranges china pieces in a showcase to hide the empty space left by one of them, which has been accidentally knocked over.

We buried him in the Jewish section of the Monumental Cemetery. It's quite the thing to be buried there but difficult because there's no room left, and fresh dead are diverted to a much larger, much less smart cemetery. My family had its own plot with a very expensive, hideous black marble monument looming on it. Thus my father was privileged; he had his place assured next to some fine Jewish gentlemen and ladies with old Italian names almost as distinguished as his own. Once, he might not have been happy about it. He might have preferred to rest as he had lived among Gentiles, provided the monument and the inscription were handsome enough.

Once, he had confessed to me to a weakness for Machiavelli's epitaph: *"Tanto nomine nullum par elogium ..."*. "No praise is equal to so great a name," but of course, nobody could use that one. Grandfather, who had been a fighter, had chosen *"Qui numquam quievit quiescit"* – "He who never rested, rests." Certainly, an epitaph in Hebrew, a language that he couldn't read, would have caused my father small satisfaction. But times had changed, and perhaps now he would be glad of the narrow, quiet, slightly snobbish enclosure of the Jewish section.

The religious ceremony was short and uninspiring. Everybody seemed in a hurry to get through it. My wife looked pale and nervous; our son Simon, who was six, rubbed his feet noisily on the ground and made clucking sounds in his throat. An old woman stood to one side and cried; she was Palmira, my nanny, who had been caring for my father and had been attached to him, but I knew her tears were for herself; my father had provided handsomely for her in his will, and she was too old to work for me, so now she faced the frustration of being useful to no one but herself.

It was early summer. Next to my family's monument, the tombstones were bright with fresh flowers; a bee fed on a yellow sunflower. The rabbi's drone faded from my perceptions. I kept looking at the bee, and when it flew away, sudden dizziness overtook me. They put a shovel in my hand. I threw the first shovelful of dirt on my father's coffin. It is considered a gesture of piety, but it seemed insensitive to me. It's like saying, "Good-bye old man, I'm putting you away, I'm piling dirt on top of you so you can never get back out."

Then it was over.

I had felt some discomfort and impatience, boredom at the uninspiring ceremony, a vague wonder at the bee's feeding on the flowers of the dead, that and nothing else. The china pieces in the showcase in my mind had been rearranged neatly, already no empty space showed, or so I thought.

I watched my six-year-old son and asked myself, is it going to be the same with us?

"Why did you bury Grandfather this way?" he asked.

"Because this is the way it's done."

"Oh, no." He shook his head. "That's not right."

"What d'you mean?"

"Dead people go to church."

"Some do. Not all."

He kept shaking his head.

"All. All dead people go to church, I know."

"How do you know?"

"It's cool in church. It's dark, and it smells nice. There're great big windows with glasses of so many colors. There're statues, lots of statues. And it's cool, and there's music and people singing and a nice smell of smoke, I know."

"How do you know?" I asked again.

Suddenly he looked shifty and evasive.

"I just do."

"Come now. You can't have secrets from Daddy."

"I can so."

"No, you can't. And anyway, it's no secret, I know already."

"No, you don't."

"Yes, I do." It wasn't difficult to guess. We had a Catholic maid; her name was Anna. "Anna took you to church."

My son stared at me defiantly.

"No, she didn't," he said at first, but he couldn't keep the lie up. "Well, I asked her, and she did."

"You asked her?"

"Sure, all my schoolmates go to church. I wanted to go too."

"Your schoolmates are Catholics like Anna. You're Jewish."

"Daddy, they say that we killed God. They say we're evil people, just a lot of money lenders, and God came down and chased us from the Temple because we're money lenders, and then we took a hammer and nails, we made a big cross out of wood, and we nailed God on it. We nailed the Child Christ, but it's the same thing; Christ is God, and we drove the nails through God's hands and feet, and we killed Him, and because we killed Him, we have to suffer forever. But Daddy, how could we kill God? How can anyone kill God?"

"You're right, Son, nobody can kill God. You mustn't listen to what they say."

"They say that sometimes when they go to church, the priest gives them Christ's flesh to eat and His blood to drink, and the priest does that because they are good and have no sins. How can that be, Daddy? Isn't eating His flesh and drinking His blood worse than killing Him?"

"They don't actually eat flesh, you know, only a wafer. And they don't drink blood, just a little water. It's all symbolic; you mustn't take it as if it were real."

"Then, they lie. Daddy, they're stupid, and they lie."

"It's not as simple as that, Son. You see, they have certain beliefs. To a believer, a wafer can be flesh and water blood; people who have such beliefs are called Catholics. We don't believe in the same things; we're Jews. But we must respect their beliefs and demand that they respect ours."

"How many Catholics are there, Daddy?"

"In Italy, you mean? About fifty million."

"And how many Jews?"

"Thirty-five thousand, almost."

"Is that many?"

"It depends. It isn't compared to fifty million."

"Then it's few?"

"You could say that."

"Very few?"

"Very few."

My son hunched his shoulders and walked away.

"Dismiss Anna," I said to my wife as soon as we got home.

"Why? She hasn't done anything so wicked. The church doesn't contaminate. She meant no harm."

"No doubt, she meant well. No doubt, she worried about Simon's soul. She wanted to make him happy, but you still need to dismiss her."

My wife shrugged.

"There's no limit to what I should accept if it were necessary to his happiness."

"You can't build happiness on such rotten foundations."

My wife poured herself a large glass of brandy. She held it in front of her face and looked at me through it. The mass of amber liquid formed a lens twisting her features into a clown's mask.

"You're not religious, so what do you care?" she said. "You've nothing to offer him in place of the cool majesty of a church, the lofty music, the smell of incense, the daylight streaming through stained glass. You've nothing to offer him except the meaningless fact that he's called a Jew. That's a burden without compensation, like some fool runner starting on a race with a haversack full of rocks on his back."

I didn't want to start the same old argument for the thousandth time.

"You're drinking too much. You know what the doctor said."

"What d'you care if I drink myself to death?" She cried.

She gulped the liquor and refilled her glass defiantly. I tried to take it from her; mine was a gentle, almost a caressing gesture, but she reacted violently as if I had struck her, and for a moment, we struggled. I was aware that the boy had come into the room.

"Stop it, leave Mummy alone!" he screamed.

My wife stood still. She stepped away from me.

"No, Simon," she said, "Daddy isn't doing anything to me."

But the boy had rushed up and bitten my right hand. My left hand tightened about the contested glass. The glass snapped. My wife looked frightened and remorseful.

"Your hand, it's bleeding!" she exclaimed.

I turned my back on her. I let the glass fragments drop to the floor but kept one sharply pointed shard. I drew it hard against the boy's teeth marks until I had made a deep jagged gash obliterating them. Now my hand bled profusely. I showed it to her.

"It's nothing. I cut myself with the glass," I said.

I thought, *It's really nothing. He misunderstood. Children don't understand it when adults pretend. He defended his mother, and that's all right, nothing to feel miserable about.*

My wife stared at me in a troubled, puzzled way.

"Silly of me to cut myself like this," I said and smiled. "It's okay, really, I'm not going to die, cheer up. Here, I'll let you give me first aid."

CHAPTER TWENTY-ONE

Our family's country house, now no longer our own, stood at the village entrance. The main road (still a dirt road) made a sharp bend there. If you let go of the steering wheel, you would drive straight into our garden, if the wrought iron gate was open, that is. But the gate looked as if it never opened. It clung stiff and rusty to two old stone pillars set in a masonry boundary wall. It must have opened for the last time with an awesome creaking, long ago, to let a funeral through. The top of the boundary wall was set with thick pieces of glass welded to it with mortar. Those were pieces broken from old wine bottles, with the dregs of ancient wines still filming their surfaces so tenaciously that they withstood innumerable rains. A wooden door painted green opened in the wall beside the gate. I pulled a handle, which shook a little bronze bell, and the door opened. I walked into the garden.

The house had two stories, a narrow front, and long flanks. It looked like a short piece of two-by-four lying on its broader side; it had once been painted pink, but its color had veered to a moldy green; strips of plaster husk hung limply from its façade. When they finished peeling off, they would feed a heap of rubbish nesting at a corner.

The new property owner was lame. He hobbled up to shake my hand and watched me curiously. He didn't seem convinced that I had no ulterior motive and was merely revisiting old places for old time's sake. Anyway, he made me sit down and gave me coffee. The brick fireplace we faced was blackened with extended use, but the walls had been coarsely whitewashed.

I felt sure that the cripple had done it himself, that the house would only get as much maintenance as his hands could manage. I knew it mourned its Jewish owners and their closed rooms with the dead's clothes and the pictures and letters and the smell of wilted flowers.

I told him that this room had once been papered in a fleur-de-lis pattern. A verse came to my mind: *"La reine a fait faire un bouquet de joli fleur-de-lis ..."* The queen has had a bunch made of pretty fleur-de-lis ..."

I asked if owls still fell down the chimney. I remembered ... I seemed to remember that they did, in my days, and then they couldn't find their way out and wandered about the house, flapping their wings. We found them in the morning, daylight-blinded, half-dead with fright. The cripple thought I was crazy, though he merely said he didn't think it possible; anyway, he'd never run across and owl that had fallen down a chimney. Still, I remembered or seemed to remember it so vividly. Could I have dreamed of it? And if so, how many of my recollections were imaginary? It was depressing to think that my memory might be cluttered with stage property looking real only to me. Those might be tinsel yearnings and cardboard regrets, a past painted on stretched canvas, as inconsistent as my imaginary fallen owls.

"It could've happened," the cripple said, but his admission was, in fact, a denial—I felt that some sort of fight had been engaged between us.

We went out into the garden. It huddled small and squalid, almost putrescent in the colors of late fall. Yellow patches, meant to be flowerbeds, were separated by paths meant to be graveled, where innumerable footsteps had ground the gravel down into the black earth. A magnolia stood dying in a corner, its trunk choked with a mossy parasite. The soil glistened black and fat, rich with organic residues, crusted with rotting fallen leaves, a happy womb for feeding earthworms' vertical threads. On one side, a boxwood hedge grew vigorously and jaggedly; next to it, a wild rose bush promised to bloom profusely come spring.

Two cypresses shot up at the end of the garden opposite the gate. I suddenly remembered that I had seen them in nightmares, seen them burning, giving off a flight of screeching hooting little birds of prey. Then they snapped at the bottom and crashed flaming on top of the house. Now that I looked at them, they were much smaller than in my nightmares. One of them had a broad charred scar left by lightning. Perhaps I had really watched fire licking up its trunk once in my childhood.

Cypresses have the shape of flames, the shape of watchfulness, and remembrance. Perhaps this is why they are planted around cemeteries, to shoulder people's burden of watching and remembering, so people can go away, forget, and not feel guilty; they have left the cypresses there much as they leave a token presence of scarecrows in the cornfields.

"We live in hard times," said the cripple. "This was silk country once. The land was thick with mulberry trees, everyone grew silkworms, and all the girls worked in the old spinning mill over there. Now silk is out—first Japanese competition and then nylon. The only mulberry trees standing are those marking the boundary lines, which we didn't get around to cutting down yet, but we will. And young people are leaving the country. I'd leave myself if it weren't for this," he pointed to his lame leg. "A war wound, you know."

As he talked, we walked on. We passed between the two cypresses out onto a grassy lane with vineyards on one side and cornfields on the other. A cloudy, gray, and opaque November light bathed the countryside. A low-lying mist blanket clung to the earth. It lifted here and there in tiny whorls like a quiet person yielding to an occasional ephemeral whim. At the end of the lane, heat steamed up from a fermenting compost heap. The tepid air rose in wavering refractions in the cold of the day, and a warm, sharp smell came to my nostrils, the bitingly strong smell of mixed cattle excrements. A narrow dirt road ran beyond the farm's boundary. Beyond the surviving doomed mulberry trees, a boy was riding a bicycle down the road. The wheels squeaked on their axles, and he whistled as if to conquer fear. I thought that the approach of winter in the country is fraught with fear. Primitives believed that spring might not return without rites and powerful magic. They perceived the running of rural spirits in these low-lying mists and felt that the exhausted earth demanded blood.

Now we walked under a thin rain made of minute drops that seemed not so much to fall from the clouds as to condense spontaneously from the moisture saturating the air. The cripple apologized for the desolation of the fields, the livid light, the mist-rain.

"You should've come at vintage," he said. "That's still a good time, no matter what."

I didn't answer. I remembered the vintages of my adolescence only too well. We had a lot of help at vintage. Young men competed to help us because our sharecroppers' daughters were the most handsome and merriest girls in the village. They were sturdy pink-skinned girls with carrot-red hair and ready ringing laughter. Our vineyards were small; we only filled two vats, two huge vats standing one on each side of a fountain where the vintagers washed their legs and feet before climbing into them.

The girls—there were four of them—insisted on crushing the black grapes by themselves. They shouted, "Go 'way! These grapes are ours because we have red hair!" They fought everyone off the black grapes vat. The boys tried to climb in for the fun of being fought off. They hoisted themselves onto the vat edge, and the girls kicked at them, harder and harder until the attackers fell off and rolled laughingly on the grass. Their faces and clothes had become all bloody from the blood-red juice.

The girls worked two at a time; they made a show of themselves up there, sweating hot, must spattered, their carrot-red hair all tousled and matted, throats bared in laughter and skirts rolled up to the top of their thighs. When they came down to be relieved by their sisters, the girls washed at the fountain, and then they disappeared into the fields—at least they did toward evening or when their father wasn't looking—and came back after a while with cheeks burning red. They picked hay bristles from their hair and bosom and went back to trampling. They were coarse girls, but I was fifteen, and whenever I thought of them, my mouth went dry, and my heart hammered.

I watched the youngest and slimmest, who was my age; I watched her when she climbed off the vat, her legs blood-red with must to above the knees and the thighs moon-white above those bloody knees. In the morning, the sharecropper's wife made her girls dress properly, but at the first escapade, they usually forgot their panties out in the fields, and when they jumped into the vat red juice, they splashed up their thighs to their belly. They laughed and raised their skirts way up in pretended dismay. From below, we couldn't see what the raised skirts revealed, but we caught the provocation of the gesture.

I followed the youngest girl to the fountain. I didn't think she was aware of me, but suddenly she turned around and grabbed my wrist. She laughed, and I understood she had lain in wait for me; she pulled me away.

"Aren't you washing?" I asked.

She bent her face close to mine; I felt the heat of her hot cheeks. She looked suddenly serious, almost fierce.

"No, I won't wash," she whispered, "it'll be better this way, you'll see. Come!"

We went behind a haystack. She made a couch of the hay while I watched her. She was fifteen too and still slim and clean-limbed; in a few years, she would turn heavy and gross like her sisters, but now as she moved, lithe muscles played in the whiteness of her thighs and her must-tinted knees and legs. There was a steely litheness to her limbs, and when she lay down on the hay, and they clamped on mine, I felt helpless. I had no strength left except in my sexual urge; I thought I could never get away if she wouldn't let me.

She smelled of sweat and must; the smell of hay rose from our couch. When I recall the mingled scents of sweat, must, and hay, it seems to me that it is the smell of life. Her lips were cool and tasted of not-quite-ripe grapes— a pungently sweet-sour taste. They opened on the tender moistness of her mouth, fresh and new when she bit me lightly, and a little of my blood oozed into her mouth, and then we kissed deeply. I thought, *I love you*. But of course, I was only a boy of fifteen making love for the first time to a girl of my age smelling of life.

Then it rained, a sudden, warm, almost summer-like rainstorm. I lay on the tepid rain-soaked hay, and I had a feeling of power, of creation. *I am a man*, I said to myself. She lay beside me, her skirt folded up to her waist, letting the rain bathe her spread-out thighs and her belly. She tilted her head, watching me, a crooked little smile playing on her lips.

"I'll let you wash the juice off my legs," she said. She stuck out her legs, and I gathered them on my lap and rubbed them gently. In the falling rain, the red juice made the rainwater pink and stained my trousers. She kept watching me and smiling her crooked smile.

"Tomorrow, I'll go with someone else," she said.

"Why?" I asked.

She shrugged.

"Oh, I like a change. Don't you want me to?"

"No."

"You want me to be faithful to you?"

I didn't answer.

She pursed her lips.

"It doesn't seem right. You're the landlord's son, the young master. I don't want you to think you own me too. Tell you what—I'll be faithful to you just for the vintage, but you must kiss my knees and ask me nicely."

I kissed her knees and said, "Be faithful to me for the vintage."

"Say please."

"Please."

She laughed, picked up her rain-soaked panties, and threw them at me.

"Here, keep these for me," she said, and then she got up and ran off.

I twisted the panties in my hand to squeeze some of the water off and followed her. That night I drank grappa. The rain had ceased. I walked out of the house into the fields. I went back to the haystack and sat on the wet hay. I had taken the grappa bottle, the grappa burned inside me, and I didn't mind the wetness.

The moon rose. The air had turned warm after the rainstorm, the countryside ripe and warm around me. It didn't sleep at all; it was alive with furtive scurrying presences. I heard rustlings and sounds, as if of subdued, not quite human laughter; I saw tiny, elusive lights bobbing in the distance.

I thought about the miraculous, shattering fact that I was a man. I had learned all that was important in life, and life was simple. It was enough to welcome it and not drive it into hiding, but men drove life into hiding. The smell of sweat, must, and hay still rose strongly in my nostrils.

I know now that this happens only once when one makes love for the first time; physical love as it should be, an unrepeatable moment of grace. But the next day, my father found the girl's panties in my room and sent me back to town.

"The vintage is a good time," the cripple had said, but I felt sure that the vintage too had withered.

We went back to the house, and I took my leave, but I had a second thought as I turned to go. I asked his permission to look upstairs. He said yes, and we climbed the concrete stairway. The steps had once been hammered to imitate stone but had worn smooth. The stairwell had a glass skylight. I recalled how a barn owl used to perch on it and sigh lugubriously down at us at bedtime. I opened the door. I stepped into a large bedroom with whitewashed walls, nearly bare, with a bed and a few pieces of square and rough furniture. A painted ochre stripe ran a wavering course near the walls' bottom as if an amateur painter had drawn it holding the brush loosely in a not too steady hand.

The cripple hadn't followed me. I stood alone in the wan light permeating the room. I perceived a humming silence outside and the smell of leaves and branches burning in the intense coolness of autumn. An old feeling came to me, of being at a crossroads, within reach of something I desperately yearned for, which I could easily grasp were there sunlight and warmth, were it springtime in the countryside and in my life. But spring would never return to me. It had left nothing behind but this disconsolate, lacerating sense of irreparable loss. I stood in the declining daylight, in the humming silence, in the smell of burning dead things. I stood alone like a wounded man dripping blood on the cold, indifferent floor.

A wind was rising as I drove away; storm clouds began to roll overhead. It began to rain hard from the blackened sky. Big drops beat down with such violence that they exploded into fragments and made a mist of livid refractions with shapes of nonexistent things. The black clouds cast large shadows across my way, like ugly flapping birds flying low. I drove almost blindly. Suddenly a half-drowned dog threw itself under my wheels, I braked hard, and the dog fled unhurt. My car skidded onto the road shoulder. The engine stopped and wouldn't start again. I lit a cigarette. The car shook and shuddered under the impact of the storm. There were no sounds in the world, but the drumming of rain and now and then a peal of thunder lightning struck so close that the car lurched each time as if a giant hand had slapped its flanks. It was dark outside now, and I was alone; no human presence, no sign of the existence of human presence anywhere.

In a while, the storm will subside, then I'll get out and look for help, or maybe the car will start of its own accord; there's nothing wrong with it; it's only afraid of the storm. I can well understand it; it's a vicious storm, an evil rain, cold and hostile. How different from the rain that washed the girl's thighs in that autumn of my spring.

My father was right. We are lost somewhere in time and space, and I have not returned because no one ever returns.

CHAPTER TWENTY-TWO

When my son asked me, "How do I know that I'm a Jew," I took it lightly. I pretended that it was a joke or at least a clever but ineffectual attempt at embarrassing the grownups. I had a smug retort ready: "How do you know that you exist, that you're a man. How do you know anything?"

"Believe me, you are a Jew," I said instead.

"This is no answer," my wife scolded me. "As usual, you have no answer. You're asking him to believe you. He doesn't want to believe; he wants to understand, to know, to be sure. And you can't help him. You should have the courage to tell him, I can't help you, I don't know what a Jew is."

"Don't I?"

"You don't. I'll prove it to you."

She took down the Encyclopedia Britannica.

"Look here. It says, '<u>Jews</u> The name came to mean the followers of Judaism,' and then, '<u>Judaism</u>: By Judaism, we mean that religion ...' and so on. Now, are you religious? No, therefore you're not a Jew."

"Oh, come! I'm a non-religious Jew."

"A non-religious Jew? What's that. Is there any such thing? According to the Britannica, there isn't."

"A great many of the Jews the Nazis killed were not religious."

"That's it. They died for something, or because of something, which doesn't exist, or at best is so abstruse that it can't be defined. The label 'Jew' is a handicap when it's nothing worse. If I claim I'm not a Jewess, and therefore under rabbinic law, neither is my son, how can you prove otherwise?"

"By your father's death," I said.

That was hitting below the belt, but I couldn't help myself.

"Is it possible that Daddy's a Jew, and I am not?" our son asked her once.

"When you grow up, you'll find out for yourself," she answered after a short hesitation.

They didn't know I had heard them, but I did, and I admitted to myself that my son hated me. Oh, I know all about the Oedipus complex, but there's a world of difference between hatred on a childish plane and the conscious, hardened, willful hatred I felt in him, which burned me every time I brushed against it as steel burns when it's frozen to brittleness. I had known it all along, though only now I admitted to myself that he hated me.

My son had gray eyes like me, not blue like his mother; he despised the color of his eyes.

"Mummy, you've such beautiful eyes. Why are mine so ugly?" he complained.

They were not ugly at all, only very much like mine, but when he looked at me, they lost all life; they became two lumps of inorganic matter, cold hard polished stone. He withdrew from them as if he feared I could read his thoughts unless he pushed them way down, far, far from me. He was very polite; since the day he had bitten my hand, he had behaved with heavy respectfulness. He hadn't forgotten that incident because years later when a viper bit him, he asked me, "Is this a punishment because of what I did to you?"

We had been walking on a mountain trail, the three of us. Bright sun had come out after a night's rain, and of course, snakes love warmth; I knew it well enough. When I slept on the Arizona desert sands, a sidewinder might crawl in to share my warmth or coil under the folded blanket I used for a pillow. In the dawn's half-wakefulness, I heard its soft rattle, and I slid gently away so as not to alarm it. I should have thought of snakes that morning. I had been looking at the empty sky, imagining an eagle's solemn flight spiraling up to infinity. That was a dizzying view, common once, but now the birds of prey had been decimated in the Alps. The *Alpini* had to be content with ravens' feathers on their hats, and the snakes flourished from their enemies' slaughter. I should have thought of snakes crawling cautiously out of their cool stone nests to enjoy the caress of sunshine. But I was staring upwards, dreaming of an eagle's soaring spirals filling the now-empty sky from peak to peak. Then my son cried out. I grabbed a stone and smashed the viper's head, but it was too late—twin teeth marks showed on his calf.

I cut a deep cross into his flesh with my penknife. He bit his lips but didn't cry. Blood flowed freely. I wanted to suck it off, but he wouldn't let me; he shoved me away with all his strength, he called out to his mother.

"Make him let me," I implored her, "I must suck away the poison," but she was under shock and merely stared at me. The boy kept crying, no! Finally, I told him, "All right, be quiet. The quieter you are, the slower your blood circulates. Be quiet, and you'll be well," and I made a makeshift tourniquet above the wound. He held on to his mother. She began to recover, and they looked at each other, an almost obscene look of love passed between them. I hoisted the boy on my shoulders. He was a dead weight crushing me down. I carried him down the path, praying that my heart wouldn't burst before we reached the motor road.

On the day of the viper, we carried him to a hospital; they treated him and kept him there. They said no danger, but I should always take serum with me, and since I didn't, why hadn't I sucked the infected blood off the wound? Had I been afraid, they enquired scornfully, had I been afraid I'd poison myself?

He went to sleep, and we left him and drove home. Home, here, was an apartment we had rented for the summer on the outskirts of Cortina. My wife was frightfully shaken, and as usual, she took refuge in drinking, and this time I followed suit. I kept thinking of my son's shoving me away when I had tried to relieve him of the poison. The hospital people had been right in scorning me; what kind of a father would be afraid of drawing the poison from his son's blood? He had rejected me though it might have endangered his life. Of course, there's symbolism, and there's a mystic to blood. Eternal friendship was sworn by sharing one another's blood; sucking another's poisoned blood is a gesture of love, and friendship or love from me repelled him. Perhaps some obscure fear had stirred in him, recalling that once vampires have sucked a man's blood, they possess his body and soul. Suddenly I remembered the ancient slander that Jews kneaded their Passover matzos with Christian children's blood. How many times a sex maniac had murdered a child, and the murderer had pointed his finger and cried, "The Jews did it!" Sometimes everybody knew who the murderer was, but no matter, lynching Jews was too great a pleasure to be foregone for the sake of mere justice, and the slaughtering of Christ's killers was an act of piety in itself. Thus a new martyr was raised to the altar to intercede for his faithful and procure graces.

Recalling all this, I wondered whether my son hadn't read some story about ritual murder or seen drawings of hook-nosed Jews sucking a Christian child's blood through long straws inserted into its veins. Whether he hadn't believed all that—was it so crazy to contemplate it? Don't people, grown-up people, well-read, politically engaged intellectuals, daily believe things about the Jews as false as ritual murder? I wondered whether he hadn't cast himself for an instant in the role of the child victim, whether he hadn't yielded for a moment to a yearning to pass over, entirely over to the other side. He was only eight; he couldn't have any such conscious thoughts, but who knew? Hatred for me could have merged in some deep dark stratum of his soul with the hieratic stained glass peace of a remembered cathedral.

"I'm sorry," my wife said, suddenly.

I didn't reply. I didn't need to; somehow, she had been tuned in to my thoughts.

"He'll grow away from us," she said.

"You mean, from me."

"From us. Sooner or later, he'll realize that in the end, no matter what, I'll go your way. He's only a child now, but someday he'll understand, then he'll reject me too. Bruno, why don't we set him free? Then everything between us would be as at the beginning; I'd do anything you want. I'd want anything you want if I didn't have to worry about my son if we'd set him free."

"You mean, baptize him?"

"Yes."

"Finish your drink and go lie down," I said. "You're exhausted."

I went out. I climbed the steep uphill meadow behind the house. The recently mown grass made a smooth carpet, but I walked painfully nevertheless. All my muscles ached from the strain of carrying my son on my shoulders. I sat on top of the hill. The night was dark. All around me, dolomite peaks rose from the valley bowl, from the blackness of meadows and fir forests; a subdued lambency coming from nowhere made them stand out against the pinpointed onyx sky, a soft rushing of torrent waters wafted from down in the valley to die at the gravelly feet of the peaks. It was warm, I was exhausted, and I dozed off. When I awoke, the sky had clouded, a storm was brewing with the customary abruptness of mountain storms. For a moment, I didn't realize where I was; my brain felt fuzzy, my head swam. I looked about me in vain; pitch darkness enveloped the landscape. Beneath me, I saw the jeweled multicolored lights of the town. Then a bolt of jagged giant lightning split the overcast, the thunder clapped awfully, the lights blinked out, and I stood alone, suspended amid nothingness.

But I felt no discomfort, only a poignant expectation.

CHAPTER TWENTY-THREE

On our visit to Israel, my wife and I ran across a boyhood friend of mine who had become a member of Kibbutz Givat Brenner. We stood on the roof of a building in the kibbutz. We could see the Judean Mountains in the east and the shimmering of the sea on the west. He was a soft-spoken man. I found his matter-of-factness almost disappointing; I wasn't used to the Israeli's shyness, his almost morbid insistence on cutting himself down to size.

"On the morning of the thirtieth December 1947," he told us, "I went to work out in the fields you saw to the right of the road just before you turned into the kibbutz. The preceding months had been quiet enough. The United Nations was debating Palestine's future, and the Arabs wished to put on a peace-loving, law-abiding front before the world. On the twenty-ninth, the partition plan was approved. A few hours later, we came under attack everywhere, but we didn't know what was brewing that morning. It was the custom for one of us to walk up the hill across the road to a small Arab village to buy cigarettes. That morning it was my turn. I pretended to balk, and there was some banter about it, which delayed me. As I was about to start, a friendly Arab sidled up to us and warned us, 'Don't you send anyone up there today. If you do, they'll kill him.' Thus it went from then on. By the time it was over, we had lost almost an entire generation of our youth."

He told us that at the worst moment, in 1948, the Egyptian armor stood at Yad Mordechai and beyond as far as Ashdod. That part of the country was Philistine land. The Philistines built Ashdod and Gaza, Ekron, and Ashkelon and Gath, so it was only fitting that the Egyptians should have to be fought there. The kibbutz was practically surrounded. I asked how they were armed.

"Oh, we'd managed to stash away some small arms and ammunition here and there, one cache opened under a cows' manger. The British did search, but they had little luck; they found next to nothing. Then, of course, we had our artillery ..."

"Artillery?"

"Actually, they were home-made mortars," he chuckled, "mere lengths of pipe with a nail at the bottom for a firing pin. We also had a 1914 machine gun, a Schwarzsole, and no ammunition for it. But it had the same caliber as the old Italian '91 rifle. The Italian forces had left behind a lot of ammo in North Africa, and some of it had made its way into Palestine. But although the caliber was right, the charge was too weak, so we opened up the cartridges and loaded the charge from every two into one. It was a tricky operation, and one of us, I remember, left some fingers in it. However, the really big guns were two field artillery pieces of the *Hagana,* just two in all the land. We kept shifting them round to multiply them in the enemy's eyes. They were venerable contraptions with wooden carriages and wooden wheels. They leaped backward whenever we fired them as if they thought, what the hell are we doing here, two rheumatic old geezers like us, ripe for the scrap heap, and tried to run away. We called them the Napoleonchicks, though I don't think they really dated from Napoleon's time. In their wanderings, the Napoleonchicks came our way. We were worried about a possible attack from Yavne's village, so we set them up and spit a few random shots in that direction. The next thing we knew, the Arabs abandoned the village."

"Was it necessary?" my wife asked.

My friend looked at her musingly, and then he laughed.

"Don't look so disconcerted. I didn't mean to preach. Come, the kibbutz will stand you a meal, such as it is."

We went to the mess hall and had a fish meal. The fish was bony and tasted definitely of mud.

"Are you happy in Italy?" my friend asked my wife.

"Yes," she answered defiantly.

I didn't contradict her.

"Then you're a good candidate for *aliyah*," my friend said.

"This sounds like a paradox."

"Oh, but it isn't. If you had problems ... *aliyah* cannot solve personal problems. When this becomes apparent, disappointed immigrants vent their frustration on the country and us. But if you are happy enough yet feel the need for something different ..."

"Such as what?"

"I can't tell you. You must find out for yourself. I can only tell you that we want you here."

"But aren't people like us a dead weight?" I asked.

He shook his head.

We had been walking in the streets of the kibbutz after our meal. Suddenly a sharp wind rose, and its dust-laden gusts slapped at us. We huddled at the foot of a huge eucalyptus tree. My wife shivered. My friend asked her if she wanted to go inside. She shook her head; she kept staring at him in a fascinated way.

"You've made some horrible suggestions," she said to him. "Is this the way you always talk to people? How do you expect ever to attract a sane person?"

"Weizman used to say, 'You don't have to be crazy to be a Zionist, but it helps.' I'm not too interested in sane persons."

"You talk about total commitment," she insisted, "which means people's lives. What do you offer in exchange?"

He shrugged.

"This is a poor country. It's said that in the days of the Bible, it flowed with milk and honey. But too many conquerors have raped it. And then we have the Arabs. They proudly call themselves the sons of the desert, and it's true, their people were born in the desert. People never cut the umbilical cord to their original environment; no matter where they go, they tend to recreate it; it isn't laziness or inefficiency. It's love for something others may find unlovable; it's an element of their culture. When some of them grow accustomed to fruit-bearing trees, they tolerate the tree for the sake of the fruit. Still, forests render them uneasy, they must destroy the forests, and when these have gone, the desert comes along pretty soon. So when we returned to our land of milk and honey, we found a ravaged, scarred, scorched earth, which it took endless patience to wheedle back to life.

"It's told that when Golda Meir was new to the country, she learned from a friend that there was an industry here, chocolate manufacture, and she was very pleased with this. She said, 'I must taste our product.' She bought a bar of that chocolate, bit off a piece, but the chocolate felt gritty. 'Why, this is full of sand!' she complained to her friend, and he replied, 'But of course, didn't you know sand is our only raw material?'"

"You didn't answer me," my wife said.

He smiled at her again.

"I wish I could persuade you. But if you ask me what we can offer ... I'll put it this way: we can offer what we have. Fair enough? Now, what do we have? A difficult life, for sure. Someday, a good death. And always, I hope, peace of the soul. Actually, you see, Golda's friend was wrong—peace of the soul is our raw material."

CHAPTER TWENTY-FOUR

Israel's sunshine burned my wife's skin to a tawny brown, but its natural pinkness still bloomed below the tan, and the blend of pink and brown achieved a glowing embers effect; it made the cool light of her sapphire eyes disconcerting as if they were two crystals of blue ice miraculously intact in the heart of a flame.

"I don't believe it," I said. "Redheads with pink skins aren't supposed to tan; they bake lobster red and blister."

"Jewish redheads tan."

She laughed, and then she looked surprised at her own words.

"I won't let you go out alone. Men will nibble at you."

She had never cared about men's admiration, but now she seemed aware of it for the first time and flattered. She walked among the hotel's guests with her head high, poised straight above her broad shoulders, with the slightly heavy muscular grace that can be the crowning charm of a big woman. She wore a clinging silk dress with garishly colored stripes, which reminded me of a festive Haitian costume. Her wrists were loaded with bracelets of all shapes, which tinkled at every gesture. She sparkled in her gay aggressive plumage; she was wonderfully bright and as disarmingly vain as a peacock, and quite as aware of her beauty—her colorful, uninhibited, sexually provocative beauty.

"The Queen of Sheba must have looked like you," I said.

She had said to me once, "Look, it's me," and I had made an inept reply, not understanding. She had stood naked in the moonlight, her arms spread away from her hips, and her hands opened flat. I know now the meaning of her nakedness and her posture and her words, and why this could only have happened in the night, in a pale silvery gleam, in the silence and the scent of wisteria, and only after we had been married. We had thought that a few words from a rabbi could make no difference because we had been sleeping together long enough, but those words in a language we didn't understand had sunk into us below the level of knowledge and awareness.

She was a big, luscious woman, but she never weighed much in my life. I did love her, but that couldn't change things. No amount of love can lend weight to light or shadow, and she was made of light and shadow; her full statuesque arms were the arms of a wraith, her strong tapering fingers were twisting feathers of smoke. She fought and thrashed in vain—there was no substance to her struggles, they went through the things of life without budging them, the things of life paid her no attention at all, but I didn't understand it. I kept pushing her mercilessly against them; I demanded that she perform the impossible feat of being real, and one day her futile struggles abated. When I looked, she was no longer there; she had slipped away from me and from the task of performing the impossible.

She's much stronger now that I have lost her. People say it's ridiculous to be faithful to a woman so long dead. Maybe they are right, perhaps it's stupid and even slightly obscene, but I can't help it. Now and then, I submit to fitful intercourse with a whore; I do it to relieve pressure and discharge my body as in defecation. It's no more important and no more pleasant than defecation; then, I wipe myself as clean as I can and go away. But if ever another woman could matter, I should feel my wife's smoke feather fingers tugging at me, now that she's gone, with overwhelming strength.

There's no need. I won't do anything to hurt you. I'm a middle-aged man, and soon I'll be old. An old man's love is a sad, disgusting thing; old men should dwindle like vapor wisps in whirling air, leaving only transparency behind. Instead, they are as hard to get rid of as plastic detritus. This is one of the crowning cruelties—an old man's faithfulness is as unattractive as his catarrhous kiss. Still, it's all he has left to give.

"The Queen of Sheba must have looked like you," I told her that night.

We drank a lot of wine, clear topaz-colored Israeli wine. Whenever she lifted her glass, her bracelets tinkled, her lips shone from the topaz-colored moisture.

"Your dress is indecent; it looks painted on you."

"Does it?" She tickled one of her breasts with a fingertip, the nipple swelled and pressed against the fabric, she laughed and stuck out her tongue at me. "Does it show?"

Men guests watched her from other tables, and she turned around to stare them down contemptuously, still with an air of ruffling her bright plumage in provocation.

"Do you have to behave like a hussy?"

She laughed.

"I'd like to stand in the middle of the room and take my dress off. I wear nothing under it. Would the men's eyes bulge out? It would be fun. I could auction myself off; who knows how high they'd go, how high would you go. You'd have to match any bids, you know, and perhaps there're some wealthy lechers in here. Imagine ruining yourself to buy your own wife back."

I shrugged.

"I don't have to buy you, though, so let's turn in."

"It took you a long time."

We went up to our room. The window stood open to the soft spring night, and we heard a soothing rush of surf and wind. The sky loomed clear and deep. A short distance away, the ground dropped. The sea had gnawed away a strip of land to form a crumbly sand bluff as on most of the Israeli shore, a warm sea breeze whipped the surf to a bioluminescent froth. My wife stood beside me, hot from the wine and excitement. Tiny beads of sweat glistened on her upper lip, and near the roots of her hair, she wore no perfume and smelled faintly of soap and sweat. I kissed the sweat beads from her lip.

"You're the only creature whose sweat tastes sweet," I said, and she laughed a little throatily.

"Now I know you're still in love with me if you can say a stupid thing like that."

She stuck out her wrists. I removed the bracelets one by one; they tinkled loudly in the quietness of the room. I switched off the lights. I opened her dress—it was so tight across the chest that it peeled off only reluctantly; it clung like a protective skin, and it rustled and gave off little sparks in the semi-darkness. She giggled; she ran her fingertips through her hair, and it sparkled too, and dangled crackling and sparking to her broad shoulders. Her skin stood out white across the tips of her breasts, and in a thin stripe above her thighs, she appeared to be dressed in a small white bikini. I hadn't realized before how very nearly nude she was when she bathed. It bothered me to think she exposed all of her body except those handkerchief-sized white areas. I told her so, and she shook her head and answered, "They make all the difference." It was meant as a playful, teasing answer, but somehow it rang earnest.

Suddenly I felt as if I didn't recognize her anymore. My hands were full of rustling silk, and I thrust it away from me. It collapsed in slow motion to the carpet, crackling softly. I stood in front of her as a thief might stand in darkness in front of a statue he has come to steal but now doesn't dare to touch; if he should touch it, he fears that something irreparable would happen; something's happening already, and he doesn't know what it is, but because of it he won't be the same man ever again.

It seemed to me that the rush of surf and wind had changed. It no longer sounded meaningless and inanimate. There were notes and voices in it, fragments of notes and voices as if someone had been singing an infinite time ago. The sea and the wind had long since broken up the song. They ground it as fine as sand and now threw random grains of it over the beach against the crumbly bluff—a spray of sound in the saltwater spray, wafting on the warm wind up to us. Something was achingly familiar about it as if the song had been repeating my memories and my yearnings: the voice of the song was my own, or perhaps a much more cherished voice telling things I had never known about myself, so dear that I recognized even the dust of it, ground from ageless time between the sea and the wind.

I heard her sigh; she heard the same sounds, perhaps thinking the same thoughts. I knelt before her, and for a long moment, I pressed my face in the warm, tight enclosure between her golden thighs. She touched one hand to the nape of my neck and otherwise stood still. I felt a stirring in her flesh as if she were slowly coming alive. I stood up, looked at her, and my eyes traveled from the red-gold froth of pubic hair to the swell of her breasts. Her face was withdrawn, hidden in a pool of darkness. Sapphire eyes glistened from the darkness.

A Star of David pendant—my gift—hung from her neck; she always wore it under her dress, and she hadn't taken it off. I pulled roughly at the chain, and the star's points drew blood in the narrow strip of white skin between her big breasts. She cried out. It was a cry of pleasure, not of pain. I wiped the droplets of blood with the tip of my tongue. She shivered and whispered, "You've hurt me," but she didn't move. She stood still, tenderly passive, blood kept oozing from the gashes in her breasts, and now I let it run down to her belly in two wavy crimson threads.

I knew that I had wanted her to bleed, and I couldn't understand it. There was never any sadism in my lovemaking, but blood was necessary tonight, and she knew it too. We stared at the rivulets gliding down the silkiness of her belly and made no move to stem the ugly little wounds in her breasts. We knew that she would wear their scars, but it didn't matter. I can't explain it, but the closest I can get to it is that we felt as if we had just been born, and making love was the first act of our lives. It was like tonight was the beginning of the world, and there's blood in any cosmogony that man has ever imagined.

Man is shy of speaking the thoughts he has when making love; they have a way of sounding silly and even shameful the morning after. Perhaps it's the morning after the time without sexual urge when one droops flabbily upon an empty self, which is silly and even shameful. Maybe lovemaking cracks the crust that man has accumulated on himself, and his core shines through for an instant, but only for a moment, then he's ashamed of what has shone through. It was too simple and too pure, too blindingly real; he feels safer when the thick accumulated crust has closed back to hide that disturbing core.

"I've never had another woman before tonight," I whispered.

But this was not what I meant and was ashamed of saying. I wonder if the future would have been different had I told her what I had glimpsed shining through my educated, well-balanced, civilized crust. Had I called her my sister, my sister-bride—only a woman of my people could be a sister-bride to me. We shared the same ancestral knowledge, the same fragments of song carrying the dust of ancient memories and yearnings. I knelt before you and kissed the enclosure between your golden things before I drew your blood and made love for the first time ever.

But I couldn't tell her those things, on the morrow. She would have laughed at me because such an attitude was the right one. We're well-balanced educated people; we came out of the bush a long time ago, and, well, it's permissible to go a little crazy when making love, to listen to your man whispering what seem absurdly wonderful things and to believe him— it's acceptable, provided the next morning you both laugh about it and good-humoredly cut each other down to size. The blazing cores of your selves have touched briefly, have given off their rending spark, but now it's over. The dull, muddy crusts have closed upon you, and you know it's all nonsense. You are your mud-encrusted selves and absolutely nothing else.

So I merely said to my wife, "I've never had another woman before tonight."

"Not even me?"

"Not even you."

Her eyes brimmed with tears.

"Even your tears are blue," I said.

"But I wear no mascara."

I kissed her, and my voice wavered a little when I told her, "I'll pay you a compliment in Biblical style: your mouth is a cup full of honey."

She laughed softly.

"Erotic folklore for tourists."

We were too damned civilized; we had to make brittle small talk even then. Only once she sighed: "It's my life ..."

But I hadn't understood what she had meant.

CHAPTER TWENTY-FIVE

The night the twins were born, a smog hung over the city, people choked and coughed in their sleep. The acrid, corrosive fumes with their sulfuric stench wiggled through every crack into the houses and settled poisonously inside. The clinic called—I hadn't been sleeping anyway. I hurried, but when I got there, everything was over. My wife lay exhausted in her bed; the two baby monkeys had been slapped into howling, washed, and laid in their cribs. They held the place of honor behind the show window because the protocol prescribed that newcomers push the days-old veterans back to an undistinguished background. But I gave them only a passing glance.

I went up to my wife's room. She lay breathing raggedly, and her face sagged on the pillow, chalk-white on white. She drooped, seemingly boneless like an outsized doll that had lost its stuffing. She waved me weakly to a chair. I sat beside the bed and stroked her hand.

"How do I look?" she asked.

"Pretty good."

"Liar, I know I look like death."

"Then why ask me?"

"It must be bad if you will lie to me."

"What did you expect? You've gone in for mass production," I said lightly.

I knew that she was trying to raise a little quarrel over nothing, but it was a pro forma, spiritless effort, and after a while, she gave up and closed her eyes. I went to have another look at the babies. They lay quietly, wide-eyed, with the unseeing, violet-colored stare of newborn babies. Behind the wrinkled monkeyish foreheads, the little computers of their brains had begun to store information. They already knew that howling wouldn't put them back into their mother's womb but hadn't yet discovered the many things it would do for them.

A nurse asked me smilingly, "Your babies?"

"Yes, and ugly as sin."

"Don't say that."

"Am I unfair to sin?"

She clucked at me.

"Pretending you're not the proud father, eh?"

I asked myself, am I? I didn't feel much one way or the other. The two little monkeys behind the plate-glass hadn't come into my life yet; I felt only concern for my wife, who was so weak she couldn't even raise a little quarrel over nothing.

I drove back home. It was daylight by now. I woke my son Simon, made him dress, and took him to the clinic. He watched his baby brothers sleepily, without interest.

"They've got hair growing down their foreheads, like apes," he said.

That annoyed me. I snapped back.

"You weren't any more handsome."

My wife had awakened, and we went to her room. The boy kissed her coldly, his mouth set, and his eyes reproachful. We talked inanities. I sensed that she wished to be alone with me, but she said nothing about it. After a while, the boy stood up and announced that he would go home; he was quite capable of going home alone, he said.

But this didn't make her smile. I didn't find it funny myself. Somehow it had made me uneasy, and I could see that it frightened her, but new mothers are often fanciful. I expected that her mood would improve as she got back her strength.

But she didn't seem to get back her strength. On the day of the babies' circumcision, she said she didn't feel up to attending. It was a schematic, squalid ceremony, with only the indifferent presence of distant relatives and acquaintances who fidgeted, cleaned up the refreshments, and escaped. But the babies didn't mind; they swiveled their button-like violet eyes about the room as gravely and good-humoredly as if they understood and made allowances. I thought they would grow into grave, good-humored children. All children's intrinsic character shows from the cradle; life may twist them, but they are there from the very first. In the end, they cried only a little in dutiful and forgiving acceptance of necessary pain.

At the clinic, I stood a long time in front of the babies' show window. I told myself that I should wait for them to return to their cribs. I was reluctant to go back to my wife. I thought of her lying in bed like an outsize doll that has lost its stuffing. Once I had read a horror story about a mad surgeon who removed the bones from people's limbs, and now she had reminded me of it. There was something unnatural and final about her limpness, something beyond tiredness or even illness.

She had always been fond of brightness and color, even noise that distracted her from herself, but there's no brightness in a sickroom. There may be sunshine beyond the windows, but it sickens as it enters, and all colors decay to gray and talk wanes to an uneasy, gloomy hush. A sickroom is a place for those who are going to die. Death has passed by and put his mark on them to show that he is busy right now, but he'll be back as soon as it's convenient. We should send people away because death will come for them and enter any house they inhabit; they must go to a place suited to their visitor. They depart in a cloud of lies and mendacious promises, and even though death may forget them for a while, they're no longer alive. Their husbands and wives, their children, their friends, have already checked them off and are secretly impatient for them to become as dead in the public registers as they already are in their hearts. I told myself that my wife's room wasn't a sickroom but a place for a new mother to rest from a happy travail. Still, the thought of her lying white and limp and alone was unbearable, and I decided that I would take her home at once.

Now the babies were back in their cribs, and they seemed to be watching me out of their button eyes. I felt sure the violet color of their eyes would veer to blue. They would grow blue-eyed like their mother, but they were baby boys. I felt a pang of regret that one of them at least wasn't a girl who might bloom into her mother's likeness and someday be fifteen and unafraid and be desired by men.

There had been a bunch of young men about my wife when I had seen her for the first time. Her face was flushed with the coolness of autumn. She dressed carelessly. She never did dress well, but her clothes achieved an attractive effect of precariousness. They were decent and even modest, but they looked as if they had been put on in a hurry and in the wrong way as if the doorbell had rung while she was in the bathtub. They looked about to slip off and made one very conscious of the statuesque body underneath. She wore wedge sandals, which emphasized her stature and, at the same time, made her funny because she perched on them so awkwardly, and now and then had to steady herself on someone's shoulder.

I lingered a little way off. It was my first day as a law student, and we were waiting outside the university building. I kept watching her; she looked forbiddingly beautiful and self-assured among the male students preening and showing off for her. Then our eyes met, and I read fear in them and an appeal for help. I thought, *Why me? There's nothing remarkable about me; I don't want to get involved with this frightened Valkyrie.* And then, she walked straight to me. It was as simple as that.

That night I found out that she was not a virgin. She told me that there had been another man, only one, before me. She asked me, did I wish her to tell me about him? I said no, I preferred him to have no name and face; then she cried a little in my arms. It was freezing in her small apartment. She lived alone, there was no one to tend the brick stove during the day, and at night one had to be careful, lest it gave off poisonous fumes. Luckily, her bed was so narrow that we had to squeeze tightly against one another and felt warm that way and delightfully cramped. That had happened a long time ago, and she had been nineteen.

I went up to my wife's room. I told her I was taking her home, and she thanked me as if I were a stranger doing her a favor—politely and indifferently. She asked how the babies were and had they suffered much.

"Once I saw a photograph of Jewish children being marched through the streets of a town by beefy, smirking Nazi soldiers," she said. "The caption didn't say where and to what destination. The soldiers carried submachine guns, and the children marched with hands above their heads, under the guns' threat. Submachine guns against children. They must have been prisoners for some time because they looked starved. They had bony, wasted small faces, little more than frames for eyes grown cavernous, and mind this, there was not a tear, not one single tear in any of those cavernous eyes. I wondered what my father would have said had he seen that photograph. He believed in God, and I know his own death couldn't shake him, but can anyone believe in a God who looks passively on such a scene? How many such scenes, because what is the number of Jewish children who have gone that way, one million, two millions? How evil can God be, to tolerate the torture of tearless skeleton children?"

"Nothing's going to happen to our children," I said.

"That's up to you. The only thing I could have done for our children was to keep them from being born. But I failed. Now it's up to you."

"You'd better get dressed."

"Right away," she said, but she made no move. She went on talking.

"It's like the story about the stranger with the parchment under the skin; you heard it once. You cut that parchment out of me one night, I felt it even then, and I told you 'It's my life,' but you wouldn't listen, and I couldn't stop you. I didn't want to stop you. The story is that the stranger recited the *Kaddish* for himself so he could crumble into a clean handful of dust; otherwise, he would have lingered on and faded away little by little. And, Bruno, oh Bruno, I cannot recite the *Kaddish* for myself or any other prayer."

CHAPTER TWENTY-SIX

Sometimes at my awakening, I hear a child's voice. It doesn't laugh or chatter; it speaks, though the words run together into a stream of meaningless sound. Sometimes its tone enquires or is edged with a complaint. Children with large wondering eyes have such voices, children who can stand still and stare gravely for hours and are easily rebuffed into silence. I know a lot about children now. I recognize the melancholy in the voice, the despair of a kind only children can feel, grief without cause and expression, as absurd, as irreparable as life itself.

There's silence in the house. My sons are asleep at this hour, but my sons don't have voices like that; it's my own voice I'm hearing. I don't fully exist in my half-wakefulness, and it can talk from the depths of me. I hear it, but I cannot answer. I couldn't answer my disembodied voice's questions or soothe its complaints even if I understood them. There's no consolation for despair with no cause, which feeds from a depth where reason cannot reach. I can only lie here and listen, overwhelmed with tenderness and pity. It's a heart-rending experience, and although it's enclosed in the infinitesimal fragment of time between sleep and wakefulness, it is beyond duration. Thus it has neither a beginning nor an end.

How can one feel such tenderness and pity for oneself? Anyway, I don't really like myself. I'm very different from anyone I could like. I can watch any suffering of mine with dispassionate objectiveness. But of course, that child is not really I; he's only a sad little creature far, far away, whom I can never reach. His thin, disembodied voice wanders to me through some freakish channel in the compounded dimensions of matter and mind. It utters incomprehensible questions and complaints steeped in a causeless, bottomless childish despair.

Once, someone told me that I could catch the moon. I asked how big is it, and she said, oh, about like this, small enough so that you can hold it in your little arms but bigger than any toy you have.

She? Of course, it was my mother. Funny, I haven't thought of her in so many years. She died when I was little. Five years old, six perhaps. I don't remember her at all. What was she like? There were some photographs once, but they told me nothing. Ladies look so strange in another generation's clothes; they should take off their costumes and put on everyday clothes, then we'd know what they looked like. Anyway, those were stiffly posed pictures, showing a vaguely handsome youngish lady staring self-consciously at the lens. One guessed that the photographer had gone over and adjusted her pose just a second before. Probably he had bad breath—one could detect a slight wrinkle of distaste to her short, slightly lumpy nose, so unlike my aquiline one. She must have smelled his breath as he tilted her head to an artistic, unnatural angle. Who knows whether she was a fastidious person or the photographer's breath smelled putrid. The photographs didn't tell you what kind of person she was.

And why did she die? I must have known, surely I was told once, but I forgot. I was only a small child when she died. Are all the women in my family doomed to die young? Well, there are none now; let my sons worry about the future, anyway. I can't picture a sunbaked, sweater-and-jeans-clad Sabra girl succumbing to anything as old-world as a family curse.

I asked my mother how big is the moon. She took my hands in hers and spread my little arms out wide and answered, "about like this, you could hold it all right, the moon's a very nice big ball, it shines but doesn't burn like glowworms, except if you catch a glowworm it switches right off, and the moon has a nose and eyes and a mouth etched on it to make it look like a fat, bald man to amuse children like you."

We stood on the balcony of our country house while the moon rose over the cypresses at the end of the garden. I remember a pervading fragrance of magnolia blossoms and how the cicadas buzzed and a man's song was dying away on a distant road

"How can I hold it in my arms if it's up there in the sky?" I asked. "I could reach it if I were on top of one of the cypresses, but by the time I climbed that far up, it would have moved away. Besides, you say I'm too little to climb trees."

She chuckled and told me there was a way. If I set a bucket full of water out on the balcony, in a little while, the moon would fall to the bottom of the bucket, then all I'd have to do would be to pour the water out. That night I sneaked out, got a bucket, filled it, and set it out. I waited patiently, shivering a little in my nightshirt as the night air sharpened. I waited until I saw the moon in the bucket, and I nearly shouted with gladness, but when I poured the water out, there was nothing left but an empty bucket. The slippery old moon hung in the sky once more.

I never told anyone about it; I guessed that they would laugh. But I felt betrayed. I remember everything about that night except for my mother's face. It's only a pale oval against the dark blue sky. She breathed deeply and sighed. Perhaps she found the fragrance of the magnolia blossoms too heady. She listened to the song dying in the distance. Maybe it was a man leaving his native village forever, or it was only a drunk staggering home—but no matter what, there was a sweet poignancy to it. She quoted, *"un canto che s'udia lontanando morire a poco a poco"*—"a song that was heard to die slowly away in the distance." But I wanted to catch the moon, and she told me how, without understanding that it meant betraying me. I don't know what she was thinking, a still-young woman alone with a child on a dark balcony in a quiet perfumed night. Perhaps her eyes moistened, and I didn't see it.

I know nothing about her. I know very little about my father, too. And because of that, they died twice. Death can begin at any moment; it starts when we become aware that nobody knows us any longer. The things nobody knows any longer have ceased to exist, which is true of persons too. But people don't realize that we have begun to die. We walk among them, carrying our growing death with us. They don't notice it because we keep playing the same game at society's table. We play the same game with the same marked cards and crazy rules, the cardboard prizes, and degrading penalties, which we began playing when we stopped being children. Then one day, it's our turn, but this time we stand still, and people say, "Look, he's dead," and they lay a bunch of flowers on our chest.

I have never taught my first son how to catch the moon. But he hates me so much; I must have betrayed him somehow. If I only knew how. On the day of his Bar Mitzvah, I listened to his reading of the *Parashah*. He read well and easily, almost disdainfully. There was a spiteful old man in the audience who used to listen to the boys' first readings so that he could prove his piety by pointing out their mistakes and demanding a rereading. But my son made no mistakes. I knew he had a good mind and learned quickly. He was tall for his age but thin, almost frail; his cold gray eyes, so very much like mine, hooded as if with fatigue.

As soon as the ceremony was over, he walked away, and I followed. I gave him a gold watch at home, a father's customary gift on the Bar Mitzvah. He thanked me lukewarmly.

"You don't seem to like it," I said.

"Oh, it's very handsome and costly, no doubt."

"That's not important."

"Aren't the most expensive gifts the best ones?" he answered contemptuously.

"You don't seem to like it," I repeated.

"I'm grateful." He put the watch on his wrist. "But why d'you always give me what I don't want?"

"Perhaps because you don't bother to tell me what you do want."

"Should I? What if I only wanted what you can't give me?"

I told him he had read well. He shrugged.

"It wasn't any problem. It's all nonsense anyway. I did it to please you, but you know it meant nothing to me. And since I'm supposed to be a man now. I'll have a mind of my own, and I'm telling you here and now, what I did today is the last thing I'll ever do to please you."

I didn't wish to quarrel.

"There'll be good reasons for anything I'll ever ask you to do," I said quietly.

For a moment, he seemed almost ready to apologize. I told him about my Bar Mitzvah. My rabbi was a very old man. He had white hair and a white beard of the purest white I've ever seen, plump waxy cheeks, and serene blue eyes which had seen atrocities in another land. He was fond of me. Whenever he taught me, his short, plump arms would shoot up in dismay.

"But you really are tone-deaf!" he would say.

He made me a present of a little book bound in parchment. He had procured a beautiful silk *tallit* for me, and on that day, he stroked it lovingly, and the palms of his age-roughened hands made a soft rasping sound as they slid over the silk. He was so old, an ancient tree with such deep roots that he was slowly dying of the long way the sap had to travel to reach his gnarled heart. Though he complained that I was tone-deaf, I read my *Parashah* without errors. The traditional chant was ringing out clearly in my still childish voice, and he was so happy he kissed my forehead. His beard tickled my nose, and I sneezed.

"But wasn't your father a freethinker?"[1]

"What's that got to do with it? So am I. Must a freethinker reject something just because others accept it? Then he's not free; someone else decides what he should think."

My father had used the same words, "I'm a free-thinker," but I didn't tell my son.

"I don't want my boy to consort with priests," he had grumbled. "What if they're Jewish priests? All priests are alike, in all religions, a scourge."

But I wanted a proper Bar Mitzvah. Other Jewish boys had talked to me about it, and they made it seem fascinating. I didn't know exactly what to expect, perhaps some kind of initiation, a rite in which mysterious truths are revealed to a boy, from which he emerges a warrior and a wise man. Finally, my father shrugged his acquiescence good-humoredly enough. But he forgot to give me a Bar Mitzvah gold watch.

Milan's synagogue had a façade with a sprinkling of gold stars on a blue background in mosaic, I think, or perhaps my memory's faulty. Perhaps that twinkling façade never existed except in my imagination, but to me, gold and blue are a synagogue's colors. There should be a ceiling painted to look like a sky with gold lettering, *"Ze sha'ar hashamaim."* But it had been built by a Gentile architect, and it couldn't help looking a bit like a church in disguise.

It was so big that it always seemed empty except on the High Holy days when it would overflow. Especially on Yom Kippur, there would be much pushing to get out when the shofar had sounded. Someone always shouted, "Stop pushing, you've already eaten anyhow," but it wasn't entirely true because the crowd would surge out and, with serene incongruousness, feed on ham sandwiches in a nearby bar, where a bewildered owner had never understood why such a swarm of ravenous people should descend on him, locust-like, once a year at a particular hour of a specific day.

On my Bar Mitzvah, the synagogue was nearly empty. My still childish voice stirred tinny echoes; the light was so dim that everything looked filmed over with dust. The clearest things were the rabbi's blue eyes staring serenely at the personal remembrance of atrocities seen in another land. I read my *Parashah,* and nothing happened. I was vouchsafed, no secrets. I emerged no more a man except insofar as any disappointment matures. The silk *tallit* and the parchment-bound booklet were soon forgotten. For many years, I never set foot in a synagogue again.

I didn't tell my son all the truth about my Bar Mitzvah. Deep down, I knew I was a fool to expect a different reaction from him and a hypocrite to demand it. My son played with the gold watch, taking it off and putting it back on. Finally, he laid it on a table. He turned away from me.

I called him back.

"You've forgotten your watch."

He took it from the table, played with it again, it slid from his hands. He didn't stoop to pick it up from the floor. Then I heard myself telling him about the way I felt in the mornings and the voice I heard in the fragment of time between sleep and wakefulness. As time passes, I said, one dies little by little because no one knows about him anymore. It was shameful to bare myself thus before my son; a boy dislikes to see his father naked, a father's confession engenders only distaste, but I couldn't stop myself, I had to lay down my defenses; this was my last chance and the only way I could bid for understanding. I went from emotion to reason. I told him that the estrangement between generations can be bridged by a continuity, a common purpose, a sharing of at least fundamental values; that this is one of the principles of Judaism, not only on the individual but on the social plane as well; that to Judaism, history's not a kind of purposeless Brownian motion but has a direction; that although it meanders it progresses to an end. I begged him not to reject his Judaism merely because his father was a Jew but to try to understand it. Then the gap between us would begin to close, and there would be continuity between father and son.

He listened in silence, and then he asked me if I was finished, and I said yes. He nodded; there was a cold little smile on his lips. He looked much older than his age; his almost emaciated face was that of a man.

"There can be no continuity between you and me," he said. "There can be nothing. 'Nessun patto fra l'uomo ed il leone, nessuna pace nell'eterna guerra dell'agnello e del lupo, e fra noi due ne giuramento ne amista' nessuna.'—No pact between man and lion, no peace in the eternal war of lamb and wolf, and between us, no promises or friendship ever.' You see, a classic education comes in handy sometimes."

My silence seemed to goad him.

"You think I don't understand what you did to my mother? That I don't remember how she cried, and her only refuge was to get drunk? You made her miserable, and you killed her. Perhaps you called that love, you call using people, 'love.' Well, I don't want your so-called love. I don't want anything from you. I wish I never see you again. You're a useless, selfish old man."

I slapped his face, then. He screamed at me.

"Thank you! Now I can tell you how much I hate you!" But his voice cracked; it was still a child's voice, pathetically treble. The awareness of this drew tears of frustration from his eyes, and the tears ran down the red marks of my fingers on his pale cheek. "I'm only a boy, and you can act the big bully. But wait, wait till I can pay you back!"

I didn't say anything. I made no move to stop him. I thought, perhaps all he has said is true, maybe I am as he sees me, perhaps what he sees is my only real self.

If you watch yourself in a mirror, you don't see what you look like to others; you need a double reflection for that, a mirror reflected in another mirror. Perhaps I see in him the reflection of my image that was in his mother's eyes, my true self to others.

There's no graver sin than to humiliate. I've always known that. But I slapped my son's face. He has the heart and dignity of a man but not a man's strength, and he couldn't strike back with his fists, only with his hatred. I have humiliated him. The marks of my fingers will vanish from his cheeks in a few minutes, but they will remain like a scar on his soul ... I have maimed my son. Could I ask his forgiveness? He couldn't grant it, not with full sincerity, and even if he could, what of it, it wouldn't cancel his scar and my remorse.

Was I like this to my father? I was indifferent to him; I didn't even bother to find out what he was. He had said, "It's so difficult to die," and I only answered, "Don't talk," a dutiful, callous answer, like a nurse's. And he had gazed at me in a half-enquiring, half-beseeching way as if willing me to do something, but who knows what that was. And when I asked him, it must have been too late because he never did reply, then a link snapped, and he lay still. The epitaph on his tombstone should have been a question: "Who lies here?" a proper epitaph, someday, for me too.

I picked up the gold Bar Mitzvah watch from where my son had dropped it. It ticked a few times. Then it quit.

CHAPTER TWENTY-SEVEN

How much should I have told my wife about myself, the self she hadn't known, I mean, that had existed before we met? I couldn't make up my mind, and then she was no longer there, and it was too late.

Of course, any woman is jealous of her man's past. It's silly to say she shouldn't be, or what does she care about the women who came before she had any rights to you? To her, "before" doesn't exist. Anything you have ever felt and done relates to the only person she knows, you as you are now, your self of today. And while it isn't true that while wounds do heal as the bow which shot the arrow slackens, they leave scars rough and thick to the touch. No woman likes to caress you, feel the thickness and the roughness under her fingers, and know that another woman has put that scar in you. Now you may despise that other woman or even have forgotten her, but because of the scar, you'll never entirely be rid of her.

I forgot who wrote once: *"Le coeur d'un homme vierge est un vase profond."* It sounds ridiculous to call a man a "virgin," yet a man's virginity can be as real and much, much more enduring than a woman's. A virgin woman is a woman who has had no intercourse, whose hymen is therefore intact; as simple as that. Very few things can be defined so precisely, but try to define a virgin man. A man can have had intercourse a hundred times. It means nothing; some go through their whole lives and make love and have children. They die virgins and never know it because a man becomes aware of his virginity only after he has lost it. And most men never were virgins;

they are too shallow. They were born with flat plate-like hearts incapable of containing the depth of virginity.

I was a virgin when I met Rita, and I lost my virginity to her. This sounds even more ridiculous, but there's no other way to express what happened; that's why I thought of her once as my first love, and there will always be in me a nostalgia, not for her, but for the depth of my virgin man's heart which I lost because of her. And I could never have explained this to my wife; no woman ever understands what it means to a man to be a virgin. When we made love for the first time, I could have told her: "I'm not a virgin either," but she wouldn't have understood.

A few days after I had returned from America, somebody mentioned Rita.

"Remember her? She's married."

"I used to be a friend of her brother's."

"Well, he's dead, but she's very much alive. Why don't you call on her? She likes to reminisce. Perhaps ... she's bored."

I didn't call on her. I kept seeing her rubbing her hand on her skirt. "Jews have sweaty hands," she had said. I thought once more that I should have killed her then. I should have placed my hands about her flower-stalk neck and squeezed. No doubt, that was the appointed fate for us, but I cheated it, and because I did, we both exist like foreign bodies in the scheme of things.

Then she called me. Her voice purred in the telephone. It sounded fuller than I remembered, a mature woman's voice. She asked to meet, and I agreed. When we met, she stared at me for a long time before speaking.

"Is it really you?" she said. "I expected you to be different. I thought I was remembering, but I suppose I was imagining another you, instead. Though you're right as you are, I see how you couldn't be any different."

"It was long ago."

She made a funny little gesture that I remembered well, with her hands.

"Long ago ..."

We talked about ourselves. She told me she was married to a much older man and had no children.

"How do I look?" she asked.

"You've grown into a smart woman. More beautiful than you used to be."

It was true.

"I used to be homely. Now I've filled out and have better coloring. I think you could call me pretty. But I'm sure you liked me better as I was a green, gawky, homely, stinking little bitch. God, what a bitch I was! But you loved me that way."

We walked along in silence. We reached the spot where we used to meet after school. Her school building showed bomb damage, but it still stood.

"Remember?" she asked.

I nodded, but I had nothing to say. I was beginning to hate that word. We started to say goodbye, and she held my hand.

"Your hands are rougher."

"I've done a lot of manual work. I'm no worse for it, believe me."

"You must take care of your beautiful Jewish hands."

"Are you trying to discover whether I've forgotten?" I said. "No, I haven't. It'd be kind of hard to forget a thing like that."

Then she clung to me; her eyes glistened.

"Take me where we can be alone," she whispered.

I took her home. We kissed. She sighed.

"It's like old times. Did you think of me all these years?"

"I tried not to."

"Do you want me now?"

"Yes."

I thought, why not, and besides what else may a gentleman answer.

It was cold in the house.

"Make a little heat, will you?" she said.

I lighted an electric stove. We sat huddled together, waiting for the warmth to rise and spread, and we sipped cognac and talked. It was a pleasant enough interlude, and I was in no hurry for it to end.

"When we were lovers," she said, "I was never certain of my feelings about you. But it was your fault. Your love for me was too intense; I felt swept off balance. I wanted to regain my footing, I needed all my cool-headedness and concentration for that, and none was left for an analysis of my own response. I'm a little woman with little feelings; my love would have been like an open faucet to your amorous flood. How d'you detect the tiny stream from a faucet in the surge of a great flood? In the end, I wanted to get rid of you. I wanted a boy who could give me a relaxed good time, who would be satisfied with what little I could give him and not overwhelm me with ... how can I put it? The Germans made total war; well, you made total love. But even getting rid of you wasn't easy, I was sure that it wasn't enough to hurt you, I had to do something so vile that you couldn't forgive me, and I succeeded, didn't I?"

I nodded because I didn't have anything to say. I felt quite numb, but pleasantly so. It was as if I had been anesthetized from pain—so old and so steady that I had lost all awareness of it and was only aware, now, of the novelty of relief.

Then the room got warm enough. She began to take off her clothes. She stood naked before me, in almost the same pose of so many years before.

"Well?" she asked.

She had a fine figure now, no longer too thin or bony, small but adequate breasts, and of course, her perfect legs.

"You're a lot cleaner than you used to be. Either you've changed your habits, or you bathed this morning, especially for me."

She laughed.

"You dog!"

I desired her but in an ordinary way. A normal young man naturally wants any pretty, young woman with a fine figure who happens to be available. We made love. It was good—nothing special, but good enough.

"How was it?" she asked afterward, as we lay relaxed.

"You know the story of the man from a provincial French town who goes to Paris in search of erotic adventure? Well, when he returns, his friends demand that he tell them all about it, and he describes how he met a smartly dressed woman, and she took him to her apartment and undressed. He keeps saying that it was quite different from anything you can find here; in our old home town, you can't find women that smart or such cozily furnished apartments, and when our women undress, their underwear can't hold a candle to that of the woman in Paris, believe me. His friends urge him to go on. All right, they want to know what happened after she took off her clothes. Ah, my friends, he sighs, what happened afterward was exactly like right here, in our old home town."

"That was pretty cruel," She said, speaking quietly.

I felt ashamed of myself. I told her so.

"I should be grateful to you. I owe you my dearest wounds, which shed such bright red blood, which gave me such exquisite pain. But you see, they've healed, leaving nothing but a mass of scar tissue which aches only now and then rheumatically, with a depressing old-age sort of ache."

She shook her head.

"Don't be silly. You haven't changed. You're not invulnerable; you've just become invulnerable to me. And it's a pity. I'd hoped I could persuade you to kill my husband, but now I won't even try."

I laughed, although I couldn't see where the joke lay.

"Oh no," she said, "I'm serious. It was quite a practical plan if I could have persuaded you that he deserves to die. He's managed to keep afloat; they say a turd always floats. He's palmed himself off as the great antifascist, but I know things about him, and I can prove them that would justify any Jew's killing him. Anyway, it wouldn't have to be crude. There could be a fistfight, and he could fall and knock his head. There'd be a lot of sympathy for the young Jew, in this case. And if it came out that the old stinker had raped the Jew's boyhood sweetheart ... blackmailing a poor innocent girl such as I was into marriage is no better than rape. Why, the jury would melt, you'd be acquitted on the grounds of self-defense, or at least receive a short suspended sentence for manslaughter with every extenuating circumstance on the books. The old swine has made pots of money in the black market, he'd leave a rich young widow, and after a decent interval, she could even marry her old sweetheart. But I suppose this last part of the program might not appeal to you."

She had been dressing, not looking at me, as she talked. Now she faced me and laughed.

"I guess the answer is no, and you're as big a fool as you ever were, and maybe I've been joking, so if you see me in widow's weeds, I've got a feeling that it won't be long now. I will wear them though they disagree with my complexion. Keep in mind that the old bastard has a bum heart and insists on drinking and whoring too much."

I laughed too. We kissed lightly. Then we had another drink. Then I sighed and said, "My father will be home any time now. I'd just as soon he didn't meet you."

"Of course."

I saw her to the door.

What I had done with her had been unimportant enough to be precisely described as "fucking." If I had told my wife, she would have argued, "All right, you didn't care for that woman. She was just a piece of tail to you, but what about the other one?"

"There was no other one,"

"Oh, but there was! The first one was much younger and thinner; she had a flat chest, she didn't dress smartly and wasn't clean, how can you say it was the same woman?"

"Well, she improved."

"No, she didn't. How can you say she improved when you loved her before and not afterward? And what do I care about the one you didn't love? It's the other one that counts."

Then my wife would have become furious and shouted and cried alternately.

"You loved her though she was mean and dirty and an anti-Semite. Besides, how could you be such a lickspittle? You've never stopped loving her because the other one, whom you didn't care for, was a different person. You said her room was a mess, and there were dirty stockings all over. I bet you picked one of them up and kissed it ..."

"I did no such thing."

"Oh yes, you did, don't deny it. I just know you did! And if I ever left my dirty stockings around ..."

"You sometimes do."

"But you complain about it; you never pick them up and kiss them as you did hers."

"I told you I did no such thing."

"You did so. You did, you did!"

How could I have explained to my wife that you mustn't be jealous of someone who never existed because you can't fight nonexistent persons, and you can't fall out of love with them? You can't hate them or despise them. You can't even kill them because they never existed. Suppose you place your hands about a flower-stalk neck and squeeze. In that case, you'd be reaching into a hallucination to kill a real someone, a stranger who has nothing to do with all this, and merely chances to stand in that spot.

My wife would have been sensitive enough to perceive my nostalgia and would have cried from frustration and jealousy. I couldn't have soothed her, for how can you teach a woman not to be jealous of the kind of disembodied love that a virgin man once had in his heart, in the deep vase of his heart?

CHAPTER TWENTY-EIGHT

As I had expected, the twins grew into two grave, good-humored children, no more alike than two brothers close in age, but because they were twins, attuned to one another. Their unspoken communication built a shell around them, a field of force to repel the outsiders. And I was one of the outsiders. They were respectful, affectionate children, but not dependent on me though motherless, very much sufficient to one another.

They called me "Father," I laughed and said, "Come on, I'm not a friar," and they replied respectfully, "Of course not, Father."

Perhaps it was just as well. There would be no painful severing of bonds when they grew up. They would merely drift farther and farther away, waving a respectful and affectionate goodbye as they grew smaller to my eye. I wondered if I would be able to wave back in the firm, cheerful way expected of a dignified old man. Of course, I would; I was good at things like that.

They were quite young when they asked me, "Father, why did God create man?"

"I don't know. Perhaps he felt lonely. The sun and the moon and the stars are beautiful, but they don't provide much company."

"Why don't they?"

"They're too perfect."

"Is that why you made us, 'cause you felt lonely?"

"I didn't 'make' you. I'm only your father. And I didn't feel lonely."

"Father, why did God create man the way he is?"

"I don't believe He meant to, you know. Not quite. The things one makes, never turn out as one expected, I think man was a surprise to Him."

"Tell us how God created man."

"Well ... I suppose He stood on top of the earth—it must have been nighttime, the most important things are done, and the most wonderful things happen at night. The sky was clear above Him, the moon and stars glittering as brightly as they could showing off before their Creator. You understand—it was all very beautiful and cold and very, very lonely. And God felt that something was missing, so he sighed because He was tired of creating, yet He must do it once more. He said to Himself—lonely people often talk to themselves, you know—He said, 'Oh well. I'll create man.' So He reached down and came up with a lump of clay and began to fashion it. I think He didn't pay much attention to the shape he was making. I told you He was tired, but then He's all spirit, and He didn't realize that shape is so important. I think even now, He keeps being surprised at the importance we attach to shape. That's why you mustn't take it literally when you hear that God made man in His image because that's true, but to God, His image is not a shape, and man's being made in His image doesn't mean that God has arms and legs and a face ..."

"What does it mean, then?"

"Well, I don't know for certain. We've been given so many explanations ... but I can guess. I believe that God stood looking down at the clay He had fashioned rather absentmindedly and thought: 'Now, what can I do that will make this thing resemble me at least a little? I'll give it intelligence, but only for its needs, and that's not very much. What, then?' He thought and thought and finally came up with the answer: the only things He could give man in an almost God-like measure were sadness and sorrow. And these he gave to man."

Once, when they were ten, my sons asked me, "In Hitler's time, when the Jews in his power were crushed worse than in Egypt, why didn't you do like Moses?"

"If I had," I said, "I should be dead, and you wouldn't exist."

But I knew that was no answer at all.

We were past reading about Moses by then, and they were crying no more over his death. The Biblical father-image had grown hazy and remote as their childhood began to wane. Still, I remained too small, and the vacant space in their world gaped as immense as ever.

"Why was Moses not allowed to lead his people into the Promised Land?" my sons asked me.

They looked thoughtful. I knew that they pictured his gaze from the top of the mountain toward Jericho, with eyes briefly endowed with a supernatural keenness, at all the places where he would never walk; places unknown yet familiar, in the way in which the songs of his people, heard for the first time, had sounded familiar on the day when he "went out to his brothers." His people's land, his own land, was denied to him. I knew that they thought it had been a cruel thing for God to do, to summon him to the top of the mountain and show him all those strange beloved places and tell him: "I have made you see it with your own eyes and there you shall not enter." Yet in that tale, one perceives no bitterness, rather the sweetness of surrender. The names of the places roll out with a musical evocativeness— the land of Gilead all the way to Dan, and all of Naphtali, and the land of Ephraim and Manasseh, and the land of Judah all the way to the Western Sea; and the Negev, and the plain of the valley of Jericho, city of the date-palms, all the way to Tzohar; and there's no record of any answer that he made to the Lord, only "... and there died Moses, servant of the Lord," a conclusion as bare as a plain slab of stone over a solitary grave.

"He must have been exhausted, you know," I said to my children. "At your age, you can't understand what it is to be really tired, just tired of being. And besides, he'd known for a long time that he could never enter the Promised Land."

Those were happy hours—no, not happy but meaningful and serene. When they asked me questions, and I answered by thinking aloud, learning as I talked, I was sometimes surprised at my own words. I knew that someday they would wave me goodbye and drift away, but that was still far in the future.

Sometimes our bedtime talks left me restless; I had to pursue some line of thought they had suggested before I could sleep. I would then go out to the terrace and stand looking down at the lighted city. I lost myself in an indefinite reverie. I seemed to float on an expanse of soothingly lukewarm, black waters; I didn't know any longer what point of time this was now. There was a door at my back, leading to my bedroom; I could turn around and open it. Would there be anyone inside? Should I find her sleeping in our bed if I went indoors now? We had had a short time, such a short time. Can time be so short, or was it all an illusion and there had never been anyone sleeping warmly and heavily in that bed, soothed by my words, lulled to sleep by my watching her?

There was a time when the twins would come to me in those hours, a time when they were afraid of the dark, or perhaps not of the dark but of sleep, of the dreams in the long sleep of the night. I didn't mind it because then they were no longer their respectful, affectionate, mutually sufficient selves. They huddled against me and clung to me as we stood looking down on the lighted city.

"Don't be afraid," I would say to them, "nighttime is a good time. Didn't I tell you that the most important things are done, and the most wonderful things happen at night? And you know, I used to have a fancy that someday I'd be standing like this, on a terrace in a warm, clear night, and a stranger would suddenly be beside me. I wouldn't turn around, but I'd know it was God, though He didn't speak, I'd know it was God, and I'd say to Him, 'I've been expecting you.' It was such a clear fancy; it felt so real that I thought it must happen someday. I was not imagining but looking, somehow, into a different portion of my time."

"And did it happen, Father?

"No, not yet, but I haven't stopped waiting. I think that God comes to every one of us once in our lifetime, and always in the night as He came to Jacob at Beth-El. But mostly, they don't recognize Him, and when they don't, He stands beside them for only a moment, and then He goes away and never returns. There's not much time left for me, but I keep waiting ..."

"Maybe tonight ..."

"No, not tonight. I must be alone, you see."

"Then we shouldn't have come."

"Nonsense, you had to come; it happens to all children once in a while; it happened to me when I was a child like you two. Shall I tell you about when I was a child and couldn't sleep either? Perhaps I was afraid of sleep the way you are."

"Yes, Father, do."

I squatted to get close to their little faces on either side of me.

"There was a small terrace, too, or rather a balcony, in the house where I lived, the house where I was born which you've never seen. It overlooked a garden, an ancient garden choked on all sides by high walls, sunk between the walls as in a pit, with two old trees; I think they were horse chestnuts or maybe plane trees. I'm not sure, with tall trunks rising out of the walls' enclosure toward the sunlight. The leaves and the branches had dropped off the trunks, and there was only a bunch of them left on top, straining upwards to entrap a little sunlight. Blackbirds lived in those trees. I never understood how they survived the winter when all the leaves had peeled off, and they clung shivering to the naked branches. Perhaps there were winters that they did not survive when their yellow beaks blanched, and they stiffened, fell to the bottom of the pit between the walls, and lay there like little toy birds made of blackened matchsticks. There were tall houses all around. It was the back of the houses that I looked at from my balcony, the higher stories where the poorer people lived. In winter, the people were as cold as the blackbirds and moaned in their sleep. I couldn't hear them through the closed windows, but I felt their moaning like a vibration that came to me in the air, over the garden's pit, from the very walls. The walls shivered, vibrated from the misery within. And in the hot season, I saw their faces at the open windows. They were white blots in the darkness, ghost-like and motionless as if the people had gone away and left those white blots behind to trick a hostile watcher ..."

But then I felt their warm little bodies going soft and slack against mine, and I stopped talking and picked them up, one in the crook of each arm.

My sons.

CHAPTER TWENTY-NINE

My son Simon told me he was leaving home.

"I could've done it a year ago," he said. "I'm nineteen now, and well, you've become such a Zionist, you can't deny that in Israel boys come of age at eighteen. They must fight Dayan's dirty war, but at least they enjoy men's rights such as they are in that kind of a country."

He spoke aggressively, but I could only think about how thin and frail he looked. His gray eyes that were so very much like mine stared feverishly from the paleness in the center of wild growth of hair and whiskers, copper-colored like his mother's hair. I told him that he was free to do as he wished.

"You bet I'm free; you can't stop me," he said.

"You think I don't know it? I'd stop you if I could."

He looked so frail. He was useful to his New Leftist friends because Israel enjoyed an enemy's status and nothing better than to use Jews against Jews. But someday it would be over, there would be other battles nearer home, or the word might come down from above to stop worrying about Israel. Then they would tell him, beat it, you dirty Jew, and how could he stand that, frail as he was ...

Life's so frightening when our children are involved. Our own life we can face, we have hardened, we can take almost anything, but becoming tough is such a painful process. The flesh must be rubbed raw and bleed before protective callus forms over it. Why should it happen to our children too? Why should they suffer for the sake of being wrong? How can we have failed them so completely that now we cannot stop them?

"When you were little, and something offended you, you'd lay down a scarf and put some underwear and toys on it and tie everything into an awkward little bundle. Then you would hang the bundle on the tip of a stick. If you didn't find a handy stick, an umbrella worked fine, and you slung the stick over your shoulder. In the tales you read then, there were pictures of children going out into the world with their possessions in a little bundle on the tip of a stick slung over a shoulder. You'd tell us your mother and me – 'I'm going away for good.' Then you'd wait, out of our sight on the landing, until we came to fetch you back."

"Boy, you're so good at the tender father act," he sneered. "You've almost got me crying."

"Only now, I won't be able to come to fetch you back."

"And I won't return."

I shook my head.

"One thing I've learned, no one ever returns. But if you ever need me, I'll be there."

"I'd have to be in a hell of shape ever to need you."

"Are you going to finish your studies?" I asked.

"Maybe. I've switched over from engineering to political sciences, anyway."

"Your mother has left a little money. It'll legally be yours when you're twenty-one. Meanwhile, I could lend you what you need, a loan you can accept from me, I suppose."

"Yes, a loan I can accept." Then he added grudgingly, "You're taking this better than I expected."

I thought, how can young people be so blind? How much time had passed since June of 1967? Only months. He had come to me, then, and put a hand on my shoulder. Then, I had thought that everything would be all right after all my little personal illusion in the grand illusion of the whole Jewish people. Now things were back to normal between Jew and Gentile and between him and me.

"Why did they have to fight?" he had asked me then. "Were there no other means?"

Of course, there were not, how could you ask?

When I was a boy, people said: "Jews are afraid of guns and horses." They said it with pity or contempt. They didn't stop to think that it isn't so strange to be afraid of things which have meant only death to your people for so long. Ho, one rides horses and fires guns to hunt or defend one's country, so brave men must like guns and horses, only Jews don't because they are not brave men; they are cowardly, treacherous worms.

People said, "The Jews are mankind's turtles; to passively withstand crushing is the only kind of heroism they're capable of."

They thought that Gentiles were daring and handsome. In contrast, windswept Jews had stoop shoulders, flabby arms, bleary short-sighted eyes, and whining voices, all outward signs of their cunning, devious souls. If a Jew's sister was raped and he got hold of a gun, at the last minute, he wouldn't shoot. He'd rather turn it on himself because a Jew might be noble enough to die but not to fight. And I had seen photographs of Jewish corpses laid side by side, after a pogrom, corpses wrapped in their tallit and lined up neatly. One recognized the military hand in such neatness of layout. Their murderers, Denikin's or Petljura's men, stood behind them leaning on their rifles, like hunters establishing a record of the game they had caught. And since the dead were wrapped in their tallit, their families, parents, and children must have been near and watched while the picture was being taken. Do you think we'll go back to that? Not ever.

"Were there no other means?" My son had asked then. "Wasn't it better to obtain justice through a social revolution, through destroying imperialism and bringing the workers to power? Better to give precedence to universal problems over our own limited ones?"

"Anything else you wish to say?" my son asked.

"No."

"Then I'll be going."

"Wait! On the day of your Bar Mitzvah, I slapped your face. I've always wanted to tell you I was sorry."

"A little late, isn't it? But I had forgotten."

"And this is your Bar Mitzvah watch. You broke it, remember, but I had it fixed, and I've kept it. Take it with you."

"I've got a good steel watch. I don't want a gold one. I don't want yours."

"It isn't mine. I've paid for it, but then I've paid for the steel one too."

He took the steel watch from his wrist and threw it down. He said, "You're right. I guess I won't worry about what time it is. Just as well, perhaps."

He turned his back on me. He walked out. I thought he walked a little skewed, like a small child with one shoulder weighted down with a bundle of underwear and toys.

CHAPTER THIRTY

One of the most relevant stories to come out of the Six-Day War is that of the German who admired military prowess and said of the Israelis: "Thank God there's still a people that can soldier," and celebrated the news of Israel's victories by standing drinks to everyone in his favorite bar. One day, although the news was still the same, he came in with a long face, and when asked what's the matter, he answered, "Oh, leave me alone, I just found out they are Jews!"

That's what happened to a good part of the world.

I had my doubts too, at one time, almost a crisis. What if there were some truth in what they said? Of course, Israel was entitled to make mistakes. Of course, no war can be fought without injustice and hardship to individuals. No one can be absolutely right; all anyone can hope for is to be essentially right. But what if Israel's stand were not essentially right? I must listen to criticism and recognize whatever truth might be in it.

A debate was being held on the Middle East by a circle of leftist intellectuals. I decided to attend. The meeting hall was small and not very crowded. The audience had a *deja vu* look; probably the same people participated in all meetings of a particular color. The first speaker, a journalist, told us that Israel was a fascistic theocratic state set up by neo-colonialism to hit the progressive Arab democracies. He said that the Jews were intruders in Palestine. They had seized it from its rightful Arab owners by force, but their presence there was now a fact. Besides, their sufferings gave them some extenuation. So a way must be found to reconcile Arabs and Jews. This was not too difficult in principle: it sufficed for the progressive forces that existed even in Israel, the Communists and the New Left, to take the helm. They should abandon the occupied territories and open the door to all Arabs wishing to return. They should also halt Jewish immigration, turn the country into a progressive state with a ruling Arab majority, and guarantee the Jewish minority's rights.

I asked, "Why do every people have a right to be independent, to be a majority somewhere, and only the Jews should be a minority everywhere? Why are the numerous Arab states a good, progressive thing, and one Jewish state a colonialist abomination? Why should self-determination be democratic for all peoples and fascistic only for the Jews? Isn't that discrimination and, therefore, antisemitism?"

The audience booed at me. The speaker replied that my questions were really out of order. Still, he wished to put it on record that it was anachronistic and unreasonable for the Jews to demand majority status or statehood. Of course, they were entitled to security. But the one road to security—speaking as the Jews' friend—was to join the fight against imperialism and bring the working classes into power everywhere. Especially, he concluded amid cheers, in Israel herself.

The second speaker was a Jew, a short fat man with frog-like eyes. He said that he could speak with some authority; he had gone to Palestine and fought with the *Hagana* in 1948. He realized that his emotions had tricked him into participating in the crime of aggression. What did it matter that technically the Arabs had initiated that war? They had quite naturally reacted to the Zionist bombing of their peaceful villages. Anyway, as Nasser had pointed out, it was undeniable that Israel's very existence was an act of aggression. However, most Jews were not Zionists; they were like him and felt ashamed when they saw oranges and grapefruit in the stores, stolen from Arab orchards. Those were the proceeds of the rape of the Arab land in Palestine.

I stood up and shouted, "You're a liar!"

The audience's boos drowned my voice. Then there was a lot of confusion. People milled around me; someone took me by the arm and propelled me to the exit. I walked out. I was furious and happy at the same time. I went into a bar for a drink to steady my nerves. As I drank, a bunch of young people came in. I thought they came from the meeting, and I wondered why they had left. But perhaps I was wrong, they weren't even looking at me, yet I had been conspicuous enough. They were boys and girls, all very young, and teasing one another and paying no attention to me. But when I left, they followed me, and there were more outside. My car was parked at a little distance. I walked toward it, and they all trooped after me, about thirty of them, I guessed. It wasn't very late, but the streets were deserted in the neighborhood. I walked slowly. I wasn't afraid, and I wanted them to see that I wasn't scared.

They began to call out to me.

"Hey, Daddy! Don't run away."

"Wait for us, let's talk some."

"You a fascist. Daddy?"

"Course he's a fascist if he's a lousy Zionist."

"A lousy Zionist fascist."

"A damned Nazi-Zionist bastard."

They surrounded me. They pushed me against a wall. We stood on a street corner. I looked both ways, and I saw nobody. They kept pushing me and surging against me, and if I didn't react, my arms would soon be pinned down, and I would be helpless, so I struck out at the nearest boy. I had to strike upwards because he was very tall. I felt the impact of my fist on his jaw; he cried out, then a blow on my cheekbone jarred me. I hit back blindly. Blows showered on me and didn't seem to hurt but stunned me, and then my arms became heavy, and I could no longer hit back. Suddenly the blows stopped, my knees buckled, my back slid against the wall, but hands held me up. I shook my head. My eyes cleared slowly. I was leaning on the arm of a policeman. I stood away from him.

"I'm all right," I said.

"Your face's bloody."

"It's nothing."

"My partners are chasing them in the Jeep. Maybe they'll catch one or two," he said.

"So what? You'll have to turn them loose in the morning, and all you'll achieve is to make big heroes out of them. Anyway, it's not important. I guess I went to the wrong meeting. Should've known better."

In a while, the police Jeep came back. There were three policemen in it and a boy.

"We've caught one of them," the driver said.

They pulled the boy out and stood him under a street lamp.

"You've made a mistake, officers," I said. "This is my son."

"Hell! Why didn't he say so?"

"Never mind. I'm all right. And thanks a lot."

I took my son's arm, and we walked to my car.

"Get in, Simon; they'll be watching us. I hadn't noticed you. You must've held back, beyond that little mob."

"Are you hurt?" he asked.

"Oh no, not really. I'll be a little sore in the morning. That's about all."

But my sight was slightly hazy, and I had to drive slowly. There was a long silence, then he said, "I tried to pull them off, but there were too many."

"Of course you did."

"What possessed you to provoke them, anyway?"

I chuckled.

"It was advertised as a debate. I expected a confrontation of ideas."

When I got out of the car, I couldn't help staggering.

"I'll help you upstairs," he said.

"Let's be quiet; your brothers are asleep."

Inside, we sat facing each other.

"There's blood on your face."

"Oh, never mind ..."

"Well ..." He fidgeted. As far as I could recall, he had always fidgeted when he talked to me.

I watched him. Although he was pale now, he looked well, fleshier than I remembered. Somehow, he had the look of having gotten himself a girl who mattered.

"Was she one of the bunch?" I asked. (What a silly question, of course, she was).

He blushed.

"Look, I'm sorry it had to be you, but whoever gets in our way, in the way of our protest against the system ... oh, what's the use!"

"Your protest!" I snapped. "What d'you know about protesting? You gave up any chance of protesting the day you walked out on your Judaism."

He got up.

"I'll be going."

I pushed him back.

"No, you'll listen. You talk about the 'system.' Well, the system wasn't created yesterday. Everyone has been a part of it one way or another, everyone except the Jewish people. The system—we could be old fashioned and call it society or even civilization—has always been soaked through with hatred and contempt for our people. Like a spider, it has imprisoned us in a web of lies to draw our blood at leisure whenever it felt like it. Do you think we could accept a system that has never stopped murdering us? I was lucky because when I went to school, I didn't know about antisemitism. I grew up in a wonderful unique island of liberalism. But even I felt my pinpricks ... I was taught how holy the Crusaders were, and then I learned that on first entering Jerusalem, they slaughtered every single Jew in the city, and their war had not been against the Jews. Didn't my teachers know about it? Come on. Then, were they ashamed or discreetly approving? I remember how a famous lawyer spent years investigating 'ritual murder' cases. He was a fair, liberal-minded man, and he concluded that all the accused Jews had been innocent. It chilled me, you know, to think that such a man should seriously investigate whether my ancestors had sucked children's blood on the High Holidays. And since many Jews had been found guilty, this lawyer asked himself, how could it happen, such an atrocious miscarriage of justice. Well, he said that's how the system could twist even a fair, liberal mind. One must consider the hostile feelings caused—caused, mind you, by the Jews' aloofness and deplorable behavior in business.

"Do you think we would defend that system? Why, every breath of a Jew who has remained alive is a scream of protest against it. Do you want to fight it? Then help us shatter the web of lies it has woven about us, instead of replacing every thread we tear with a fresh one. That web fell apart in '67, but not for long. Oh no, too many hands got busy weaving it back, and now it's there again more impenetrable than ever, hiding us from the sight of the honest little people who have no ax to grind, everywhere, and that's a victory for the system.

"You don't realize it, but you young people are not fighting the system; you're doing a job of face-lifting on it. You talk about a revolution against oppression, but your leaders don't mind oppression; they just wish they were the ones doing the oppressing. They're after fat oppressors' jobs for themselves. What you call revolution is only switching of roles in the same old pantomime. But Zionism is a true revolution. You wish to be a revolutionist? Then come over to our side; it takes revolutionists to stand up against those who have the oilfields. I don't think your friends would. I shouldn't be surprised if a little oil money went into the 'debate' of tonight."

My son jumped to his feet.

"Shut Up, shut up!" he shouted. "To think I felt guilty because you bled and staggered, or was it an act? Anyway, it's no use. I've always hated you, and you know why and now get out of my way!"

He tried to push past me, but I grabbed his shoulders. I felt his body straining inadequately in my grip; he was not strong enough to pull free. A wave of frustration rose from his straining body, washing sickeningly against me. He hit me with his elbow in the pit of the stomach, I hardly felt the blow, but I pretended to gasp and fell back. I let him go. As he went out, he looked back, the smirk of triumph on his face wounded and consoled me.

Then I was alone. I felt a stinging pain between my nose and eyes as if I were about to cry. There was a light over the door, and as he was going out, it shone on his wild copper-colored hair. It was such long hair that I might almost have been looking at the back of his mother's head.

I imagined her voice asking me, what have you done to my son.

I don't know; I don't know.

Please don't be angry at him.

Angry? How could I be?

You see, it takes a kind of courage to voice one's fears. You were very brave that way. But I think he has inherited your fears and not the courage to express them, and I can understand it. The fears that are not our own, which come from someone else's past, must be unbearable. I can only guess how painful from the livid shadow of them, which I saw on his face.

He had told me, "I tried to pull them off, but they were too many." And I had replied, "Of course you did." But he was lying, and I wonder if he knew that I knew he was lying. I think he stood a little way back from the edge of that mob while they were beating me. There was no mark on his face and hands, and there would have been if he had tried. A while ago, I felt his inadequate strength as he strained in my grip, and I think I know why he stood back from the edge of the mob: because it would have repulsed him so easily. He would have made no headway in the writhing mass of angry, violent young people, and he couldn't have stood the humiliation. Besides, on the morrow, he would have been on trial before his friends. So I am his father. That would be no excuse, not even an extenuating circumstance, for he has certainly told them that I'm a fascist swine. Anyway, the family is shit, a rotten institution, a tool of the system.

And then his girl was there, in the mob. I vaguely remember a pretty, dirty face with wild light-colored eyes. I wonder if it was she. I wonder whether her fingernails made these deep scratches in my cheek, which still ooze serum. Perhaps he's gone back to her and is telling her lies about how he got away from the pigs. He can't confess that he let me cover up for him and that he helped me upstairs because I staggered a little. Perhaps she's telling him, 'I got to the old bastard, you bet I did. My fingernails raked his shitty face. What a shame the pigs came too early.' And he's replying, 'I got to him too, just one blow to the stomach but a good one.' Then she'll want to make love, but I don't think he can, not tonight.

How does it feel to worship violence or pretend to worship it and to be weak? How does it feel to be driven by fears, paralyzed by fears which come from someone else's past and which, therefore, cannot be exorcised? To watch one's father being beaten, for all one knows, to death, and be rooted to a spot at a little distance from the edge of the mob and not to know why; to be convulsed with a helpless shame from which there can never be the relief of confession?

In the Jewish cemetery of Prague, there is the tomb of the Holy Rabbi Low. Jewish children used to scribble their wishes on scraps of paper. They folded the scraps into tight little packages and slid them into a crevice of the tomb so that the holy rabbi would know about the wishes and intercede for them to come true. And when they cleaned the grave, they found papers which had lain there since the days of Hitler. Jewish children had scribbled on them in wavering infantile hands: please Holy Rabbi Low, please protect me from being taken away, let me stay at home, let me live. But for a Jewish child to ask for life was a presumption beyond any intercession. Maybe the holy rabbi didn't even try to intercede. So those children joined millions of others, despite their wishes scribbled in wavering infantile hands and consigned to the holy rabbi's tomb, together they went up in smoke.

You cried when you read about it. You said, "Now do you understand why I don't want children?" But you could talk about your fears; you were lucky that way.

If he had told me, "Father, I was afraid. I'm not very strong, you know, I couldn't have helped you anyway. The truth is I didn't try because I was afraid, and I felt so sick when I thought you'd been badly hurt ..." If he had been able to tell me that, everything would have been all right between us. I would have said to him, "Of course you were afraid, but there's no shame in it. It's not your own fear, it comes from someone else's past, and you can conquer it if only you'll stop being ashamed." And I would have said, "What's this anyway, since when does a father rely on his son's help? Old men are tough, you know, you'll become tough in time, but it's a slow, painful process, then you'll talk to your children the way I'm talking to you." But he could never confess his fears to me. He must go on pretending to worship the violence that sickens him and that in his hate of me, there is no love.

You cried over Prague's Jewish children who went up in smoke despite the tightly folded scraps of paper bearing their wish for life.

"Nothing's going to happen to our children," I said, and it was a glib, empty promise. It's so easy to promise.

The next day the twins asked me, "You'll never let Simon come back, will you?"

"He doesn't wish to," I said, "but if he ever should, he's my son."

"You love him more'n you do us," they cried. "He hollered at you, and he hit you, and you'd take him back."

I tried to soothe them.

"He didn't really hit me, you know, it's difficult to explain, but he was hitting out at himself, and I think he hurt himself very much, not me at all. And as for loving him more than I do you … it's nonsense, yet there's a grain of truth in it, and there should be. A father can't help feeling a special tenderness for the weakest son, the helpless one, who needs him most."

"We need you too," they said.

Of course, they did. It was a measure of my blindness that they had to tell me, and my good luck that they did tell me. Why is it so easy to recognize love behind the mask of hatred and not behind that of affection? I had thought them mutually sufficient, but how could they be, two twelve-year-old children? Perhaps I was unconsciously taking mean revenge in advance for the day when they'd drift away from me.

"Of course you do, and I love you as much as your brother, but you mustn't be jealous."

"We heard you last night, we pretended to be asleep, but we were listening and watching. We saw him hit you, and we'd have fought him if he hadn't run away so quickly. He's wicked, and we hate him."

I shook my head.

"No, you don't, you don't even know what it is to hate."

"Do you?"

"Perhaps not. It looks like we're a silly inexperienced bunch, all together."

They laughed tearfully, and I laughed with them.

One of them told me, "I remember when we were very little, and you bent over our cradles, our funny twin cradles. You looked enormous. When we grew up a little, we thought you were one of those fairy tales' giants, you looked a lot bigger than other men, but that's not true. I guess you're not very big, and there are many men bigger than you."

The other one listened and nodded.

"Now, what made you say that?" I asked.

"I don't know."

Well, I knew.

"I want you to understand that I did right. I want you to understand that your brother is not wicked. Perhaps this is big talk for small children like you, but it can't wait because I'm glad you know I'm not a giant, but I don't want you to think I'm a dwarf. You see, it's tough to be a Jew. As long as you're little, your parents do it for you, well or badly, but they do it. But then you grow up and have to be a Jew all on your own. Man believes what he wishes to believe. If he cannot believe it, he pretends to. He runs away from painful truths, from responsibility, from admitting he's not doing his duty. And the weaker he is, the faster, the more blindly he runs into the arms of the nearest consoling illusion. He seeks to be put asleep by a lullaby of soothing lies and forget the painful reality in which he is caught. Well, don't hate your brother, don't even blame him for being weak."

But the twins remained silent, tight-lipped. Their hard blue stares meant we do hate him, and it's either him or us. That they were respectful, affectionate children were no reason to love them less. They deserved forgiveness for being too young to forgive.

Then for no reason at all, I remembered a morning long before, when their brother was only a small child, perhaps five or six. His hair was a lighter color when he was little, a pale golden hue, and always a bit too long. His mother liked it that way; at the slightest touch of sunshine, it became luminous, the only striking feature of a frail, not unhandsome child. The morning light kindled his hair, but it made his pale gray eyes so much like mine look flat and dead. I recalled his standing there in the morning light, staring at me out of pale eyes. He had spread his little legs apart to lend stability to a tense, feather-light childish body.

I could see myself in a mirror if I turned my head. I had been shaving, and my chest was bare, my face half-covered with soapy foam; there was a nick on my chin, and it reddened the foam. A few drops of blood, thus diluted in the foam, gave the illusion of a lot of blood. He was very little, so he tilted his face upwards to stare at me. I must have seemed a giant to him, a strange wounded giant, and the drops of blood from the tiny nick the obscene red gushing of a not quite human body liquid.

He held a toy gun in his hand and aimed it at me. The weapon was made of plastic, gaily-colored plastic, yellow or green. I'm not sure, the morning sunlight fell on it and made its smooth surface gleam gaily, but my son's eyes stared flat and dead as he aimed the toy gun at me.

"Well? Are you going to shoot me?" I asked him and laughed.

He lowered the gun slowly, but the tenseness didn't go out of him. He bit his lip in concentration. Then he rushed out. I closed the door and resumed shaving. After a while, he was back. He opened the door stealthily and stood poised on the threshold. I turned to him. He held a toy airplane in his hand. The plane was made of sheet metal, enameled a bright red. Slowly he raised the hand to shoulder height, aiming the toy plane at me. He watched me almost hungrily, a tight grimace on his face, ready to break into a smirk of triumph at my expected fear. But in a way, he looked funny, and I laughed again. He kept watching me as if he couldn't quite believe it that I was invulnerable even to this, obviously his ultimate weapon. He sagged in defeat; he dropped the toy and walked away.

But why had he threatened me? Why did he want to hurt me? I had no idea then, and I never found out. Was it anything I had done to him, a thoughtless act, perhaps, like my laughing at him just now, or was it merely that I existed, a bulky giant with loud, overbearing manners, capricious commands, and an incomprehensible hold over his mother, a grip which could be broken only in pitched battle?

Perhaps that is the meaning of all the children's tales about knights who rescues damsels from dragons. The knight is small, boy-size, the dragon huge and repulsive, its body covered with slimy scales as the father's body is with hair. Perhaps to a boy, the identification is unequivocal. The tales serve as wish-fulfillment dreams, but a day comes when dreams are no longer enough, and then the boy goes in search of a weapon to slay the dragon. It doesn't matter that the dragon has done nothing to him; it suffices that it exists. But real-life dragons are invulnerable; in real life, the knight goes down to defeat, all he can do is huddle in a corner nursing his bruised soul, but even that doesn't work. The bruises never heal; they only grow scabs that rub off at the first friction and hurt and keep hurting through life. And with time, the knight grows into a dragon too, but it doesn't help; by then, it's too late: the past's truth is immutable, so even while he has become a dragon to his own children, and while they fight him as such, within his soul he remains the knight. He keeps fighting the battle of his childhood against his old dragon, as gigantic and invulnerable as ever. But the dragon may have turned into a toothless, whining, helpless old man.

That night the twins went to bed without kissing me goodnight. They were still angry at me for loving their brother too much. I went into their bedroom and stood looking down at them. I thought that there must be a moment when the barrier between father and sons dwindles; if we only knew, if we were ready for it. They had been sleeping sweetly, peacefully. Suddenly their eyes snapped open. I met their blue stare and smiled.

"Were you pretending to sleep?"

"No, Father, we did sleep, but even in our sleep, we felt you come in, or perhaps we're still asleep, and we're dreaming that you've come in to kiss us goodnight."

I sat down between their small identical beds.

"Fine, then I'll talk to you, and tomorrow you won't know whether I did it, or you just dreamed it," I said. "As I looked at you, I wished that though we're father and sons, we were of the same age. It must have been my wish that woke you up or made you dream that you woke up and brought me into your dream. So, you see, now our souls can touch as if we were neither children nor grownups but were free from age and time, and it doesn't make much sense to wonder whether it's a dream or reality. Our father, Jacob, saw God at Beth-El, and the Torah says he was dreaming. Still, I believe that it was one of those moments in which all borderlines break down. We face reality, unlike all reality that we call a dream because we have no other word. Now, remember that Jacob was our father, and then he was called Israel, and we're Israel, too, so that night at Beth-El belongs to us. We've drifted away from it, but we've never abandoned it, we've never lost it altogether, and that's our faithfulness and the meaning of our being Jews."

They climbed from their beds and onto my lap, and I held their small warm bodies tightly against mine.

"Remember when you were smaller and afraid of the dark, or perhaps not of the dark but of sleep, and you came to me, and together we looked down at the city lights?"

"When was that? We've forgotten."

"Oh, it wasn't so long ago."

"We can still see the city lights through the window panes."

"Of course, the lights haven't changed. You have changed."

"And you. Father?"

"Remember when you cried over Moses' death and the moment before his death when he looked from the top of a mountain at all the places where he would never walk, his own land, denied to him? Remember the names of the places? 'The land of Gilead all the way to Dan, and all of Naphtali, and the land of Ephraim and Manasseh, and the land of Judah all the way to the Western Sea, and the Negev, and the plain of the valley of Jericho, city of the date-palms, all the way to Tzohar.' The names of familiar places never visited. Don't you think you'd recognize them too?"

They tilted their faces to mine; they looked like little birds waiting for a feed.

"Once that land was green with forests and fields. The forests teemed with animals, tame and wild, and the Jews grew their crops in the fields. Then the Jews went away. The land withers if it isn't loved. So the trees died, the animals died, the minute organic life within the soil died, and the soil dried up. It crumbled to dust so that the wind was no longer filled with vegetable scents and wandering germs but with choking yellow dust. Of course, wise men will tell you that the soil chemicals remain in the dust. If you water and fertilize it and sow seeds, life will grow once more, only in its hardiest forms at first, but life breeds life. In time the dust will coalesce once more to hummus. Man can plant trees and grow crops from the hummus, so it's only a matter of water, fertilizers, and seeds, or if you wish, money and labor. All very plain and not very exciting, but you see, not the whole truth. Because those wise men don't know that the forests and the fields of the past had never ceased to be, they were still there, ground to tiny particles in the dust. You see, what has happened can never cease to have happened and, therefore, to be. And all of our past and all we can ever be has always been in that dust blown in the wind, we are that dust, from that we can bring ourselves back to life, from that dust and nothing, nothing else."

CHAPTER THIRTY-ONE

I went to say goodbye to my old nanny. She looked so ancient that I knew I would never see her again.

"How old are you, Palmira?" I asked.

She shook her head.

"I won't tell you, *Signorino*."

"Come on, why d'you keep calling me *Signorino* when I'm over fifty?"

She stood at the window and gazed outside. Her room nested at the top of a square turret set high above the roofs, and we could see far into the distance.

"I saw the lightning strike at midnight, a storm broke out, and everything up here shakes, so during a storm, who can sleep? The lightning struck near the Church of the Madonna del Carmine. You should've heard the crash. Holy Mother, what a crash!"

"Were you afraid?"

Sometimes she had the trick of not answering questions; perhaps she had grown a little deaf.

"Come over here, *Signorino*. I want to show you something."

I joined her at the window. It was early morning, and many of the tightly slatted shutters in the neighboring houses stood closed. It hadn't stopped dripping from the night's storm; rooms and garrets lay asleep in darkness striped with light seeping between the slats. The shutters of an attic in front of us opened, and a woman leaned out to push them against the wall.

She looked young but no longer a girl; she had dark tousled hair and wore a dirty, scuffed sweater with a torn shoulder. She rubbed her eyes, hugged herself shivering, and withdrew.

Palmira said, "There ..."

"Who is she?"

"Nobody. A servant. But she's me, in a way, she's me a long time ago. You see, there's no running water in that garret. There're very few people left who have no running water. She'll wash from a pitcher if she washes at all. The way I did when I was a girl. I worked for a seamstress. She insisted on cleanliness, so on winter mornings, I broke the ice in the pitcher and poured water into a basin, and then I threw it away. She heard the swishing and was satisfied. Then she gave me a bowl of hot chicory, but she wouldn't let me warm my hands on the bowl; she said that touching hot things with chilled hands gave one cold sores, and if I grew cold sores, I couldn't work properly. I didn't mind, though. I was out of the orphanage, at least. In the orphanage, when I broke the rules, the sisters made me drag myself on bare knees over crushed nutshells. I still wear the scars on the skin of my knees."

"You're not cold up here?"

"I have everything I want. I have a nice stove and plenty of coke to burn in it. Anyway, winters aren't so cold as they used to be. Oh, sometimes sunrise finds a layer of frost on the roofs, but it melts quickly. Only old people like me who don't need much sleep ever get to see it, and all that reaches down to street level is a little wetness."

The room had a window on each side. From one of them, I looked down on a bare patch of ground between walls, covered with sickly grass and rubbish, what had once been my garden.

"They've cut down the trees. I didn't know. How long ago?"

"Oh, I forget. They had dried up and threatened to crash down on the house."

"Where have the blackbirds gone?"

"Who can tell? I haven't seen them in such a long time. Maybe they flew away."

But I knew they hadn't. How could they know that there was a world outside this pit between ancient walls which had once been my garden, that there was anything to perch on, besides the branches of those rotted trees? I could picture them flying about and whistling. Blackbirds cannot whimper and then let themselves fall into the pit, all the way to the sickly grass at the bottom. If they did, they would lie there, grow matchstick-stiff overnight, then crumble away. Maybe if I searched, I might still find a shred of a black feather. How very much like some Jews I had known.

"I've come to say goodbye; I'm going away," I said.

She looked at me calmly.

"Forever?"

"Forever."

She was silent.

"You're not asking where I'm going."

She shook her head.

"I still have my wits, *Signorino*. You're a Jew, aren't you? Where else would you go if not home?"

"Of course, where else, if not home ... how simple ..."

She nodded.

"But there's some sadness in leaving, is that it? You have suffered here, but you were fed the love of this country with your milk and how greedy a baby you were, by the way," she chuckled.

"It's a beautiful country. And her people are as fine as people come."

"Of course. All you have to do is look out these windows."

I knew what she meant. She meant, they say that this city has no beauty, but how can it be, when this is where I was born and where I'm about to die? Somewhere in this city, the blood from my torn knees still clings to the stone flooring of some orphanage, the blood I shed when the sisters made me crawl over crushed nutshells because I was fifteen and had giggled at prayers; the blood has seeped into the cracks between granite slabs and put a faint rustiness in their eternal grayness. Granite orphanage floors never wear out; how could they while I'm alive? No, it's all still there, someplace I cannot quite remember, in this city. Perhaps now and then, the old rusty blood turns fresh again; it turns bright red and flows in the cracks with the merriness of my fifteen years. Don't tell me it's impossible. Of course, it's a miracle like that of San Gennaro, but what of it? If his congealed blood can melt and flow, why not mine? Why shouldn't a tiny miracle bloom from my few drops of blood, which nobody notices and nobody would care about?

This city where I suffered and bled cannot be but beautiful. It isn't dark and sooty as they say. What if the roofs don't flaunt the red brashness of furnace-fresh tile? They have stood the harshness of our northern weather and have mellowed as good men mellow from the harshness of life. And when the air is as clean as it is today, the pealing of the church bells sounds so close that it must be meant especially for me. I feel it beating at my windows, and I open them to let it in. Then the air wings in from all sides, and it's as fresh and pure as the sound of the bells. I am enveloped by freshness and purity; there are no walls around me anymore; I feel weightless, suspended in space above the city. I look down on its soot-mellowed tiles and further, into the recesses of its oldest streets, its narrow, winding, sunless streets full of secrets that only someone poor and alone can really know.

I love this old city in which I shall soon die, and perhaps dying is like now, a dwindling away of enclosing walls, a dwindling away of all matter, and only freshness and purity remaining, the pealing of bells, love and resignation, not trying to understand anymore, forgetting, surrendering ...

I looked around. The room had been built to house servants, to put distance and narrow passages and stairs between them and the gentlefolk. The elevator stopped at the turret's bottom, so one had to cross a tunnel-like corridor and then climb a steep, tight flight of stairs, marking the transition between two worlds. The room had a flooring of cheap tiles and bare walls whitewashed over a rough mortar finish. It was furnished with an enormous couch covered with threadbare cotton damask, a rickety table with two matching chairs, a small gas range, a cast-iron stove, and a roughly-painted chest.

A door led into a cubicle serving as the bedroom. Bells chimed from the church where the lightning had struck at midnight. The sun had risen above the houses in the east. I sprawled on the couch and felt at peace.

"When I came to work for your family, I was a young woman," she said. "The seamstress had died, and I had been out of work and very hungry. Somebody told me, 'Watch out; those people are Jews.' Your grandfather was alive then. When he looked at me with those eyes of his, bright as live coals, he frightened me out of my wits. Once he said to me, 'Don't you know we have hooves instead of feet?' I didn't really believe him, but I thought, perhaps, who knows ... He laughed and told me, 'Watch, I'll take off my shoe and show you my hoof.' He wore high buttoned boots, the way old men used to then. It took him a long time to undo all those buttons one by one. I stood rooted there, not daring to take my eyes from him, then he pulled off the shoe and sighed. He said, 'What d'you know, I've got regular feet now, somebody must have prayed for me.' Then he put the shoe back on, he came near me and stared at me with those live-coal eyes of his. He snapped, 'You stupid girl, you were ready to believe anything! Now mind, don't ever be so stupid again.' I muttered something about having been told ... and he interrupted, 'Lies, I don't care what kind. Always remember that the purpose of all lies is the same, to make slaves of all who believe them.'"

She fell silent.

I thought, how could so long a life produce so small an accumulation of things? Once, she had shown me where she kept her "papers." She had tied them into a little bundle with a lavender colored ribbon. All she had were receipted bills for trifling sums and a few postcards. There was something holy about such a simple, naked life, about having wanted nothing but food and shelter, finally reaching this dingy, threadbare haven, and sighing, "I have everything I want."

I sat there in silence and felt at peace. And I thought, of course, this too is part of being a Jew—feeling at ease in the company of an insignificant, harmless life. There's a fundamental kinship between us and little people everywhere, the little people who have not made society, who have not made politics, who have not made revolutions or reactions or any part of history, but who bear society and politics, revolutions, reactions, history on their bowed shoulders. Their fight is our fight, whether we like it or not. And that's why we are so dangerous to all the domineering crude oil bladders of this world; that's why they blow and will keep blowing so hard on all the trumpets that political power can command and oil money can buy, because we have told them, never again. And unless the little people can be persuaded that we have horns and hooves, someday they will think: "The Jews did it, why not we?"

"I'll make you a cup of chocolate," the old woman said.

She poured some cocoa powder into a pot, let water drip in, stirring carefully, and then she put the pot over a gas fire. She muttered as if to herself, "There is some sadness in leaving."

"But that's the best way to go," I said, "not away from something but to something."

She nodded. She poured the hot chocolate, and I drank it.

"Can you point out the window of the room that was mine in the old house?"

"You can see every window of the old house from here, now that the trees have been cut down. But I can't tell you which one was yours. It was so long ago."

"Perhaps it's just as well."

"You ought to remember, though. God knows you spent enough time at that window. There were nights I had to drag you to bed. But as you grew up and didn't change, I just gave up. I let you stand there and wait for the morning."

"Where I'm going, we call the morning star 'the doe of dawning.' The sky's so deep and clear, and the starlight so bright that there seems to be life up there. It would be right if something alive, something all grace and motion, should leap over the horizon. And the sunrise comes like a promise and a blessing as if God said for the first time: 'Let there be light.' It's a country where you may not believe in God, and still you feel His presence. You don't know exactly what kind of a God He is, certainly not the bigots' bureaucratic God. Yet, He's everywhere, and you may not believe in Him, but you strain to hear His voice when the wind comes in from the sea. And if you lie in the cleft of a narrow *wadi* and gazelles leap across outlined against the sun, or you stand aside to let a family of partridges waddle by, mother in front and chicks in Indian file, or you stand near a field dotted with peacefully feeding storks—if you watch such graceful, harmless, apparently purposeless lives, there as nowhere else you understand the absolute holiness of all life, and how easy it is to be a man, after all, and never to be afraid."

She stared at me in a puzzled way. She could understand my going "home." Perhaps she remembered the past more keenly than I; maybe it's easier to forget the harm we have suffered ourselves. But she could not understand my traveling so far to search for God. Why, if one needed Him, He was so close at hand, a few hundred yards away from where the lightning had struck at midnight.

I chuckled.

"Never mind, I was thinking out loud."

And then I took my leave. But before going, I asked her, "Did you ever hear anything when you came to me at night?"

"Anything?"

"A sound. Like a man's sobbing. I never could decide whether he was far away or was close by and choked his sobs into a pillow. The sound was faint, but I kept hearing it, you know, night after night when there was quiet, and I listened keenly."

"No. I never heard it."

"Perhaps I wasn't meant to hear it," she added as in an afterthought.

CHAPTER THIRTY-TWO

I let the twins pack their two identical suitcases, then I told them, "I'll put you to bed."

"Don't treat us like children," they protested, "we'll be Bar Mitzvah soon."

Of course. Adolescence was bringing them gawkiness and pimples and independence. They chattered excitedly about tomorrow.

"We're metamorphosing, like insects shedding their skins, flying out of their old skins."

"Yeah. I've never seen homelier butterflies, though."

They attacked me playfully with their small fists. But it was past midnight, and they were exhausted with excitement. As soon as I got them to crawl under the sheets, they dropped off to sleep. I watched them for a while, and then I went out on the terrace. I heard a drone overhead. I could see nothing because of the overcast, but a plane flew low in the low gray clouds. As I lifted my face upwards, a tepid droplet fell on it, and I fancied that it might be condensed steam from one of its engines' exhaust. The drone was unmistakably that of a propeller plane, not even turbo, regular piston engines. It was a mechanical antique, grinding and rattling its way low, where the air is thicker. An aircraft like this only carries freight; it's entrusted with no human lives except the pilot's necessary, expendable one. The pilot sits before a fuselage full of silent, lifeless objects to be carried by ancient motors, grinding and clanking in the clouds. It flies at night when one can always find a nearly deserted airstrip for landing.

Perhaps they're older men who don't know how to pilot a jet plane, who should hold armchair jobs. Still, flying cargo pays better, and they need the money. When they land on nearly deserted strips, their plane is serviced by the older mechanics. Or perhaps they are the less skillful ones who cannot balk at getting an undesirable shift. An aircraft like this one, you could board it and fly at the edge of the clouds without knowing exactly where to. It wouldn't matter because all clouds are alike, and all nearly deserted landing strips look the same in the dark. And this is all a lonely man can find in a city night—a drone of old engines overhead, and the fancy that the tepid drop falling on his forehead is condensed steam from a plane engine's exhaust.

Yet if I were alone, I should like to get on a plane like this one and fly at the edge of the clouds, fly all the way home, get in so low from the sea as to skim the surf, then land apologetically at the most remote corner of the airfield, and get off and walk away and melt into the country so quickly that no one would notice me, just another Jew in a land of Jews. If I were alone, but although I feel alone, I am not.

When I was little, I never felt alone. I felt that somebody always watched me. That was when I looked at things; in the split instant, when I focused my eyes, they arranged themselves. They struck a pose meant especially for me, meant to hide their secrets from me. They hid the very fact that they were alive, that all things are alive. I asked the grownups, was it real, and they laughed: "of course not, there's a big difference between live creatures and inanimate things. Inanimate things don't move unless we make them move and have no secrets to hide. Come on, you mustn't be so fanciful, Bruno, or you'll be getting nightmares, and those shadows under your eyes will deepen. You might become very, very sick."

But I didn't believe the grown-ups. In a room of the old house, there were two iron brackets in a wall. I never found out their purpose; they had lost it or possibly never had one. Anyway, they stuck out from the wall, and each had a projection like a big nail on its tip. I imagined that the projections were dwarves, tiny, tiny dwarves, standing very still, pretending to be what adults called inanimate things (all inanimate things were live creatures standing still) frightened into stillness by the presence of men. I knew that men like to kill anything too small to strike back. Because they're clever at inventing extenuating semantics, they tag what they kill "vermin."

I thought, *come on, little dwarves, you should know I wouldn't hurt you; anyway I couldn't. I'm a giant to you yet too small to reach you, and besides, you see, I love you, little dwarves. Can't you hear my thoughts? And if you do, why don't you trust me?*

I sat in the room, hummed to myself, pretending to be engrossed in playing, and pointedly looked away from the brackets. When I thought I detected motion at the very edge of my field of vision, I swiveled around, but they were too quick for me, there they stood looking for all the world like two pieces of iron no bigger than big nails and utterly motionless. They were two pieces of iron, and I imagined life in them and loved them.

What happened to the child I was? How did he turn into me? Did it happen in a single moment so painful that I have compelled myself to forget it? Only a vague screen-memory remains, of a wanly lit room, a humming silence outside, the smell of dry leaves and branches burning in the pungent coolness of autumn, a feeling of crossroads, of a season which will never return, a disconsolate, lacerating sense of irreparable loss? Or has it been going on all the time? Does every human life start with a flight aiming upwards, then level off, then dive to a final impact and infinite stillness? Is that all there is to me, for good or bad, that I am a man? If only we understood our purpose, the meaning of this parabola that is repeated and repeated without end. Does God Himself know it, or is He making us this way because it's the only way He knows?

When I was eighteen, I thought I was in love and growing into a man. It's a task to be in love at eighteen, and it's a task to grow into a man. But when you do, it's the moment of discovery, and the pain which goes with it is like a bite merging into a kiss from a beloved mouth. Every boy should pour all his being into that moment of discovery, of love and growth, knowing that it's unique, a moment granted but once. But not I. My love flowed into the ground like the contents of a shattered vase. I did not grow into a man; I mutated into something less than human, and to mutate back was to be a long and painful process.

Meanwhile, my brothers were dying. I should have forgotten about myself, about my love and my manhood, because they were small, petty things, particles of dust blown about the slope of a mountain. But I did not forget. My mind told me that I was unimportant, that my love and loss of love were nothing, that friends and country's betrayal was nothing, but deep down, I did not accept what I knew. It took me a long time to accept it and look at myself with the absent-minded compassion one might feel for a dead cat thrown out into the gutter.

Because of this, I lived as if my brothers were not dying. I did not go to them; I stayed outside their martyrdom. I got up in the morning and worked to procure food, I ate and slept, sometimes I satisfied my sex urge, all as if my life's parabola had a right to be like other men's. And this was a sin, the sin I've had to live with as I live with contempt for myself and the knowledge that no matter what happens to me, I deserve no sympathy. Because I am a Jew and a Jew has to survive but to survive your brothers is a sin. I have to carry my guilt and hate myself for doing what it was my duty to do because I am a Jew.

The drone of the plane's engines had died away. It must be very late; there was silence even here in the heart of the city, in this night black under the clouds.

There was a time when if I opened that door behind me and went inside. I would find her sleeping warmly and heavily in our bed, but now the bed is empty, and opening and closing doors, going from one place to another, all are useless—my aloneness follows me everywhere. We had such a short time; her arm was linked with mine, but all I had to do was to look away for one instant, and when I turned back, she had vanished. Now it's hard even to recall her, to do more than conjure up a shadow—my sister-bride. Our first honeymoon night smelled of wisteria, a real honeymoon night, though.

Sometimes on moonlit nights, I smell that same scent, and I stretch out my hand, but there's nothing there. I am an old man sleeping alone, dreaming of a scent that existed in another life. My sister-bride, I gave her a Star of David pendant, and once when I tore it from her neck, the points of the star drew blood from her breasts. She cried out in pleasure, not in pain.

"Nothing's going to happen to our children," I promised her, but it was an empty promise. One of them watched me being beaten and stood away from the edge of the mob because he was afraid. He pretends to worship violence, but he's weak and frightened, bowed with shame from which there can never be the relief of confession. I didn't say to him, "Come, there's nothing to be ashamed of," and embrace him as I so much wanted to. And now, I'm leaving him behind, and I'm betraying him once again, my son. I'm taking the others home, to orange-scented winds and a deep luminous sky, to a fearless life, to wholeness, to the nearness of God, but I'm leaving him behind.

The drone of the plane's engines had died long since, and it was very quiet. How much time had passed, how long had I stood on the empty terrace? The night must be very deep. It had gotten chilly. I shivered, I recalled other nights and how I had shivered in my nightshirt, a little boy leaning on a wrought-iron balcony railing, watching whitish face-like blots at other windows, listening to the smothered sound of someone's crying, obstinately waiting through the night for I didn't know what.

Suddenly it seemed to me that I was no longer alone; I felt a Presence at my side. I didn't turn round, but I knew that the Presence was there, and I whispered, "I've been expecting You, ever since I can remember I've been expecting You."

I hadn't thought those words. I had spoken them and heard their sound, a clear sound though I had but whispered, the night was so still.

Why didn't You come to me when I was young and intact when I walked the streets in the rain and felt the sorrows of the people locked behind slatted shutters and heavy wooden doors? I wanted to step into their houses, to climb their stone stairways, knock on their doors, and watch them open slowly to let me in. If You had come then, nothing would have mattered anymore. I should have smiled at my lover's rubbing her hand on her skirt, and I should have gone to my brothers, and now I shouldn't have to live with my guilt.

Or earlier, why didn't You come to me when I could love even two pieces of iron, and I hunted the moon with a bucket full of water. I waited through the night, not knowing that I was waiting for You. Then I shouldn't have become what I am, I shouldn't have let my sister-bride vanish from my side, and I shouldn't be leaving my first son behind to fear and humiliation. But of course, You could come only now. I had to walk alone, to become what was in me to be, only at the end of the road becoming aware of You. This is what my awareness means that I have come to the end of my road."

Then I had nothing more to say. I stood there and cried, I who never cried as a child. I cried softly, and I recognized the sound of my crying, seeming far or perhaps near but smothered like a man's sobs choked into a pillow. After a while, a gray glow gnawed at the edge of the sky. The night had passed as swiftly as if I had slept and dreamed and remembered only the end of the dream. I went inside and into my sons' room. I shook them gently.

"Get up," I called, "get up and shed your old skins."

They snapped awake and laughed.

"Like butterflies."

MASTER SARGEANT ETTORE (EDGAR) LUZZATTO

I was about nine years old when my father one day said to me, "Americans are decent people. You should remember that." He had a way of saying things, no matter that I had no clue what he was talking about and why. He simply would come up with a statement and make sure that I memorized it for the future. It wasn't until years later that I got the whole story, which I had only heard in bits and pieces before.

My father, Edgar (aka Ettore) Luzzatto, grew up in Milan, Italy, in the fascist era. With the publication of Mussolini's racial laws, he decided that he wouldn't put up with the discrimination against the Jews. He applied for an immigrant visa to the U.S. but didn't know that in late 1938 the State Department was restricting the issuance of visas to Italian Jews. His application was denied; he was summoned to the U.S. embassy for an interview with a vice-consul, who offered him a visitor visa instead. My father, who was young and headstrong, disdainfully refused and got up to leave, but the vice-consul, who obviously knew more than he was allowed to say, stopped him. "Take the visa I'm offering you, and use it immediately!" he said. My father was so impressed by the tone of his voice that he took it and left Italy after a few days. Had he stayed longer, he might have never been able to leave.

Edgar Luzzatto's 1938 Visitor Visa

Knowing my father, I'm sure that he would have found a way to get himself killed had he stayed in Italy. Instead, he took a boat to New York City. There he met other decent people who didn't know him from Adam but still vouched for him. They even signed supporting affidavits, without which he would have been shipped back to Italy or some other deadly place in Europe. With the support of those decent people, he left for Havana, where he eventually obtained an immigrant visa and returned to NYC.

My father naturalized as an American and decided that the best way to pay his debt to the country that had taken him in was to enlist in the army. He served for almost five years and participated in the liberation of the Philippines. He was honorably discharged in 1946 with the rank of Master Sergeant.

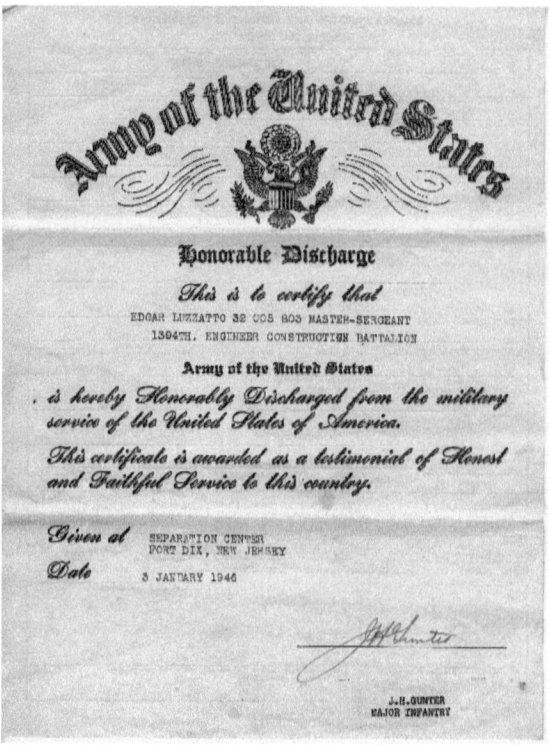

I have heard only a handful of stories from him about the war and the army. It took one of those envelopes that came in the mail now and then from the Veteran's Administration to make him talkative on the subject. Then he almost always opened or concluded his remarks with the same statement: "Americans are decent people."

www.ingramcontent.com/pod-product-compliance
Lightning Source LLC
Chambersburg PA
CBHW020641260626
47157CB00008B/2855